New look, old evil

Deacon stalked to the door, marched over the threshold, and disappeared. Minutes passed. Minutes that seemed like hours, with Rose writhing and moaning, her screams no less pitiful and painful with the leather strap in her mouth. Then the door burst open, and Deacon came in, leading a shirtless man in blue jeans and bare feet.

Deacon had the man's arms trapped behind his back, and the man didn't say one word. The reason why was easy to see—he had no mouth, just smooth skin where the orifice should be.

I'd never seen the man before, but I knew him instantly, and not only because Deacon held him with such furious certainty. Six black dots lined each side of his face, three tracking beside his nose and three curving under each eye. I knew those marks, had watched those dots as they seemed to float above his skin as life faded from me.

Lucas Johnson had found a new body.

TORN

BOOK TWO IN THE
BLOOD LILY CHRONICLES

JULIE KENNER

ACE BOOKS, NEW YORK

THE BERKLEY PUBLISHING GROUP
Published by the Penguin Group
Penguin Group (USA) Inc.
375 Hudson Street, New York, New York 10014, USA
Penguin Group (Canada), 90 Eglinton Avenue East, Suite 700, Toronto, Ontario M4P 2Y3, Canada
(a division of Pearson Penguin Canada Inc.)
Penguin Books Ltd., 80 Strand, London WC2R 0RL, England
Penguin Group Ireland, 25 St. Stephen's Green, Dublin 2, Ireland (a division of Penguin Books Ltd.)
Penguin Group (Australia), 250 Camberwell Road, Camberwell, Victoria 3124, Australia
(a division of Pearson Australia Group Pty. Ltd.)
Penguin Books India Pvt. Ltd., 11 Community Centre, Panchsheel Park, New Delhi—110 017, India
Penguin Group (NZ), 67 Apollo Drive, Rosedale, North Shore 0632, New Zealand
(a division of Pearson New Zealand Ltd.)
Penguin Books (South Africa) (Pty.) Ltd., 24 Sturdee Avenue, Rosebank, Johannesburg 2196,
South Africa

Penguin Books Ltd., Registered Offices: 80 Strand, London WC2R 0RL, England

This is a work of fiction. Names, characters, places, and incidents either are the product of the author's imagination or are used fictitiously, and any resemblance to actual persons, living or dead, business establishments, events, or locales is entirely coincidental. The publisher does not have any control over and does not assume any responsibility for author or third-party websites or their content.

TORN

An Ace Book / published by arrangement with the author

PRINTING HISTORY
Ace mass-market edition / December 2009

Copyright © 2009 by Julie Kenner.
Excerpt from *Turned* copyright © by Julie Kenner.
Cover art by Craig White.
Cover design by Annette Fiore DeFex.
Interior text design by Laura K. Corless.

ISBN: 978-0-441-01797-3

ACE
Ace Books are published by The Berkley Publishing Group,
a division of Penguin Group (USA) Inc.,
375 Hudson Street, New York, New York 10014.
ACE and the "A" design are trademarks of Penguin Group (USA) Inc.

PRINTED IN THE UNITED STATES OF AMERICA

10 9 8 7 6 5 4 3 2 1

For Jess and Aaron . . .
Thanks for going with me into the dark.

ONE

My name is Lily Carlyle. Except that it's not. Not really. Not anymore.

I'd gone out one night intending to kill the son of a bitch who'd stalked and raped my little sister, Rose. I failed, though, and instead of killing Lucas Johnson, I'd ended up dead.

Not exactly the result I'd been hoping for, I'll admit. And it just got weirder when I woke up in someone else's body.

Since that day, my name's been Alice Elaine Purdue.

Which pretty much makes my name a metaphor for my life. Because nothing in my life is what it seems. For example, I thought that I'd been brought back to life to kill the demons who were trying to open the Ninth Gate to Hell. I thought I was stopping an army of demons from crossing over at the next interdimensional convergence. That I was preventing Armageddon. That I was doing Good, with a capital G, and when all was said and done, I'd walk away with a nice shiny halo and a great big A+ on my permanent record.

Um, no.

The truth is a lot more complicated. The truth, for that matter, pisses me off.

I was duped. Told I was battling the Big Bad, when really I was doing Evil's bidding. My mission wasn't to keep the Ninth Gate locked up tight and hold back the demonic horde—it was to keep the good guys from doing that very thing.

I hadn't prevented the end of the world; I'd facilitated it.

The Ninth Gate is wide-open, and in less than two weeks, an army of demons is going to cross over. Life as we know it is going to end. And the cliché "hell on earth" will no longer be a figure of speech.

At least, that's the demons' dirty little plan. I, however, don't intend to let that happen. They made me a warrior, and by God it is time to do battle.

I'm going to figure out how to lock the gate tight.

And the more demons I have to kill to do that, the better.

TWO

Like a caged panther, Deacon paced the length of the rank motel room. He wore jeans and a white T-shirt, and the look would have been almost casual were it not for the dark glasses that he sported despite the single dim lamp and the predawn hour.

With those glasses, he looked like the consummate bad boy. Which, frankly, was exactly what he was. A demon. A Tri-Jal. One of the worst of the worst.

More than that, though, he was a demon allied with a demon hunter—me. The irony made me smile even as a nugget of worry settled in my gut. Because this was a dangerous game I was playing. If I'd made the wrong choice in aligning myself with Deacon, I could very well end up paying the price for eternity. All I knew was that I couldn't deny him. Couldn't push him out of my life, out of my head, or even out of my heart. He'd claimed me once, gotten right inside my head, and announced that I was his. *Mine,* he'd said.

And as every day passed, I feared that he was right.

Feared it and fought it, but at the same time, I welcomed it.

I didn't know where he'd found the dark glasses, and I didn't ask. What I did know was that he wore them because of me. Because if I couldn't see his eyes, I couldn't get into his head. And in his head was where the real bad boy lay. The images of past deeds. Of memories too horrible to share.

I wanted to see them. *Needed* to see them. Needed to know the heart of this man who compelled me. But he wasn't letting me in, and the glasses were just one more way of telling me not to even try.

Honestly, it pissed me off. Then again, these days, it didn't take much to irritate me. I was walking a knife-edge. Tilt one way, and I fell into rage. The other, and I slipped into despair.

"It's almost dawn," he said.

"You have somewhere else to be?" I asked. I was on the bed, my sister Rose's head cradled in my lap. And, yeah, I was tired and cranky. Too much had happened too quickly, and my head was spinning. My body might not need sleep anymore, but right then I craved a nap.

As for Deacon, I honestly didn't know what he craved. Until now I'd never been with him for any extended period, and I found myself wondering what he did with himself during the day, or during the night for that matter. I thought about asking, but since I wasn't certain I'd like the answer, I kept my mouth shut.

The truth was, I didn't want him to leave. Didn't want him to tell me he had to disappear and that he'd come back when he could. I needed help. And, selfishly, I wanted Deacon with me. Wanted the comfort that his presence provided, even a supercharged presence that looked like it was on the verge of exploding.

We'd been in our cracker-box motel for almost six hours, having holed up in the aftermath of a nasty little battle during which Lucas Johnson had shoved part of his demonic essence into Rose before we'd gotten her the hell out of there.

She'd screamed in pain and terror, then passed out cold. She still slept, and to be honest, I was beginning to worry that she'd never wake up. Deacon, however, had assured me that she would regain consciousness soon, albeit with one hell of a headache. I didn't ask him how he could be so certain about the particulars of demonic possession. That was just one more thing I didn't want to know.

Add on top of all that the fact that I had, only hours prior, managed to single-handedly facilitate the imminent arrival of Armageddon, and you can probably see why I was a little stressed.

"They'll start looking for you soon," Deacon said. "We need a plan."

The "they" he referred to was actually a "he": Clarence, in particular. My amphibious handler. A toad-faced little demon who'd run the con on me and whom I despised all the more because I'd actually been starting to like him.

"I have a plan," I said, stroking Rose's hair. "I already told you." For that matter, we'd talked of nothing other than my plan for hours. With me alternating between berating myself for failing both Rose and the world, and fantasizing in glorious detail how I would kill not only Clarence but every other demon I came in contact with.

The fantasy alone was cathartic, but not nearly enough, and I couldn't wait for the real deal. I wanted the satisfaction of the kill. The strength I gained. And, yeah, I wanted the hit of power. I drew it in when I killed them. The demon's essence. Its darkness. Its fury.

And, yeah, I was happy to embrace the homicidal happiness. Ironic, I suppose, since without all this demon-assassin prophecy bullshit, I wouldn't be having warm, fuzzy, murderous thoughts. I wouldn't be spending every day of my life trying to suppress the demonic essence that got sucked into me with each and every kill.

And here's an interesting tidbit: You'd think that since I'd been unknowingly working for the bad guys, I would have been out there killing *good* guys who I'd been duped to whack. If that had been the case, then I'd be filled with goodness and light, about as sweet and charming as they come, because I would have sucked in the essence of a boatload of near-angelic souls.

A nice theory, but not even close to my reality. Because Clarence and crew didn't want me sweet; they didn't want me nice. And they'd had me training on real, true, badass demons. Sacrificing their own kind so that I'd become more like them. More badass. More evil.

Apparently, it had worked. Because the darkness writhed within me.

I wanted to be over the top, and I wanted to end them all.

"We can't simply waltz in and kill Clarence," Deacon said.

"'We'?" I replied. "No, no, no. This one's personal. This is all me."

"Fuck that."

"Fuck *you*," I countered, demonstrating my keen skill at argument. "He's my handler. I can get close to him. Close enough to shove my blade through his heart." My plan was to go back to Alice's apartment, call Clarence, and pretend like I was the good little soldier. It didn't matter much if he believed me; it only mattered that he came over. But if Deacon was standing there beside me when he walked into the apartment, we lost the element of surprise, and what could have been a nice, clean kill would become a bloodbath.

And as much as the thought of seeing Clarence waste away in a pool of his own blood left a nice warm feeling in my gut, for this job, I preferred the subtle approach. Grab him by the short hairs, and drag my blade across his fat little throat.

"Besides," I said, "I have to get close to him, and you know it. Unless I get inside his head, this thing's over before it's even begun."

The problem with swearing on all that is holy that you are going to go forth and lock the door to hell is pretty fundamental: Doors require keys. And without knowing where this particular key was, we were pretty much screwed.

Deacon and I both knew damn good and well that there was no way Clarence was going to reveal the incantation for finding the legendary key that would permanently lock tight all of the nine gates to hell.

To be honest, we didn't even know if Clarence knew the incantation, but I had to poke around and find out. And if he did know it, then we could use the spell to raise a map to the key's location on my skin. A rather handy but bizarre side effect of being Prophecy Girl.

"The moment he knows you're poking around in his head, he's going to gut you like a fish," Deacon said. "And he may be shaped like a frog, but I'm betting he can move fast. He gets you down and injured, and you might find yourself in pieces or trapped in a tiny pine box forever."

"I think I can handle Clarence," I said, even though I knew he was right. Yet another of the perks of my über-chick persona was immortality. And the idea of spend-

ing eternity awake but six feet under was definitely the
stuff of my nightmares.

For that matter, if I came up against a demon with
telepathic powers, I could also end up the victim of
permanent brain-fry. And since Clarence had just such
a skill set, I had to consider the possibility that he'd be
able to whup my ass without lifting a finger.

"You're important, Lily. Don't risk yourself."

The irony was inescapable, and I bit back a laugh.
"Important," I repeated. "I think Clarence once told me
that very thing."

"I'm not him," he said. "And I'm not using you."

I was about to argue but kept my mouth closed. The
truth was, despite the inexplicable bond I felt with Deacon, I still didn't trust him. For that matter, I didn't
trust anyone. I'd learned my lesson with Clarence, and
until I had a peek into someone's mind, I had to assume
their agenda was their own, and I was only a pawn.

Needless to say, that wasn't a role I much liked.

"You have to trust me sometime," Deacon said. He
was looking straight at me, and I could see my reflec-
tion in the black lenses of his glasses.

"No," I said. "I really don't." I'd work with him. Truth
be told, I'd do a hell of a lot more with him. But that
didn't mean I had to trust him.

"Dammit, Lily," he said, grinding my name out like
a curse.

That frustration in his voice irritated me, snapping

the final taut string that had been holding my patience in place.

"No," I snarled as I slid out from under Rose and moved across the small room to stand in front of him. I hadn't taken off my knife, and the pressure of the thigh holster against my leg gave me a sense of confidence. Of power. "You told me you had a vision of the two of us closing the Ninth Gate. Well, good for you. But in case you've forgotten, I've already played the we-need-you-to-save-the-world game once, and I lost big-time."

I'd been told my mission was to stop a demon priest from opening a portal to hell. Instead, I'd been duped into stopping a real priest from sealing that very thing. And in only two short weeks, that portal was going to be filled with incoming demon traffic, busier than a freeway during morning rush hour.

"I screwed up," I said. "I'm not going to make the same mistake twice."

"Trusting me isn't a mistake," he said.

"Since you won't let me look in your head, I have absolutely no way of knowing if you're bullshitting me or not."

He stopped pacing and turned slowly toward me. Too slowly, actually, and I longed to see his eyes, to have a hint as to what he was thinking. Beneath the thin shirt, his muscles tensed. An animal readying for the kill.

I took an involuntary step back, my hand going automatically to my blade even before I realized what I was doing.

"You are not going inside my head again," he said, his voice slow and deadly.

"If I want to, you can't stop me."

"Believe me, Lily," he said. "I could stop you."

"Wanna prove it?" I said, feeling pissed off and grumpy, and yeah, I wanted to hurt him. Wanted to pick a fight. The demons inside me were stirred up, gunning for some action. Violence. Pain. Sex. One at a time, or all at once in a singularly wild erotic moment. I didn't care. I just needed the release. The catharsis.

"Back off, Lily," he said, his jaw firm and his muscles tense. He turned and deliberately looked toward Rose. "Back off and get a grip."

I exhaled, loud and long, frustrated and ashamed. "At the end of the day, I don't know a damn thing about you except that you're a demon. A Tri-Jal." I knew that, and yet I also knew that I wanted him. Knew that I'd seen the two of us together, wild and naked, in his mind. But I'd seen blood there, too. And pain. And the promise of a redemption that he hadn't yet achieved. "You're asking me to take a lot on faith."

"Yeah," he said, "I am."

"I don't have a lot of faith left in me."

"Lily . . ."

"Dammit, Deacon. Let me in. Let me see. Let me have one true thing in this completely whacked world I live in now. One thing that I can feel and touch and say, 'Yes, I know this is real.'"

He moved so fast I never saw the hand that reached

out and jerked me toward him. He slammed me back against the wall, his arms caging me even as my palm closed around the hilt of my knife. He was hot and hard and right there, and I could hear the blood rushing through me, could feel my body tighten in reaction to his proximity. I heard myself gasp and hated myself for it. At the same time, I wanted nothing more than for him to close his mouth over mine and make me forget everything else that was going on in this freaked-out world we were living in.

"You want true?" he whispered, leaning in close to my ear, his breath making me shiver. "Then hear this. I'm going with you. I'll wait in the back. I'll hide in a fucking closet if that's what it takes. But if it looks like Clarence is going to get the best of you, then I'm coming in and I'm taking him out. And that, Lily, is the truth."

His hand dropped down to cover mine, which was over my still-sheathed knife. "You didn't draw your weapon, Lily," he said. "I'd say you have some faith left in you."

I drew in a breath, long and deep, determined to regain a sense of control. "You can come," I said, knowing that I was conceding this round. "But we take Rose, too."

"Risky," he said. "She's your Achilles' heel, and Clarence knows that better than anyone."

I looked toward the bed, toward my little sister, curled up, broken and battered. Her once-dewy skin was sallow, and dark bags hung beneath her closed eyes. Her blond hair was dark with oil and stringy from not having been combed or washed. She looked like a street urchin instead of a princess, and I wanted the princess back. She deserved it, and I was determined to make it happen.

"She comes," I repeated, "but we make sure he doesn't realize she's there. I'm not leaving her alone."

He cut a glance across the room to the bed, then moved toward her and slid an arm under her back and another under her knees.

"What are you doing?"

"Carrying her."

"Now? We're going now?"

"You have a better idea?"

I shook my head. He was right, of course. The time for hiding in dark rooms was over.

From his arms, I heard a small mewling sound.

"Rose?" My throat was thick, my voice barely functioning.

Deacon turned, shifting her body toward me. Even despite those damned glasses, I could feel his eyes on me, watching me, gauging my reaction.

I moved closer, unable to speak from the hope that was filling my chest and my throat.

"Lily?" Her voice was weak. "Lily, what happened?" Her eyes fluttered open, her features slack but aware, and I drew in a breath, realizing the tightness in my chest was because I'd stopped breathing.

"Rose. Thank God." She was okay. She was Rose.

Whatever he'd done to her, she'd fought it off. It hadn't stuck. This was my baby sister, and she was going to be just fine.

Two seconds later, she proved me a liar.

"Lily," she said, her voice sharp and panicked. "Lily, what's happening?"

"Deacon!" I cried, because I didn't know. Rose's body was convulsing in his arms, her eyes rolling back in her head until only the whites remained. I screamed her name, screamed at Deacon to do something. And then I slammed my mouth shut in horror when I heard her speak again.

"Sweet Lily," my sister said, in a voice not her own. "I'm fucking your sister. Again."

THREE

I recoiled in horror from the vile words. And Deacon, who I'd never seen rattled, tossed her forward, dropping her on the bed even as he stepped sideways, his body moving between the bed and me.

"This time, I'm filling her up, from the inside out." I knew that tone. That sound. That lazy cadence.

I knew him, and the urge to eviscerate the beast inside Rose nearly overpowered my reason.

Lucas Johnson. He was right there, deep inside the person I loved most in all the world.

"Get out!" I screamed. "Get the hell out of my sister!"

Without thinking, I leaped toward the bed, then kicked and flailed as Deacon grabbed me around the waist and held me back. "It's still Rose," he said, his voice icy calm. "Hurt him, hurt your sister."

On the bed, my sister's body shifted, sitting up on her knees, then tossing her head back and breathing deep. Her breasts rose beneath the sacrificial silk gown they'd put her in, nipples straining against the material. I watched, revolted and helpless, as the demon inside her forced her hand to slide down, over her breast, then down farther until he cupped her crotch. "Pretty, pretty," he said. "And so soft and sweet. I bet she's all wet inside. What do you think, Lily? Is your sister wet for me?"

I hacked back a wad of phlegm and let it fly, hitting him—hitting Rose—square on the face.

The hand on her crotch lifted, and he used the back of Rose's hand to wipe away the spitball. "Now, Sugarlips," he said, "is that any way to treat your kith and kin? We're close now, you and me. Real close."

"Get out of her," I said again, slowly and carefully. "Get out of her right now, or I swear I will end you."

"You try that, Sweetpea. You go ahead and try." There wasn't the slightest hint of worry in his voice. I was no threat to him, and we both knew it. Even so, he took his hands off my sister's body.

Why?

I watched through narrowed, wary eyes, wondering what was to come. Why he had given in so easily?

His actions gave me no clue. Instead, he eased back against the headboard and breathed in deep. "Haven't been inside a girl in at least a thousand years," he said. Then he chuckled. "Well, 'course we both know I've been *inside* a girl. But this—this here's different. This way, I'm touching her everywhere."

I heard a low, feral growl, then realized it was coming from my throat. Deacon's arms around my waist tightened, making sure I didn't do something stupid.

"Aw, see, now you're going to hurt my feelings," Lucas said. "Make me feel unwelcome."

"What do you want?" Deacon asked.

Rose's head lifted, slowly and deliberately, until her eyes—with Lucas behind them—faced Deacon dead on. "I don't converse with traitors," he said. Then he smiled, and the expression was all Rose. "I find that kind of behavior unbecoming," he said, but this time he used my sister's voice.

Hot tears trickled down my cheeks, and, behind me, I felt Deacon's body stiffen with rage. I reached up and held fast to his arms around me. It was my turn to hold him in place.

"Goddammit," I hissed, "answer the question. What do you want?"

"What do you think I want?"

I was afraid to answer, fearful that he wanted Rose. That he wanted to crush the life from her. That he wanted her fully, body and soul, and he wanted to thumb his nose at the fact that I'd failed her on so many different levels.

"I said, what do you think I want?" he snarled.

I squeezed my eyes closed, releasing more tears, but refusing to put voice to my biggest fear. "I don't know. How the hell can I know what a monster like you is thinking?"

"I want the key, you ignorant bitch. The key, the key, the fucking key." His voice took on a manic, singsong edge.

"Yeah? Well, join the club."

"Not the key you seek. I seek the *Oris Clef*—the key to *open* the gates—all the gates. The masses await, and on the night of convergence, Kokbiel will rise above all others, allowing entry only to those who swear fealty to his grace."

Since I didn't have a clue what he was talking about, I only gaped. Deacon, however, was right there with the program.

"All this time, and you still serve Kokbiel?"

"I am his most loyal servant. Wherever I have wandered, it has always been Kokbiel that I have served." His eyes narrowed as he looked at Deacon. "And you, Deacon Camphire, whom do you serve?"

"I serve no master."

"Oh, but you have," Johnson retorted, making Rose's sweet voice hard and harsh. "Have you told her? Have you told the little girl whom you've served? What you've done?"

I jerked out of Deacon's arms and turned, needing to see his face, but it gave me no clue.

Johnson laughed. "The powerful Camphire, the—"

Without warning, Deacon lunged, knocking Rose back, his knife at her throat, his knee hard on her chest.

"Deacon!" I sprang forward, my own blade drawn, and pressed the tip firmly against Deacon's temple. "Don't you even think about it."

"I know about you," Johnson hissed. "I know everything. Every stinking thing."

"I sincerely doubt that," Deacon said, his voice icy calm.

"She doesn't know," Johnson said with a low laugh. "She doesn't have a clue what you've done."

I could see Deacon's muscles tighten. "Deacon . . ."

"Lily wants this body alive," he said, ignoring my blade. Ignoring me. His sole focus on the body beneath him. "I don't. I suggest you keep that in mind before you provoke me again."

Rose's eyes closed, and Johnson barked out a laugh. "What an impasse. What a pretty predicament. She really doesn't know, does she? She doesn't know what you are. What you've done. What you're capable of." Rose's mouth pursed into a little moue. "Does the widdle boy just want to impress the pwetty girlie? Or have you got another agenda to be with the bitch?" he asked, ending with a harsh accusation. "One more suited to your nature."

Deacon's lip curled, and his arms flexed.

"Don't fucking move," I said, fearing he'd press down with the blade. And in case he didn't get the message, I thrust forward just hard enough to draw a drop of blood. It trickled down in front of his ear, the scent of it enticing, making me edgy and ready for a fight. "Pull back, Deacon. Pull back right now."

"I can tell you, Lily," Rose said sweetly. "I can tell you everything I know about him. And I know lots. Dirty things. Dark things. Red things. Cruel things."

"Shut the fuck up!" I snarled. Because the truth was I did want to know—I *did*—but I didn't want any truth that came from the mouth of Lucas Johnson. More than that, I feared if I gave in—if I let Johnson tell me—then Deacon really would kill my sister, and I might not be fast enough to prevent it. "You want something from me, fine. You want my attention, you've got it. Now, get on with it and tell me."

I dropped my blade and took one step back. "Let him go," I said to Deacon, and when he hesitated, I repeated myself. "Let. Him. Go."

Deacon pulled back, his knife still out, his jaw tight.

I focused on Rose—on Johnson. "Now, spell it out for me, because I'm tired of playing twenty questions. Start with the *Oris Clef*. Where is it?"

"Isn't that the question of the hour?" Johnson said.

I faced Deacon. "You, then. Tell me."

"No one knows," he said, looking at Rose rather than me. "The *Oris Clef* was forged in secret by Penemue."

"Who?"

"An angel. He wanted power, and he secretly created a key that would force all nine gates open—and would instill the gatekeeper with power and dominion over those who passed through the gates."

"So what happened?"

"The archangels discovered his treachery before he could use the *Oris Clef*," Deacon said. "He was cast out of heaven, transformed into the vilest of demons, and the key was dismantled. Broken into three pieces."

"Since Penemue made it, only he could destroy it," Johnson said. "So those holier-than-thou fucks were stymied, weren't they?"

"And that's the key you want," I said, shooting a scathing look toward Johnson. "So that this Cookie demon you work for will be the big demon on campus."

"Well, well, not such an idiot cunt after all," he said, the words so harsh from my sister's mouth.

"What does this have to do with me? With Rose? I don't know where your damn key is."

"But you will." A wide, sweet grin split Rose's face. "And when you get it, you'll give it to me."

"The hell I will."

"Oh, you will." He fell backward onto the mattress, Rose's arms out to her sides. As I watched, Rose fell silent, and her body relaxed. Her eyes opened, slowly, as if she'd awakened from a long sleep, and she started to sit up. "Lily?" she said, her voice confused and frustrated. "What's going on?"

I rushed toward her. This was Rose; this was my sis-

ter. That thing inside her had gone away. "It's okay," I
lied. "It'll be okay."

She screamed, the sound so loud and piercing I
thought my eardrums would break.

"Get him out! Get him out!" She started brushing at
her body, ripping at her clothes, as wild as a child who'd
sat down on a fire ant mound. "Lily! Lily! Off! Off!"

I couldn't answer. I couldn't speak for the tears in
my throat. Instead, I pulled her to me, held her even
while I looked helplessly at Deacon. He was rage. Pure
rage, and there was nowhere for him to direct it.

"I will," I managed to whisper to Rose. "I'll figure it
out. I'll get him out."

But I don't think she heard me through her screams.

I held tight, rocking her back and forth, and watched,
mystified, as Deacon stalked to the bathroom. Moments
later, I heard the mirror shatter.

As if that was a signal, Rose jerked out of my arms.
She fell back, her whole body convulsing.

"Deacon!"

He raced back in to find me shoving the belt part
of my thigh holster into her mouth, holding down her
tongue to prevent her from swallowing it.

Beneath me, Rose writhed and lurched, and nothing
I did could calm her. "I can't let her ride it out," I
yelled, my face wet with hot tears. "This isn't a seizure.
It's him. He's gonna kill her. If I don't agree to find this
fucking key, he's going to kill my little sister."

Deacon stood watching, breathing hard, nostrils flaring. The glasses had come off, were hooked to his T-shirt, and his eyes flashed red with fury. "She's a pawn, Lily, and we're playing on a celestial chessboard."

I could only shake my head, my throat thick with tears. "No," I finally managed, spitting out the word. "Don't you even fucking *think* it."

"Let her go, and his hold over you is over. It's done."

"No!" I screamed the word, wanting to hit, wanting to pound, but I had to hold my sister. Had to keep her safe.

"He's near," Deacon finally said, his voice low, his head cocked as if he'd just figured something out.

"What? What?"

He held a finger up. "What if he goes too far? What if her little body can't handle it?"

"Oh, God. Oh, God, Deacon." I could barely speak through the tears. What the fuck was wrong with him? What the bloody hell was he talking about? Why wasn't he *doing* something?

"Safety net," he said, then met my eyes. "He's nearby. He'll need to have someplace for this piece of him to go if she dies."

I still didn't understand, but his lip lifted into a snarl, then he stalked to the door, marched over the threshold, and disappeared. Minutes passed. Minutes that seemed like hours, with Rose writhing and moaning, her screams no less pitiful and painful with the leather strap in her mouth. Then the door burst open, and Deacon came in, leading a shirtless man in blue jeans and bare feet.

Deacon had the man's arms trapped behind his back, and the man didn't say one word.

The reason why was easy to see—he had no mouth, just smooth skin where the orifice should be.

I'd never seen the man before, but I knew him instantly, and not only because Deacon held him with such furious certainty. Six black dots lined each side of his face, three tracking beside his nose and three curving under each eye. I knew those marks, had watched those dots as they seemed to float above his skin as life faded from me.

Lucas Johnson had found a new body.

FOUR

Deacon held his blade pressed tight at Johnson's neck. "One wrong move, and I will drop you into a bleeding pile of waste."

On the bed, Rose stopped convulsing, and for the briefest of moments, hope flared in my belly. Then she started laughing, and hope died once again.

"Laugh it up," Deacon said. "But I kill you, and your essence is going to leave this body. *Both* bodies."

"Fool," Johnson spat, in Rose's voice. "I would have thought you above all would know better. You kill that body—that shell that holds the bulk of me—and I will move entirely into the girl. I'll become her. Meld with her."

He ran Rose's hands over her body, sliding down to stroke herself at the crotch and sighing with ecstasy as he did so. I shivered, my body sore from the effort to keep from leaping upon him and knocking his fucking head off.

"She'll be me, and I'll be her, and there will be no going back. And it'll be on your hands," he said, Rose's eyes staring hard at Deacon. "Do you think your pretty Lily will want you then? Do you think she'll let you touch her if you've killed her sister?"

"You're bluffing," Deacon said, the knife pressing hard enough by then to leave a line on the grotesque, mouthless man's throat.

"Deacon—" My voice was not my own, squeezed small by the paralyzing fear that had gripped me.

"You want to find out?" Johnson asked in Rose's soft, sweet voice. "Go ahead. I'm growing tired of that body anyway. So thick and clunky. Nice to have something new. Something young. Something nubile."

I swallowed and realized my head was shaking, back and forth, back and forth. "Deacon," I whispered, my voice filled with a plea.

In his arms, Johnson pulled back toward Deacon's body and away from the knife. Deacon reacted in a flash, jerking the knife away, but then slamming Johnson's mouthless body to the floor. I heard the crunch as his nose broke, then saw the blood when he rolled over.

My nose twitched, my mouth filling with saliva. *Blood.*

I wanted it—craved it.

And I hated myself for this weakness I didn't want and hadn't asked for.

Johnson pushed himself up onto hands and knees, his eyes on me as if he knew exactly what I was thinking. Beside me, Rose leaned closer. "Taste," she whispered. "Take and taste. You know you want to."

"Shut up!" I screamed, pressing my hands to my ears, fighting the urge to lash out, to send her flying across the room. I *didn't* want blood. Didn't, didn't, didn't. And I sure as hell didn't want the blood of Lucas Johnson.

"Take," Rose whispered again. "When you taste, you'll know. I can be your greatest ally. Taste . . . and see what I can offer you."

"Never," I whispered, but dammit, I wanted to. The blood. God, the lure of the blood . . .

I still wasn't used to the bloodlust, and to have it forced on me so unexpectedly was horrific. I didn't have the strength to fight. Not then, not after all that had happened.

And what if he was right? What if I could catch a glimpse of him through the blood? What if I should drink in order to understand? To see? To learn how to defeat him?

I knew—*knew*—that it was the bloodlust talking. That I would learn nothing from him but would only sink further toward the demonic side of me. That it was peeking out. Calling to me from where I'd hidden it.

Open the door, and the essence would burst through. I'd give in to the nature of what I'd killed, what I'd consumed.

Do that, and I couldn't protect Rose, much less the world.

Do that, and I really would become that which I abhorred.

And yet my strength was waning. I wanted . . . I craved . . .

And without even thinking, I found myself on hands and knees, moving over the bed toward the scent to Johnson's blood.

As I approached, Deacon lashed down with the knife, striking the butt end of it against the back of Johnson's head. Johnson fell to the ground, and Deacon whipped off his coat and tossed it over the lifeless form.

I reared back and howled. I was like an animal, complaining that the hunt had been taken from me, the prey plucked from my path, and like an animal, I snarled at the man who'd taken it from me.

"Don't," he said, his voice suggesting that whatever beast might be keening within me was no match for what lived day to day within him.

Right then, I didn't care. I would have leaped on him, would have attacked without another thought, if Rose hadn't sprung from the bed to do that very thing. She launched herself at him, moving with inhuman speed, her hands clawed and her fingernails going straight for Deacon's face.

I grappled to catch her from behind, on the one hand terrified that Deacon had killed the body and all of the monster was deep inside my sister, and on the other hand afraid that Rose would kill Deacon with her bare hands.

"He's alive!" Deacon said, hands up, feet in a fighting stance. His glasses were still off, and his eyes burned red—and right then I had no doubt that he would rip Rose's head off if she came anywhere close to him. "The bastard's alive. I only knocked him out."

I relaxed only slightly. Rose did not.

"You swear?" I demanded.

Deacon's lip curled into a snarl. "Don't you think she'd be the first to tell you if I was lying?"

"This is my sister," I said, my voice low. "Do not ever forget that."

"Until we get him out of her, your sister might as well be dead."

I shook my head, finally letting go of Rose, who crawled backward onto the head of the bed, then crouched there on the pillows, looking forlorn and lost.

"You think that's her, peeking out, looking scared? That's what he wants us to see. And the sooner you acknowledge that, Lily, the better this will go."

"Better?" I retorted. "How the fuck can any of this be better?" I drew in an angry breath, because of course it could be better. If Johnson were out of Rose's body. If the demonic essence of every demon I'd killed would leave my body in a puff. If Deacon would confide in me and share his secrets so that I knew whether I could trust him.

And if we could lock the Ninth Gate before the demon horde came rushing through.

Accomplish those things, and yeah, things could be better.

But seeing as I didn't see signs that any one of those things would happen anytime soon, I was reveling in the fucked-up-edness of the situation. Not to mention my own dark pity party.

I pressed my fingers to my head and tried to beat back the blackness. Compartmentalize. Shove all that demonic stuff back into a corner of my mind. One breath, then another. When I felt centered, I faced Deacon. "How do we know he's telling the truth? How do we know we can't kill that freakish, mouthless body without hurting Rose?"

It wasn't a chance I intended to take, but I needed to understand how this stuff worked. And right then, Deacon was the only one who could tell me.

Deacon drew in two noisy breaths through his nose, as if by the mere act of doing so he could calm a rage growing wild inside him. "When a demon invades a body," he finally said, "it's generally an all-or-nothing thing. A demon *can* send a small piece of himself into a human and try to tempt the human to do his bidding.

But in those instances, the demon has no voice except inside the mind of the human he's possessed. Here, that portion speaks." He nodded toward the body at his feet. "And the body has been robbed of that ability."

"How do you know all of this?"

He looked at me, his eyes flat.

I licked suddenly dry lips. "Right. So. That means he's different from, well, other demons," I said, shooting Deacon a sideways glance.

"So it would seem."

"So we have to believe him," I said, nodding toward the body on the floor. "Until I can figure out a way to get Rose free"—I turned to face my sister, who was crouched on the pillows—"and I *will* figure out a way, then Johnson's body stays alive. Tie it up."

"My pleasure," Deacon said, taking his knife to the pull cord for the curtains, then using the cut strands to bind the Johnson-body's hands and feet.

While he did that, I turned back to Rose. To Johnson. To the thing that had invaded my sister. "You," I said. "Talk. What are you doing, and what exactly do you want?"

"Why, Lily," Johnson said in a singsong Rose voice. "You sound so serious. And here I thought we were having a nice little family reunion."

The urge to lash out threatened to overwhelm me. I wanted to bloody up that sweet face. To make him shut the fuck up. Because the more I talked to him, the more I forgot that Rose was in there, and I *couldn't* forget.

Couldn't sacrifice my sister. There I was—trained, bred, created, whatever—to fight.

But right then, I had nothing to fight against.

"I want you out of her." Yet another understatement.

"We all want something," Lucas countered.

I seriously considered ripping my hair out. "In case *you* haven't been paying attention, I don't know anything about your damn key. So how the hell am I supposed to find it for you?" It pissed me the hell off that he was tying my sister's safety—hell, her *sanity*—to me handing over some stupid thing that I'd never even seen, much less had my hot little hands on.

"Patience, Lily," he said. "You don't have it now, but you will soon." Rose's perfect Cupid's bow of a mouth stretched into a distended grin. "It's why they made you."

I shook my head. "No. They made me to kill a priest. To keep him from closing and locking the Ninth Gate. And in case you missed the memo, they got what they wanted."

"Well, there's the thing, Sugarlips—you've only fulfilled the first stage."

"What are you talking about?" Deacon asked.

My sister might never have been a drama queen, but the same could not be said of Johnson. He crawled to the center of the bed, then sat cross-legged, back straight, arms balanced over her knees.

"And lo, it came to pass that the Ninth Gate of Hell

burst open, and those who dwelled below crept forth, bringing desolation and darkness to the land. To the righteous shall fall the task of sealing the gate, and woe to those who seek to secure the maw, for their champion is neither alive nor dead, neither friend nor foe, neither wicked nor pure, not thus until her allegiance be claimed, making fealty sworn, and bound until the end comes nigh. Great shall be the power of her blood, with power to see the hidden and the lost, and she shall consume her enemy and become one."

He bowed his head, then slowly looked up at me. "Nice to know they got you by the balls, isn't it?" Johnson said. "And they do now. They really do." He spread his arms wide. "Fealty sworn, babe. You're one of us now."

I shook my head, refusing to believe, even though so much of the freakish words rang true. *A champion*—that was what Clarence called me. *Neither alive nor dead*—and wasn't I immortal, not to mention that I'd died, and yet I lived? And oh, yeah, there was that little bit about consuming my enemies. Didn't much like it, but couldn't avoid it.

And, yes, my blood had led Clarence straight to Father Carlton.

And let's not forget that "hidden and the lost" part. Because hadn't Clarence used my very skin to find the location of the Box of Shankara? Hadn't the location of Father Carlton's ceremony been seared upon my forearm?

It described me, all right. The prophecy described me to a T.

I'd always known I was Prophecy Girl, but I'd never known what the prophecy said. Now that Johnson had recited it for me, I can't say that I was particularly happy with the knowledge. Especially not the knowledge that I was someone karmically locked on the demon side of things. "No," I said, not willing to believe it. "I never made the choice. They tricked me. It can't possibly count if they tricked me."

"Tricked you?" Johnson repeated, only this time he spoke in Rose's voice. "Is that what you tell yourself so that you can sleep at night? Poor little baby was tricked. Poor you, how horrible."

"Dammit, Johnson, I never made the choice."

"The hell you didn't. You made the choice every time you embraced the rage. Every time you clung to the darkness. You made the choice, bitch, the day you tried to kill me."

I shook my head and took an involuntary step backward, then stopped when Deacon's hand closed over my shoulder, warm and comforting.

Johnson, however, didn't stop. He crawled forward on the bed, his eyes on mine. "You know it's true. You feel the darkness in your soul. Eating away at you. You won't even have one before long. Just the blackness, warm and sweet, filling you up. Don't fight it, Lily. Embrace it."

Behind me, Deacon's hand tightened, but I jerked

away, the pressure no longer comforting but confusing. Was he trying to reassure or to drag me down? Had I found an ally in the man, or was he truly my enemy, secretly serving his demonic master?

"Overwhelming, isn't it?" Johnson said. "The power at your fingertips. The solidarity."

"Fuck you."

He laughed. "Not me you should hate, Sugar. I'm not the one who brought you, turned you. Tricked you into choosing sides."

Hatred filled me, and with it, the image of one man. "Clarence."

"Well, this is your lucky day," Johnson said. "Because I'll tell you a little secret. I hate him, too."

"Clarence works for Penemue," Deacon said. "Damn, of course he does."

"And a pat on the head to the little demon boy," Johnson said, earning a low growl from Deacon.

I turned to Deacon. "Clarence works for the guy who invented the *Oris Clef*? And this Penemue dude doesn't much like Kokbiel, I'm thinking?"

"Kokbiel and Penemue have been brutal enemies since the early times," Deacon said.

"And Penemue wants his key back," I added, thinking aloud. "Which means Clarence is going to be searching for this *Oris Clef* thing, too."

"Clever girl," Johnson said.

"But if all this is true, why didn't they have me going after the *Oris Clef* from the very beginning?"

"Had to stop the threat," Johnson said. "That bitch-spawn priest was going to lock the last open gate, and if the gates are sealed when the convergence comes, then the Riders can't cross over." He shrugged. "One gate's better than nothing, and even though Armageddon would come faster through nine doorways, it can still make it through one."

My stomach roiled, and I feared I'd throw up. So close—the forces of good had come so close to locking out the dark—and I'd single-handedly mucked it all up.

"More than that, they had to make sure you were aligned to their side—and what better way than to send you on so easy a quest? Killing an old, fat, human priest. No challenge, none at all. But now it's over, and there's no turning back. You're marked, girlie. Heaven's no longer an option. You get that, right?"

I took Deacon's hand. "I'll never believe that," I lied. "Never." But so help me, I did believe it. I could feel the evil inside me, after all.

"He lies," Deacon said. "That's what he does. What he is. A walking lie. Even his body's not his own."

"And yours is?" Johnson said. "How many bodies have you held over the course of your existence? How many lives have you thrust aside because you coveted their flesh?"

Deacon ripped his hand from mine, then stalked toward Johnson. "I will end you," he said, his voice low, dangerous. "Before this is over, you will burn, then you will disappear." Never once did Deacon raise his voice.

Never once did his tone change. But death and destruction dripped from every word. I saw fear spark in those too-familiar eyes, and I wanted to applaud. Because he'd made a dent. Deacon had actually scared the creature I hated most in all the world.

"Big talk," Johnson said. "So long as I'm in this body, I'm safe." He turned to me. "Then again, maybe I'm not. What do you think, Sugarbritches? Would he betray you to avenge himself? Would he kill your sister if it meant ending me?"

"Enough," I said, my voice as low and harsh as Deacon's had been earlier. "You're picking on the wrong girl. Because there is no way I am going back to work for that scum. Your *Oris Clef* is staying lost, and I'm killing that bastard. Clarence dies, and I'm doing it today."

Rose's eyebrows lifted in mock surprise. "The moment you do, your sister dies. So make your decision, Lily. And make it good."

"That's bullshit," I said. "You hate him, too. Why the fuck do you care if he dies? Go find your own damn key pieces."

"He needs Clarence," Deacon said. "He's an Incantor, isn't he?"

"A what?"

He nodded toward my arm. "A demon who can recite the incantations to raise the map. And he's a servant of Penemue. That gives him special insight."

"What's it going to be, Lily? You do your job—do what you were made to do—or your sister dies."

I drew in a breath, prolonging the moment. But there was never any doubt. How could there be when Rose's life was on the line? "Fine," I said. "I'm in."

"No." Deacon reached out and grabbed my upper arm so firmly I feared for finger-sized bruises. "You can't do this."

I cut my gaze toward Rose. "Yeah. I can."

"We're going to talk," he said. "Alone."

On the bed, Johnson chuckled. "Go on, then. I'll stay here, toying with your sister's life."

"Are you crazy?" I hissed, as soon as the motel door closed behind us.

He held up a finger instead of answering, then moved us down the walkway to the stairs. Only after we'd made our way to the brownish green pool did he speak.

"You cannot do this," he said.

"Watch me." I turned to walk away, but he grabbed my arm and jerked me back. I countered, taking my free arm and landing a solid uppercut on his jaw. His head snapped back, and when he steadied himself, his face was contorted with fury.

"Do not push me, Lily. Not now. Not about this."

"Ditto," I said, my blood boiling and my body thrumming. I was itching for a fight. Itching to smash Lucas Johnson's face in. But if I couldn't have him, maybe Deacon was the next best thing.

"Two weeks," Deacon said. "The convergence is in two weeks. What happened to us locking the gate?"

"What happened?" I repeated, my voice rising in bafflement. "Try Lucas Johnson. *He* happened."

"Dammit, Lily, we're meant to lock the gate."

I shook my head. "Hold up there, cowboy. You may have had a vision about us locking the Ninth Gate, Deacon, but that's been all shot to hell."

"No—"

"Yes," I said. "Visions aren't the future, dammit. They're a possible future. A possible future that I completely screwed up when I destroyed the Box of Shankara."

"I don't accept that. We can still lock the Ninth Gate. We can lock all the gates."

I ran my fingers through my hair, completely frustrated. "Dammit, Deacon, you said yourself this superlock is only a legend. We don't even know that it exists."

"There are other ways, too, Lily. There are ways to lock each of the gates."

"Yeah? How?" He was silent, and I raved on. "That's what I thought. So don't talk to me about chasing some damned phantom. Not when my sister's life is on the line."

"It's the Apocalypse, Lily. Everyone's life is on the line."

"That's the point! We don't have time to play games. At least if I get this *Oris Clef*, then we'll have something to bargain with. You think I'm going to give it over to a lunatic like Johnson? Or even to Clarence?

I'm not. But I need time to figure out how to get that bastard out of my sister."

"I can't let you do this, Lily."

"Dammit, Deacon, I don't have a choice."

"You always have a choice."

I planted my feet and shifted my stance, my arms crossed tight over my chest. "Fair enough," I said. "I choose Rose. I'm not failing her again."

"Lily—"

"No." I held up a hand, cutting him off. "You figure out what the lock is, where it is, how we find it, and we can have this argument again. Until then . . ." I drew in a breath. "Until then, I guess I'm a goddamned double agent."

"You're playing right into their hands."

"I have to," I said. "If I don't, Rose is dead." And at the end of the day, that was the bottom line. If I didn't help Johnson, my sister would die. To me, that made this a total no-brainer. Everything else was just window dressing.

"You don't get it, do you?" Deacon retorted. "She's dead anyway if we don't shut the gate. Kokbiel and Penemue—you don't want to be in their cross fire. They're strong. Stronger than you can imagine."

I lifted my chin. "Then I'll have to make myself stronger still."

He shook his head. "Not even possible. Not even if you killed every demon that already walks the earth. And once you have the pieces for the key, there will be no bargaining. No winning. Only death and failure. Accept it," he said. "Rose is collateral damage. Accept it, and help me find the only key that matters."

But I couldn't. I could never accept that.

And so I walked away from Deacon and aligned myself with my enemy.

FIVE

"You wanna tell me where you've been?" Clarence said. He was sitting cross-legged in front of my apartment door. "I've been calling and calling, and you're not even answering your damned cell phone."

"I turned it off," I said. "Sorry. I didn't think. I—" I ran my fingers through my hair and made an effort to look frazzled. It really wasn't hard. "I've had a rough day."

"Day? You've been gone for more than twenty-four hours. I've been pacing a damned path in this shit carpeting they've got in your hallway."

And the weird thing? There really was a worn pattern in the carpet. Not, I'm sure, because he was pacing with worry. More likely he was afraid his newly sworn Pawn of Evil had gone AWOL.

I slid my key in and opened the door. He slouched inside ahead of me, then plopped himself down in one of Alice's armchairs. "Make yourself at home," I mumbled.

He sighed, then kicked his feet up on an ottoman and took a long, slow breath. "Can't help it," he said. "I'm too damn relieved you're okay." His fedora was slanted down over his bulgy eyes, and stretched out like that, he looked less froglike than usual. He looked casual. He looked comfortable.

And I hated him all the more for waltzing into my life and looking like an ordinary guy. Because he wasn't ordinary. He was evil. He was the frog-faced little worm who'd gotten me into this whole mess, and before this thing was over, I would see him dead.

Not now, though, I thought, even as the weight of my blade in the thigh holster tempted me. *Not now, because I've made a deal with an even worse devil.*

What was it they said about the devil you knew?

Briefly, I wondered if I wasn't screwing up big-time by not telling Clarence what Johnson was up to. Tell Clarence, and get him and Penemue working behind the scenes to figure out a way to get Johnson out of Rose. And they'd do it, too, because I was Prophecy Girl. The über-warrior chick with Rand McNally blood.

More than that, there was no way they'd want Johnson and Kokbiel to succeed with their plan.

I was tempted. So, so tempted.

But in the end I kept my mouth shut.

Being a double agent was one thing, but I wasn't sure I had it in me to be a triple agent. More than that, I simply wasn't willing to take the risk. Because if I took it and failed, I'd pay with Rose's life. And that was unacceptable.

So instead of saying anything to Clarence, I did what I was supposed to do: I played it cool.

I drew in a breath and tried to act like a girl whose entire system of reality hadn't once again been turned askew. A girl whose sister hadn't been violated by a demon.

A girl who wasn't slowly, with every kill, becoming the thing she most despised.

"So?" he said, his arms tossed out to the sides, his shoulders rising in a deep shrug.

"Uh . . ."

"Your story? Where have you been? Egan's dead," he said, referring to Alice's uncle. "There's evidence of a ritual in the pub's basement, and you're nowhere to be found. So, yeah. I've been worried." He exhaled loudly. "Damn glad to see you're okay, but you scared the crap out of me. So where the hell have you been?"

Where I'd been wasn't a topic I intended to delve into in depth. Instead, I wanted to scream that I wasn't okay. That it would never be okay until I got my hands around Johnson's neck—*his* neck and not Rose's—and squeezed until I felt every last drop of life ooze out of him. I wanted to take a knife and gut him. I wanted his blood spilled, and I wanted to be the one to spill it.

"Yo? You gonna answer my question?"

I blinked, realizing that Clarence had not only stood up and moved to the window, but that he'd been talking, and I hadn't been listening. "What question?"

"I talk, talk, talk. But do you listen? Nope. I'm only Clarence, your handler, your mentor. Not like I'd be worried about you. Not like I'd—"

"*Clarence.* What question?"

"I asked where you've been. I asked what happened. Bodies all over the damn pub, and I can't find you anywhere."

"Bodies?" As far as I knew, there was only one body, Alice's uncle Egan, aka the man who murdered Alice. Once I'd figured that out, I wasn't terribly inclined to show him any sympathy. And, yeah, I killed him.

Not that I wanted Clarence to know that. Fortunately, Deacon and I had come up with a story that mixed fact with fiction. I only hoped it would fly.

"I've been with Rose," I said, keeping a keen eye on him as I gauged his reaction.

"Rose? Your sister Rose?" The shock on his face seemed legitimate, but I'd learned not to trust anything tossed at me by the little beast. "I thought I made it crystal clear that you gotta cut yourself off from your old life. You can't be Lily anymore. You need to let it go, kid."

"I did," I lied. "I have."

"And yet you went flouncing off to the Flats?" he retorted, referring to the Boston neighborhood where I'd grown up. "Doesn't sound to me like you're walking away from the old Lily."

"Rose came to me," I said. "She came to the pub." I paused, both for dramatic effect, and also because the truth still ate at me. She'd come to the pub looking for me. "She came, and the demons got her."

"What the fuck are you talking about?" Clarence asked, sounding genuinely perplexed. "I send you out to kill a demon. I don't hear from you for more than a day. And now you come back with some story about how the demons snatched your sister?"

"It's not a story," I said. "There were three of them, and they had Rose in a room in the basement strapped to a slab, and she was about to be some demon ass-hole's sacrifice."

"You're sure?"

"I was there," I said. "Hard to miss." I managed an offhand shrug. "Not like this is coming out of the blue, right? I mean, the pub's always had a freaky reputation." The Bloody Tongue—now half-owned by me in light of Egan's untimely demise—has been around for centuries and is a staple on Haunted Boston tours. Before I dipped my toe into the wonderful world of demons and hell and darkness and light, I'd assumed that was all hype and hoopla.

I'd assumed wrong.

Turned out that Alice's family had been deep into the dark arts for generations, and though Clarence had assured me that Egan scorned such devilish things, the

truth was exactly the opposite: Egan was in tight with
the demons, going so far as to pull homeless girls and
runaways off the street and sell them to the demons, a
little fact that had pissed off his sister, Alice's mother.
Her mom had been trying desperately to extricate herself from the family business, and her efforts were not
appreciated. When it became clear that she was going
to be trouble, Egan murdered his sister.

When the demons insisted that Egan provide them
with a specific girl for a sacrifice—his niece Alice—
he'd gone along, undoubtedly fearing their wrath more
than he loved his niece. What the demons didn't tell
him was that Alice was part of a whole big scheme to
create a fancy, schmancy warrior. All he knew was that
he sent his niece off to be a sacrificial lamb one Satur-
day night. And on Monday evening, her body came
strolling back into the pub for her shift. Granted, the
new Alice was me, but Egan didn't know that.

To keep Egan from asking a bunch of messy questions, the demons did what I actually considered a pretty
smart thing: They told Egan the sacrifice had failed, that
Alice was tainted goods, and that Egan needed to provide another. When Rose had wandered in looking for
Alice, Egan had snatched the opportunity and delivered
my little sister to the demons.

"So tell me exactly what happened," Clarence said.
He was leaning forward, his brow furrowed, which had
the effect of making his eyes bulge out even more than
usual.

"Rose called while I was fighting the demon priest." *There* was a big fat lie. I'd killed a priest, all right, but he hadn't been demonic. "And by the time I checked my messages, it was too late. She'd already left her house."

"What was the message?"

"She was going to the pub and wanted me to meet her there." Not an outright lie, but the real truth was that I'd already learned about the sacrifice and was racing to the pub to stop it when I got Rose's message.

"And she was there," Clarence said.

"I didn't see her right away, but Deacon Camphire was there."

"The filthy demon got ahold of your sister," Clarence said, instilling so much fury into his voice that I almost broke out into applause at his stellar acting abilities.

"Guess so," I said, saying a silent apology to Deacon, despite the fact that he and I had planned out my cover story for Clarence long ago. Even when I'd been planning to kill Clarence, I'd still needed a solid story. Because to kill a beast like Clarence, you had to be sneaky. And you had to get close.

"I know for a fact Deacon killed Egan," I added. "I saw him over the body, but he took off. Got away before I could slam my knife through his slimy, black heart." Okay, maybe that was pouring it on a little thick. "Anyway," I continued, hurrying on before he could put too much thought into my story, "Egan told me that they'd taken a girl downstairs. And when I ran down, I found two demons standing over Rose, and there was someone else escaping out the back."

Once again, I saw surprise flash in his eyes. "Do you know who?"

"I'm going to go out on a limb and guess it was a demon."

"Lily, this is—"

"She's staying with me," I said, my voice flat and firm and designed to brook no argument.

"No. I don't think—"

"She stays," I said. "She stays, and I protect her. She was supposed to be sacrificed to demons, Clarence. You think they're just going to give up on her? She's in their sights now, and no way am I leaving her unprotected."

Clarence was shaking his head slowly from side to side. "I can't agree to that."

"It's not your choice," I said firmly. "I killed the demon priest before he could open the gate, right? I think I'm entitled to a little leeway here. And what I want is to keep an eye on my sister."

"She has a father. You can't just pull her away—"

"Joe isn't going to give a flip," I said, my heart light in my chest. Because my alcoholic stepfather really wouldn't care. I'd won. I knew it, and Clarence knew it. All I needed was for him to acknowledge it.

"It's not a good idea."

"It's a great idea," I countered. The point was non-negotiable.

"I can't allow it."

I smiled broadly, pretending I hadn't heard him. "Then it's settled. I'll keep doing your kill-the-demon errands, and you let Rose move in with me."

"I don't like it," he said.

"Get used to it," I countered.

He stared at me, hard. Then his head tilted slowly to the side. "What else have you been up to?"

I swallowed, hoping my face didn't show my guilt. "Nothing. What do you mean?"

"You're thinking one hell of a lot softer these days, Lily," he said. "What did you do?"

"Oh?" I pretended shock. "No way? You mean you really can't get into my mind anymore? I don't have to sing 'Conjunction Junction' in my head to keep you out of my thoughts?" From the first second I'd known him, Clarence had had the ability to poke around in my head. An ability I'd thwarted by going out and killing a Secret Keeper demon—a fortuitous kill, as that was how I'd learned about the plan to sacrifice a girl in the pub basement.

I had no intention of telling that to Clarence, however.

"I didn't do anything." I shrugged, hoping for casual. "Maybe it's a little present to me for a job well-done. The Big Boss giving me my privacy."

His lips thinned, but his expression was thoughtful. Maybe my suggestion wasn't outside the realm of possibility.

"What's the matter," I pressed. "Don't you trust me?"

I waited one beat, then another. Finally, he nodded. "Of course I trust you. I'm just used to hearing all the prattle from your mind buzzing around me. It's damn quiet in here now."

I rolled my eyes, my entire body sagging in relief. "And Rose? We're cool there, right? She stays with me."

I held my breath, waiting for his response. Finally, he nodded. "But you're Alice," he said. "Not Lily. You're not that girl's dead sister."

"Sure thing," I said. "No problem."

"Did she see the demons? When you killed them? Did she see them melt away?"

I shook my head. "She'd passed out by then. No worries about explaining demon goo to my little sister."

"What about explaining who she is to Rachel? Alice's sister will wonder when you bring a young girl home. And what about taking care of her while you're at the pub? Finding someone to watch over her while you're off fighting demons?"

"Well, listen to you," I said. "You've really got the lowdown on child care. But she's fourteen, not six. And I swear I'll work it out." Of course, I was going to have to break the news to Johnson that he would have to fake being fourteen. I stifled a wicked grin. Finally, something I was looking forward to.

"I suggest you put some thought into the care and feeding of your sister. I need you focused, Lily."

"See, this is what I don't get," I protested. "When

you first sold me this gig, you told me I was the girl who could prevent the gate from opening. That I'd stop the Apocalypse. You said that was my mission. My purpose."

"And it was," Clarence said, his expression slightly concerned, as if he wasn't sure where I was going with this.

"I did all that," I said, working to keep the rage and self-loathing out of my voice. Because I *didn't* do that, as Clarence damn well knew. "So why aren't I done? Lily Carlyle," I said in a newscaster-style voice, "you just saved the world. What are you going to do now?" I peered hard at Clarence. "I should be going to Disneyland, not working harder."

"You locked the Ninth Gate, kid," he said, his lie making me sick to my stomach. "And a big high five to you. But you think that solved all our problems? You think the world is all peachy keen now?"

I had to agree it was not, and I tried not to hold my breath as I waited for him to tell me about my new mission, searching for this funny little key that would *lock* the gates shut. Yeah, right.

"Like I said. We got work. We got demons on the streets, infiltrating themselves into the lives of the innocent. And, yeah, we got demons plotting another Armageddon."

"The fun never stops," I said. "What are they up to?"

"The other eight gates," he said. "They're running

around trying to figure out how to open them before the convergence."

I grinned. Score one for the cynical girl.

"Is that even possible?" I asked, keeping my face serious, my expression concerned. "I thought they were locked tight."

"It's not easy," he said. "But it's possible. And we need to make sure it doesn't happen."

"How?"

"They're looking for a key," he said. "The *Oris Clef.* This one unlocks all the gates," he said. "The three pieces are scattered, but once they're assembled, we're talking some serious mojo."

"Oh," I said, actually impressed that Clarence wasn't trying to hide the basic nature of our quest from me. "So what's our plan?"

He grinned at me, then said exactly the words I wanted to hear. "Give me your arm, Lily. Because we're going to find those pieces first."

SIX

I used my own knife to slice my palm, then smeared my blood over the flat edge of the blade. As Clarence muttered an incantation, I ran the blade down the soft interior of my right forearm, causing two strange symbols to rise on my flesh, the pain as my flesh was seared making me grit my teeth and squeeze my fingers and toes together. A second swipe of blood cooled the pain, though, and I opened my eyes to peer down at the symbols, the first, an Aztec-looking circle. The second, a series of lines and squiggles crammed tight into an area roughly the shape of a triangle.

"I'm running out of arm," I said, knowing we still needed the third symbol for the third piece of the *Oris Clef*.

"No worries. We've got your whole body to work with."

"Great. If the demon-killing gig goes under, I can always join the circus."

He tapped my other arm, and I held it out, ready for yet another demonic tat. "You gonna let me do it this time?"

"You know how to call up the symbols?" he asked.

"No," I admitted, though I realized it would be a good idea for me to figure that out. I wasn't sure where one went to learn basic body-map-symbol-raising skills—maybe a Learning Annex course?

Wincing a little, I once again smeared the flat edge of my blade with the blood, then passed the blade to Clarence, who drew the blood down my forearm, all the while muttering the strange, foreign incantation. I cringed, anticipating the familiar burn as the blood seared a new locator into my flesh, then exhaled as another swipe of my blood over the by-then-visible design quelled the pain.

"What is it?" I asked, peering at the strange, geometric marks now burned into my flesh. An odd square, the lines inside seeming to collapse in on themselves as with a spiral descending to a point. A triangle in which another upside-down triangle was embedded. And a design that seemed to resemble a tic-tac-toe board, with dots in the outer squares and the image of an eye in the center.

"The three pieces," he said, voicing what I already knew. "Each design represents one of the three pieces of the *Oris Clef.*"

"And all three images rose on my arm," I said thoughtfully. "So that means the pieces still exist. That they're in this dimension." My learning curve about the Rand McNally me thing was pretty steep, and one of my first lessons was that my hyped-up blood could only latch onto things that were in this dimension. No locating lost relics that had been hidden forever within the demon realm.

I scowled down at the image burned onto my flesh. This next bit was the part I really didn't like. "You ready?"

"Go on in," he said.

I nodded, disconcerted by the fact that Clarence was now my anchor back to reality. Before, I'd believed he worked for the angels. Now I knew the true nature of the creature who was watching my back.

No helping it, though. Trying not to think about what could go wrong, I closed my palm over the square, then waited for the sharp tug near my navel.

It didn't come.

I looked up at Clarence and shrugged. "You sure you got that incantation right?"

"I did," he said, bouncing a bit in agitation. "I know I did. Try again. Try again right now."

"Right." This time, I went with the next image—the triangle. Again, nothing. "No way," I said, thinking of

Rose and the way Johnson was surely going to freak out completely if I returned to the motel without even a solid lead. "Something's wrong. You did something wrong."

"Try the last one," he said, his voice tight.

I wasn't expecting anything, but I did what he asked, slapping my hand over the tic-tac-toe board—and getting yanked off my feet by the hard jerk of an invisible thread pulling me down, down, down into the board.

"Clarence!" I called out as I clutched his hand tight. I'd done this twice before, and I still wasn't used to it. I knew that when I was finished on the other side, I could touch my arm again, and the portal would reopen and Clarence could pull me back. I'd never actually *done* that, having missed my return journey both times before. But I knew how it worked, and intellectually, I was with the program.

Emotionally, though, I felt all alone and lost in the rush of wind as I moved through dark, swirling mists and thick, velvety blackness.

This was the scariest part. The nothingness. The loneliness. This was where I feared getting stuck, and until I passed through to the other side, I was pretty much a wreck.

In front of me, the darkness began to move. At first, the changes were difficult to discern, but the mist moved as well, and soon I could see the mists mixing with the black, faster and faster, until the mists and the blackness formed a vortex, and I was sucked in, closer and closer, until I was finally thrust through the middle and emerged into a blinding white light.

I blinked and realized I was looking at a huge expanse of sky. I shifted, rolling over, and discovered that I was floating above rocky terrain into which someone had carved buildings. I tried to shift to get a better look, but I couldn't manage. Not this time.

I was looking—or trying to look—at the place where one of the pieces of the *Oris Clef* had been stashed. On my last two trips I'd been dumped unceremoniously into the middle of the target location. This time, however, I couldn't even get a clear view, much less get close. Somehow, the relic was being protected even from me and my supersecret decoder skin. And didn't that suck the big one?

I frowned, trying to find some additional clue. Because if I couldn't get there through a portal in my arm, I was going to have to use the old-fashioned method of taking a plane. But to where? Buildings carved into rock weren't common, but they also weren't rare, and without some idea where exactly the key was, I could be bouncing all over the globe trying to find my vision. Good for frequent flyer miles, not so good for my sanity. Or my sister.

Trouble was, I saw nothing. I was too far above the site, and yet I had no range of motion. Nothing, that was, except for flipping over and looking at the sky again. And since I had no better idea, that was what I did right then. Maybe the sky held a clue. But when I looked, all I saw was a whitewashed blue that shifted to black as the sun set before my eyes.

The stars came out, winking and twinkling, and I lay there, floating on a current of air and thinking that I had never once in all my life seen the stars so clearly. After a while, they didn't even look like stars anymore. They looked like drawings. Like sketches. And soon all that was left as I looked was a square chunk of space that was filled with what looked like a hand-drawn map of the very stars I'd been watching.

And that, I thought, was weird.

I tried to commit the image to memory, but visual recall was never my strong suit, and before I could even take a second look to bolster the image in my mind, that damn tug was back, as if a giant hook had emerged from my gut, grabbed hold of the skin around my belly button, and pulled me back inside. Hard and fast, and there was Clarence, both hands holding tight to my own, and his face beaded with sweat.

"What?" I asked in alarm. "What happened?"

"Felt like I was losing you a couple of times."

"I couldn't get a good view," I said. "It was like the place was protected or something."

Clarence ran stubby fingers through his sweaty mass of hair. "So now we know. We're more careful next time."

I swallowed. *Next time.* And there would be no avoiding it. I had to play along because if I didn't, Rose was dead.

"Could you see anything?"

I told him, trying hard to describe the strange image in the sky and the unusual buildings in the hillside. "They were all carved into the stone," I said, my eyes closed so I could picture it better. "But one building seemed to emerge from the top. I think I recognized it."

His eyes lit. "You know the location?"

"No, I mean the type of building. It was one of those—what do they call them?—like in Chinese action imports. *Once Upon a Time in China* and all that." Movies & More, my place of employment before I got into this new demon-killing gig, had a huge collection of Asian action flicks, and I loved them all. For that matter, with my sword and magic map arm, I almost felt like a character out of one of them. The tragic heroine trying hard for redemption, and in those movies, the good guy always won.

The thought gave me a moment of peace. At least until I remembered the demons whose essence I absorbed daily. Maybe I wasn't so much the good guy after all.

"So that's it," I said with a shrug. "Like I said, I couldn't get close. Is it enough? Can you figure out where it is? Do you have a jet? A private plane?"

"I think perhaps a bridge will do the job better."

I frowned. A *bridge* was the name he'd given to the way I'd always gone through my arm to end up at a place. "I just told you it didn't work."

"That doesn't mean we can't conjure another bridge.

A stand-alone. Using the map on your arm as a destination marker."

"That will work?"

"Possibly," he said thoughtfully. "Possibly."

"Oh." I wasn't sure what to say to that. On the one hand, I wanted to get the damn relics and get it over with. On the other, I didn't want to be walking a bridge through other dimensions if we weren't absolutely sure where I was going to come out on the other side. I mean, I'm a big fan of Space Mountain and all, but the dark on my freaky arm bridge isn't just an absence of light; it's an utter void, without time or space or light or anything, and you're all alone, trapped with the thought that if the other side of the bridge closes off, you'll be stuck there forever, lost in nothingness for eternity.

Talk about your scary bedtime stories.

"Clarence," I said, this time more urgently. "You won't do it unless you're certain, right?"

"Hmm?" He looked up at me, distracted. "Oh. Right. Of course." He tapped my arm. "The protections are a bit troubling, but on the whole they were to be expected. No, it's the other two images I'm worried about. Or the absence of images." Without asking, he yanked my arm toward him.

"Hey!"

"Touch them again."

I did what he asked, even though I wanted to smack him for bossing me around. Then again, bossing me around was what he did best.

We both looked at my arm. Nothing.

"Maybe there's an order," I said. "Maybe after we get the piece from the buildings in the hill, the other images will pop to life."

His eyes went wide, impressed, and he tapped the side of his nose. "Listen to you," he said. "You just may be right." He puffed out his cheeks and exhaled noisily. "Okay, I'll do some research, find the location, and we'll put together a game plan for going in."

I cocked my head, taking devious pleasure from the fact that I was about to antagonize him. "How come we need a game plan? The pieces are under guard, right?"

"We presume so," he said, looking puzzled. "It is also possible they are simply well hidden."

"Oh." I hadn't considered that maybe the pieces were basically buried treasure. "But if they are guarded, then aren't we on the same side as the guards? We're all the good guys, right? Trying to keep the pieces away from the demons?"

Uncertainty played over the lying little frog's face. Then it cleared, and he sucked in a breath, going, "Ohhhhh. I see your confusion."

I crossed my arms over my chest, wanting so badly to tell him that I knew the truth that my stomach hurt. I wanted to scream at him. Instead, I said, "Confusion?"

"If they exist, those who guard the pieces will be neither good nor bad, neither friend nor foe."

"Huh?"

"They have one purpose only," Clarence said, "and

that's to keep the pieces safe. Warriors," he said, "who would not give up the pieces even to the Archangel Gabriel himself."

I hated the fact that I didn't know if he was telling me the truth. Because what he said sounded perfectly reasonable. "But then why are we even going after them? Won't these warriors keep the pieces out of the demons' hands?"

"With the approach of the convergence, the demon population is desperate. Many will be willing now to try anything to obtain the *Oris Clef* and the power it wields. Their assault will be brutal and deadly, and if the relic is there, the demons will find it, warrior guards or not. Make no mistake, Lily, either as to the extent to which the demons will go or to the breadth of their power." He drew in a breath. "The only way to protect the pieces is to take them. Take them, and destroy them."

I knew damn good and well that he had no intention of destroying them, and his smarmy "beat the demons" attitude made me want to gag. At the same time, it occurred to me that Kokbiel and Penemue probably weren't the only ones looking. Surely there were other big-shot demons looking to be king of the universe. An inconvenient fact that still brought a smile to my face. Bring them on. The more I killed, the more powerful I'd become.

Except how did those demons know where to look? The question turned my smile to a frown, and I posed my question to my demonic froggy handler. "I mean, they don't have my arm," I said in conclusion. "So what are the demons using to find the relics of the key?"

"You," he said. "The demons will seek out you."

I swallowed. I was strong—and getting stronger—and I had that nice immortality thing going for me. But that didn't mean I was invincible, or impervious to pain. And being immortal didn't mean I couldn't lose. It only meant that if I did lose, I'd have a long, long, long time to think about it.

Not that I intended to show any fear or doubt in front of Clarence. Instead, I shot him my best haughty look. "I'm ready."

"Probably," he agreed. "But we're not taking any chances. You're too important," he added. "That's why you're not doing this solo. Lily, my girl," he said, his eyes bulging with pleasure, "from here on out, I'm teaming you up with a partner."

SEVEN

"A partner," I raged, bursting into the cheap motel room. "I can't pull this off with a partner watching my every move."

Deacon and Rose both looked up at me, his face hard behind dark glasses, hers soft and worried.

I focused on Deacon. "You're here." I'd expected him to be gone. I'd expected to walk into a room with a mouthless Johnson and my possessed sister.

As pissed as I'd been at him, I have to admit I was a little relieved. "Is she—"

"Normal," he said. "Right now, anyway. Hasn't said a word, but she's awake. Alert. And I haven't seen a hint of our friend since you left."

I snorted. "'Friend.' Yeah, right. Yours maybe." And though it was a joke, I was certain I saw Deacon flinch.

On the bed, Rose shifted. "Lily?"

I rushed to my sister and pressed my hands to her cheeks. I almost looked into her eyes, but at the last moment remembered and shifted my focus, staring instead at the pattern of six freckles on the curve of her nose. For a second, I considered going for it—peeking inside her mind. But I feared that if Lucas was in there, he would share the vision. Might even be able to get a grip on me mentally. I didn't know if that was an ability the demon bastard had, but I did know it wasn't a risk I was prepared to take. I was sickened enough that he'd gotten his hooks into Rose. No way was he getting them into me, too.

"Lily, what's going on? What's wrong with me? What did he do to me? I can feel him, in there, in me, and it's . . ." She trailed off into sobs, and there wasn't a damn thing I could do except hold her and pat her and promise it would be okay.

I'd made promises to Rose before. Promises I hadn't been able to keep. About this, though, I was determined.

"Where is he?" I asked. "Is he listening? Is he inside, watching it all? Laughing at us?"

"He's dormant," Deacon said. "And there's no way to know if he hears."

I squeezed my sister tighter, determined not to treat her differently. Determined not to think about the fact that when I was touching her, I was touching Lucas Johnson.

As she pressed her face against my shoulder, I looked up at Deacon, suddenly realizing who we were missing from our little party. "Where's the rest of him?"

"Gone," Deacon said, his expression as dark as his tone.

"Are you insane? You let him go?"

He pulled off his glasses, and for the first time I saw the dark bruise rising over his left eye. "*I* didn't." He shifted his steely gaze from me to Rose, and as he did, my stomach did a complicated acrobatic move as I realized that Rose—or rather Johnson—had freed the mouthless body.

"Out of respect for you, Lily, I didn't hurt her body. But rein in your new pet, because if that prick touches me again, I swear I will tear through the body to get to the beast inside."

I shivered, because I believed him. I even sympathized with him. But if he touched a hair on Rose's head, I knew that I would end him.

Impasse, much?

I blew out a noisy breath, then pressed a kiss to Rose's forehead before getting up and pacing. Because I had to move. I couldn't think if I didn't move, and right then I really needed to think.

"I'm serious," I said, deciding the only way to deal with Deacon's threats against my sister's body was to push them aside and hope we never got that far. "It's one thing for me to play double agent if I'm working by myself. I can pretend to lose a battle. I can wing it. I can somehow figure out a way to keep my cover without killing the good guys."

"You can't do that with a partner."

"I know." Even though Clarence had assured me that those guarding the relics would be neither good nor bad, I didn't believe him. Why would he tell me the truth about this one thing when everything else had been a lie?

I couldn't think of a single reason, and that suggested to me that my suspicions were true: The guards were innocents, and I was meant to kill them.

Collateral damage, I thought, my stomach twisting at the words. Wasn't that what Deacon had called Rose? Collateral damage.

She wasn't, however, collateral to me.

I'd killed before to keep her safe. I could do it again.

"I'll make it work," I said aloud. "I'll figure out a way not to kill." Or I'd try. But if push came to shove, I was doing whatever it took to stay alive. To get the *Oris Clef.*

To get back my sister.

"Dammit, Lily . . ."

"No," I said, shaking my head. "It's worth it."

His eyes cut to Rose, and I could see the frustration envelop him like a dark cloud. "Rose can't be your first priority," he said. "Not now. Not anymore."

"You know what, Deacon," I said, moving to stand in front of him. "Fuck you. Fuck you and your visions

and your redemption. You think you're the only one
who's been to hell? I'm living here, every single day.
I've got demons breathing down my neck, pulling my
strings like a puppet. First Clarence, then Johnson, and
now you. It's my decision, dammit. Mine."

"Then make the right one."

I lifted my hand to slap him, for no particular reason
other than that I needed to blow off steam.

He caught my wrist and held it, and damned if he
didn't look me right in the eyes. I felt the pull of the
vision, my breath ripping out of me from the force of
it. And then, just as the vision was about to suck me in,
I heard Deacon's harsh, "No," then felt the shock of his
mouth closing over mine.

He took me—claimed me—the intimacy overwhelming despite the fact that we touched nowhere except lips
and hands and wrists. His mouth was heat and male
and delicious sin, and I wanted to drown in it. Wanted
to forget the freak show that was my life.

Wanted to forget that my sister—and a demonic
invader—was sitting not five feet away, watching with
slack-jawed wonder.

I jerked my head, breaking the kiss, my eyes finding
Rose, who was, as I'd imagined, staring in our direction, her expression a mixture of awe and longing.

I drew in ragged gasps of air as I faced Deacon, my
head shaking. "I can't do it," I said. "I can't do what
you want. You prove to me the lock's really out there,
and I'll consider it. You figure out a way to get Lucas

out of Rose, and I'm totally open to other game plans. But until then, I'm working this gig. Until then, I'm protecting my sister."

"This is about more than your sister."

"Maybe," I admitted. "But I can't save the world. I tried that once, and I failed. But I can save Rose, and I'm not going to walk away from that."

He stared at me for a moment, then nodded. "You've made your decision."

"I have."

"And I've made mine." He put the glasses on and took a step toward the door.

I hurried toward him. "What are you doing?"

"I told you," he said. "I'm not standing around and watching you do this. You want to play welcoming committee for the Apocalypse, you do it by yourself."

He paused in the open threshold, his body silhouetted by the afternoon sun, the light making him look like exactly the kind of angelic helper I needed.

Too bad he was just the opposite.

"I do have one idea," he said, but he wasn't looking at me. He was looking at Rose, and my heart lightened just a bit.

"An idea?"

"Maybe. It's risky. But maybe . . ." He trailed off with a shake of his head, then stepped out onto the sidewalk.

"Wait!" I hurried forward. "That's it? You're leaving?" My heart twisted at the thought. I might not completely trust him, but I wanted him around. And not just because Deacon Camphire had gotten under my skin. I wanted him watching my back, and it irked me that that wasn't going to happen. "You're really walking out on me?"

His smile was grim. "I'll be around, Lily." He shot a quick glance toward Rose. "There's no way I'm letting Kokbiel get his hands on that key. So I'll be back. But you may not be happy to see me."

EIGHT

I sped through the late-afternoon traffic on my vintage Triumph Tiger, Rose's arms around my waist and her face pressed tight against my back. There was fear in her grip, and so help me, I was glad. Glad to be scaring my little sister by going too fast on the motorcycle she'd never liked and had always refused to ride.

Because so long as she was scared, she wasn't Johnson. And so long as she wasn't Johnson, her touch didn't nauseate me.

"What are we doing, Lily?" she asked, as I idled at a red light.

"Alice," I said. "You have to call me Alice. And I told you. I have to make things right with Joe."

"Oh. Right. I remember." But her words were fuzzy, as if she was picking over complicated memories. I fought the urge to ditch the bike, pull her into my arms, and promise her that I'd get things back to normal. I couldn't, though. That was all I'd ever done—make promises. Now I had to act on them.

I reached our shabby neighborhood of run-down clap-board houses with neglected lawns and beer-can yard or-naments. Once upon a time, our house had been tended, our mother making sure the paint was crisp and clean and the plants watered and blooming. A comfy swing with plumped-up pillows once dominated the front yard only a few yards away from a neatly printed sign that announced, *The Carlyle Residence—Welcome!*

Now the sign was weathered and nearly unreadable, and the swing was stained with rust, the cushions dot-ted with mildew. The place felt dull and lifeless, and for the first time I was truly happy to have a new life. A new home. Even a new me.

I killed the bike's engine. "Come on," I said to Rose.

She dragged her teeth over her lower lip. She was nervous. She was Rose. And I couldn't be happier about that.

As we walked toward the front door, I wondered vaguely why Johnson had retreated. Had I done some-thing to make him pull back? Could I do it again on purpose?

Not that I had much time to ponder these inscrutable questions. Our house is not a mansion, the approaching sidewalk not a private drive, and we had reached the porch in six long strides. "Will he be home?" I asked, for the first time remembering that Joe had a job. An easy thing to forget considering that, after my mother had died, he'd spent more time on the couch than he had framing houses and installing drywall.

Rose shrugged. "Usually is, 'specially since you died." Her forehead creased at that, but she didn't look too freaked.

I grimaced, guilty once again. My decision to go out and kill Johnson that night had affected more than just my life. I'd been selfish, and now I was paying the price. Big-time.

We climbed the steps, and I rapped hard on the door with my left hand. My right hand was otherwise occupied, as Rose had snaked her fingers through mine and was squeezing tight. I understood why; she wanted this. Wanted to leave with me even as much as I wanted her by my side.

Joe hadn't always been a shit—when he'd married my mom, he was actually kind of cool. I remember him giving me piggyback rides and taking me and Mom for long rides in his convertible.

All that had changed after my mom had died. The Joe I'd liked had been replaced by the Joe who drank. The Joe who sometimes hit. The Joe I would have completely walked away from but for the fact that Rose was stuck living with him, and I'd promised my mother that I'd look after my little sister.

I was beginning to think he'd actually sucked it up and gone to work when I saw movement behind the glass of the front door. Moments later, I could make out his form, distorted through the frosted glass. "Whaddya want?" he demanded.

I cocked my head at Rose, silently giving her the floor.

"It's me. I'm, um, I'm back."

The lock rattled, and the door creaked open, revealing Joe in filthy jeans and a stained wife-beater. I'd expected him to at least appear relieved. To look at Rose with concern, silently checking her out for cuts and bruises. She was only fourteen, after all, and she'd been gone for over a day.

He did none of that. Instead, he hocked back a wad of spit, then let it fly into the yard. "You forget your key, little girl?" He swung his head toward me, the motion exaggerated from the drink I could now smell on his breath. He looked me up and down, and I shifted uncomfortably, realizing that it might have been a good idea to change clothes. I was still in grimy jeans, an equally filthy tank top, and my red-leather duster. As a rule, the coat hid the knife I had strapped to my thigh. Right then, though, because of the way I was standing, I could see the hilt peeking out. Joe probably could, too.

He met my eyes. "I know you?"

"I'm—I mean, I *was*—a friend of Lily's."

"Huh." He looked between the two of us. "Well, come on in."

Rose looked at me, and I shrugged. Then we followed him inside, though "follow" isn't exactly accurate, as he was already down the long hallway to the living room. By the time we reached it, he was in his favorite chair, his feet on the ottoman and a football game playing on the screen.

He saw me staring. "Classic," he said. "Cowboys trampled the Redskins. A goddamned thing of beauty."

"Right. Um, listen. There's something I wanted to ask you."

"Shoot," he said, lifting the remote and increasing the volume.

"I want to take Rose home with me for a while. I, um, think Lily would have liked that. And I think it would be good for Rose," I added, continuing my spiel at the speed of light, afraid that if he interrupted with a question or an argument, that I wouldn't have a good response, and I'd lose before I'd even begun. "I mean, she's got some pretty nasty memories here—her mom, then that stuff with Lucas Johnson, and now her sister getting killed. And I think it would be really good for her to get some distance, and I'm completely responsible and my apartment's in a good neighborhood. She'll have to take an incomplete this semester from school, but I really think it's for the best and, well, that's it."

He hadn't moved a muscle during my speech, just kept his eyes glued to the television, his finger resting over the pause button on the remote. For a moment, I feared he hadn't even heard me, and I was going to have to go through the whole spiel again. More likely, he'd just say no. After all, he didn't know Alice Purdue from Adam.

But then he pressed the button to freeze the screen, and he turned to me. "All right, then," he said, before unpausing the picture and sliding back into his game.

That was it: "All right, then." And I wasn't sure if I should be happy it went over so easy, disgusted that he cared so little for his own daughter that he would wave her out the door with a near stranger, or sad for this man who had so little capacity for dealing with the blows that life had dealt him.

Not that I was inclined to hang around philosophizing. He'd handed Rose to me on a platter. Time to get out before he changed his mind.

I found her in her bedroom, shoving clothing into a duffel bag. "Don't take too much," I said. "We can always come back and get more."

She looked up, her expression bland. "We can always buy more," she corrected.

She stood and started to zip the bag. She stopped, though, then moved across the room to the small wooden desk that we'd painted the summer before she'd turned twelve. A cluster of framed pictures littered the desktop, and she picked one, moving back to the duffel so quickly I barely caught the image: Me, Rose, our mom, and Joe. Happier times.

I met Rose's eyes, and she shrugged. Not really a whole lot we needed to say about that.

"Ready," she said, hauling the duffel up onto her shoulder.

I reached out and took it from her, easily hefting its weight. "I've got it."

She pressed her lips together, and I saw tears glistening in her eyes. "I know you do."

I opened my mouth, wanting to say that I was sorry—sorry for every horrible thing that had happened to her, sorry for failing to protect her, sorry for not being the sister to her that I knew our mom wanted me to be.

I didn't say any of that, even though I knew damn well the opportunity might soon be lost, that Johnson might be back any second. Instead, I just smiled, and said, "Come on."

With the duffel strapped onto the back of the bike and Rose crammed in behind me, I gunned the engine and took off down the road. Twilight had fallen while we were inside, and the world was painted in shades of gray, apropos of my mood.

Rose squeezed me tight around the waist but didn't complain, and I had the feeling she wanted away from that house as much as I did. There are all kinds of demons in the world, and not all of them come from hell. Those just happen to be easier to fight.

I rolled to a stop at a red light, idly revving the engine in time with my wild thoughts. The light changed, and I kicked the bike into gear, ready to peel out of the neighborhood.

I didn't make it.

Because suddenly this dim, empty street at the edge of the Flats wasn't so empty anymore. Suddenly, there was someone standing in the middle of the road.

He was huge—his head shaved bald, his face a mass of strange tattoos through which I could barely make out the cold, hard gleam of his eyes.

He stood, legs spread and arms flung out wide, and around him I swear the air seemed to ripple.

Then he reached back and pulled the most big-ass sword I'd ever seen from a scabbard on his back.

Holy shit. I didn't know what kind of demon this was, but I wasn't inclined to hang around and find out, not with Rose on the back of my bike.

"Go," she hissed, though I was already turning the handlebars to swing the bike around. "Leave."

I realized then that she wasn't Rose anymore. She was Johnson. And Johnson wanted out of there at least as much as I did.

I gunned it, the back tire fishtailing on the gritty street. And as I accelerated down the road, willing the bike to build up speed, I heard the beast behind me release a loud, hell-shattering war cry.

I didn't turn around, though I wanted to. Wanted to see this thing I was escaping. But I knew that if I *did* turn, we wouldn't get out of there. I had to keep going, keep moving, and I was trying—trying so damn hard— to will the bike faster.

No use.

We were about a block and a half away when the cry echoed again, this time followed by an odd *whoosh* and then the sharp *clank* of metal on metal.

The sound confused me, and it was only when we were skidding out of control that I realized the source— the warrior demon had heaved that sword, sending it flying down the street to intersect with the back tire of my bike.

Of course, by the time I realized this, there wasn't a damn thing I could do about it. The back tire locked up, the bike jerked, and though it all happened so fast that the details are a blur, somehow Rose and I ended up on the side of the road, with the bike on top of us—and our view down the street unimpaired.

A view that was dominated by that massive warrior demon, marching straight toward us, the lust for the kill shining bright in his eyes.

NINE

"Get it off! Get it off!" Rose screamed, even as I was scrambling to do that very thing. "It's burning me!"

Her leg was wedged under the exhaust pipe, and I was trying to move fast, but even über-girl-superchick strength wasn't instantaneous, and I'd landed at an off angle, meaning I was wasting precious seconds.

I twisted at the waist, leaving my legs trapped, and closed my hands over the gas tank. With one deep groan, I shoved up, ordering Rose to scoot backward as I did.

She didn't hesitate, and soon she was clear of the bike, the smell of burning denim and flesh wafting in the air as she moved.

"Lily! Hurry!"

In my peripheral vision, I could see her climbing to her feet, looking at something back the way we'd come.

I didn't need to turn to know what it was—the warrior demon was coming closer.

I drew in another breath and shoved again—hard—lifting the bike enough to free my own legs. I dragged myself back over the rough surface of the street, gravel cutting into my hands, my head twisting only once to gauge my enemy's approach.

Immediately, I wished I hadn't.

That sucker moved fast, and I grabbed Rose's hand, yanking her to her feet with me. "Run!"

She didn't hesitate, didn't argue, but she was limping, her burned leg slowing her down, and the demon was coming. Closer, closer . . .

"Go, Lily! Just go!"

"Are you out of your mind? I'm not leaving you."

"He'll come out," she said, and I knew she was referring to Johnson. "He'll come, and he'll fight. I'll be okay," she added, but from the pure terror on her face, I knew she didn't believe it.

Me either. In no form or fashion did I consider Johnson popping up inside her to save the day a good thing. No way, no how.

I yanked hard on her hand and pulled her behind me. I didn't want to do this—didn't want to fight with Rose right there—but he was coming too fast.

Time to make a stand.

I closed my hand around the hilt of my blade and

pulled it from its sheath. Behind me, Rose was saying, "No, no, no," over and over again.

"*You* run," I said. "I'll be okay." I steeled myself, holding my knife at the ready. "This is what they made me for." And, dammit, I hoped that was true. Because this demon was more fierce, more bold, more *everything* than any I'd faced before.

"No," she said. "I'm not—"

"Dammit, Rose, *run!*" She gawked at me, nodded, then scampered down the street, favoring her injured leg. I only watched for a second, then turned back to the warrior, now about three houses away. It had slowed its pace and was watching me, head tilted to one side as it took my measure.

"Come on, you son of a bitch," I murmured. "Let's get this over with."

And then, as if it had been waiting for the invitation, the demon rushed me, his strides eating up the pavement, moving so fast, I swear he was only a blur. I heard a sharp screech and smelled burning rubber, and as I thrust my knife forward, trying to find a damn target and fearing that I was about to be soundly and utterly destroyed, I had the absurd thought that the demon was moving so fast he was burning up the soles of his shoes, and that was the pungent odor that had caught my attention.

"Get in!"

Not his shoes, I realized. *A car.* It had careened to a stop behind me, and now the female driver was shouting at me through the open passenger-side window. I didn't hesitate, instead turning fast on my heel and diving headfirst through the open window, pushing a pile of weapons across the bench seat even as the demon reached out and grabbed my foot.

I kicked hard, then yanked my legs into the car. And into safety.

The girl hit the gas, and as I righted myself in the car, I saw the demon in the side mirror. He was standing there, his face a mask of fury and frustration beneath the blue and black tattoos.

"Rose!" I said, pointing to the side of the road, and my sister, now hobbling toward us. I thrust my leg over to the driver's side of the car, and slammed on the brake.

"Are you crazy?" the girl shouted as Rose yanked open the back door. The driver kicked my leg away and accelerated, but the pause had been enough—Rose was in the car, the door hanging open, but inside and safe.

I climbed over the seat and into the back, hanging half out of the speeding car as I grabbed for the door and slammed it shut.

"Is he still on us?" the girl asked, her short-cropped hair a pink blur as she whipped around to face me.

I pivoted to look out the back. "No." But only moments after I answered, the car shook, rubber burning on the asphalt as the car inched backward. "What the fuck?" I whipped back around to face the girl. "What the hell are you doing?"

"Me?" she retorted. "I thought you said he'd given up on us."

I looked back and saw that, sure enough, the demon was standing stock-still in the middle of the road, his arms outstretched, the air between his hands shimmering as if from a rising heat wave.

This wasn't good. This really, really, *really* wasn't good.

"Do something!" the girl shouted, as Rose cowered in the corner.

"What? What the hell am I supposed to do?"

"Distract him. Stop him. Slow him down. Something," she howled. "But do it now, because we're going nowhere fast, and he's getting closer."

Distract him? What the hell was I supposed to do? Strip naked and do the hula?

Probably not the best option, and instead I hung over into the front seat, scouring the weapons cache I'd barreled into when I'd first jumped into the car. I found a crossbow, hefted it, and pulled it into the backseat with me, along with a handful of arrows.

"Hurry!" the driver screamed. Beside me, Rose was still silent, but she'd turned around and was facing the back window, her expression worried.

I clenched my jaw, determined to wipe the fear from her face, and leaned out of the open window, the crossbow at the ready. The car was thrumming, vibrating, and it wasn't easy to aim, but I got the demon in my sights, aiming for the broad expanse of chest. I said a prayer and let the arrow fly, and it wasn't until the shaft was zipping through the air toward him that it occurred to me to wonder if that strange shimmer between his hands was impermeable. If it was—if the arrow bounced back uselessly—then I was going to have to go hand to hand with the big guy. And *that* idea was really not rocking my boat.

Figuring I was better off being proactive, I reached to reload the weapon—planning this time to aim for his face. A smaller target, but possibly a more accessible one.

Turned out my caution wasn't necessary, though, because even before I'd managed to slide the second arrow into place, the first struck home—and struck hard.

The demon released an earsplitting howl as the arrow slid through flesh—and as his hold on our car weakened. I felt a lurch, heard a *pop*, and suddenly we were free, and my mystery driver was shooting us like a rocket down the street.

"Holy shit, holy shit, holy fucking shit!" she kept saying, over and over, her eyes flicking up to meet mine in the rearview mirror every few seconds. Or maybe she wasn't looking at me. Maybe she was checking to see if we had a tail, something I kept doing, too, twisting around to look down the street behind us. So far, he wasn't coming. And so far, the car was still moving.

I took that as a good sign.

The driver spun the steering wheel, making a hard

right, then an immediate left, taking us onto a straight-away that she blasted down, going at least sixty miles over the posted speed limit. After a few minutes of that, she blew through a red light, careened into a parking lot, slammed on the brakes, then twisted in the seat, looking back at me and breathing hard.

"Whoa," she said. "I think we lost him."

"Yeah." I took a tentative glance out the back glass again. Nothing. Beside me, Rose had her eyes on the driver and one hand tight on the door handle.

"Hell of a way to meet," the girl with pink hair said, thrusting out a hand to me. "I'm Kiera. I'm your new partner."

TEN

"Partner?" I repeated. Okay, probably I should have guessed that one. After all, most Good Samaritans would at least blink at the sight of a behemoth demon attacking two girls in the street. And though a Samaritan would, by definition, stop to help, the odds were that said do-gooder wouldn't be transporting a weapons cache in the front seat of a battered Pontiac.

Then again, I was no longer Trusting Lily. By then, I was Edgy, Suspicious Lily, especially since I had Rose to protect.

I eyed her warily. "How'd you find me?"

"Clarence," she said. She shifted in the seat, leaning up against the driver's door and stretching leather-clad legs out on the battered bench seat, revealing an ankle holster sporting a very badass knife. "Said you were going to go see some dude about keeping a girl." She stretched, craning her neck so she could see over the back of the seat, then peering hard at Rose. "That the girl?"

"That's the one." I fought the urge to scoot protectively toward my sister. Then I wondered why the hell I was fighting. I slid over and pulled her close.

"Huh," Kiera said.

I bristled. And, yes, I know she'd saved my ass, but right then I wasn't entirely sure I liked her. "Huh, what?" I asked testily.

"Demon scent," she said, then flicked her eyes up and looked at me. Just looked at me, waiting for me to say something in response.

What the hell was I supposed to say? I went for the obvious: "Excuse me?"

Kiera's nose crinkled. "She's got some on her." She leaned closer, her nostrils flaring, as Rose shrunk back against the upholstery. "Huh. Can't get a handle on it."

After a moment of that, I pressed Kiera's shoulder and pushed her back. "Do you mind?" I said, hoping my voice sounded level. "She was strapped to a slab while the bastards did a number on her. Do you really have to go and remind her?"

"No shit?" Kiera cocked her head, and I kept my expression firm. Obstinate. Because she had to believe me. If she didn't—if she could tell that a demon was inside Rose—then I'd have to plead shock and ignorance. I might even get away with it. But Rose . . .

Well, she'd be in deep doo-doo. Because if Kiera

was a demon hunter—and she damn sure looked the part—then she'd take Rose out.

Or, at least, she'd try to. And that wasn't a battle I was keen on fighting.

"Bastard marked her," Kiera said, crossing her arms on the back of the bench seat and staring me down. "Lousy demon fucking marked her."

"Marked her?"

She lifted a shoulder. "Sometimes, all they want is a sacrifice, and any old body will do. Male, female, virgin, slut, doesn't much matter. But sometimes, the demon gives a flip, and he marks his prey." She leaned forward again, breathing deep. Then she looked up, her green eyes fixed on me. "Oh, yeah. If she got the scent after getting strapped down, then she was marked. Who is it? Who wants the girl?"

"I don't know," I said, reinforcing the lie by meeting her eyes dead on. "All I know is she was strapped down, and it was gnarly."

"Huh."

"Shouldn't we get moving again?" I looked backward out the window, but didn't see our warrior-demon buddy. "He might come back."

"Oh, he will," she said. "But he'll regroup first." She shifted her neck from side to side, sighing a little as it cracked. "But you're right. I'm ripped."

"Me, too," I said, happy for the opening to get on with the program and get out of there. I mean, I was thrilled she'd saved our butts—and, yeah, she seemed to be who she said she was—but I was double-agent girl now, and I was towing a demon-infested sister along beside me. Really not the time to play get-to-know-you with the new girl at the office. "Can you take us back to my bike?"

Her eyes went wide. "Good God, are you bagging on me?"

"No," I said. "I mean . . ."

"I think we both need to blow off some steam." She smiled wide, perfect white teeth flashing. "And Little Bit there can come along for the ride. Can't you, girl?"

Rose looked up at me, but I just shrugged, a mixture of acquiescence and befuddlement.

"So we're settled," Kiera said. She turned back around, jerked the car into gear, and peeled out of the parking lot.

She cruised around, getting deeper and deeper into the kinds of neighborhoods even I used to avoid—and we're talking even back in the days when I wasn't above selling a little smack to make an extra buck. She slid the Pontiac into a space in front of a hole-in-the-wall diner with a sputtering neon sign out front announcing they served "Good Food," but only the G, an O, and a D were lit up.

Personally, I doubted God dined there. Unless God was keen on salmonella poisoning and rat droppings in the hamburgers. But then again, what did I know? We clambered inside and slid into one of the booths, Rose and I on one side, and Kiera surveying us both from the other.

She lifted her arm and snapped, then pointed her finger at the table. Moments later, an emaciated waitress with matching nose and eyebrow rings delivered us water and coffee. I took a sip, discovered the coffee wasn't nearly as bad as I'd expected, and settled back against the mutilated vinyl booth.

"Okay, partner," she said. "Tell me all about you."

I glanced sideways at Rose, who was staring at Kiera, her elbow on the table and her chin propped on her fist. I shifted my gaze back to Kiera and shrugged. "Not much to tell."

Her brows lifted in an obvious expression of disbelief. "Uh-huh," she said, but she didn't press. Instead, she focused on Rose. "So how you doing, Little Bit?"

Rose tilted her head down and mumbled to the table. "Okay. He's hiding."

"He?" Kiera's sharp eyes found mine. "Who's he?"

"I'm guessing our friend with the supersuction hands," I said, and as Kiera lifted her arm and waved the waitress back over, I willed myself not to shoot my little sister a look of deep recrimination. At the same time, I couldn't help but wonder about her words. Why would Johnson disappear around this girl? The way I figured it, he'd want to stay around. Learn about his enemy's assets. And from what little I knew of Kiera, I already considered her a pretty strong addition to Penemue's team.

I cocked my head as a theory played at my mind. "So you can smell demons, huh? Just your generic demon, or can you pick out a particular one?"

She took a long sip of coffee, then rolled her shoulders. "Depends on how good a whiff I get, and whether I've met the little bastard before. This one," she added with a wave toward Rose, "whoever that was didn't stick around long. Marked her and skedaddled. Not a lot of scent there."

"Too bad," I said, trying to keep my voice steady. "I would have liked to know what demon had a hard-on for her."

She shrugged. "You work with what you got."

That you do. And right then, I was working with some very gnarly theories, starting with the jumping-off point that Johnson had disappeared, or at least that he'd buried himself deep, deep, deep inside of Rose. And now I had to wonder if he was afraid that Kiera and her demon-sniffing nose would recognize him.

I remembered what Johnson had said about no matter where he wandered, he still served Kokbiel, and the pieces began to fall into place. I might be the current double agent in tonight's little drama, but I had a feeling that dubious honor had once fallen on Johnson's head. More to the point, I was thinking that he'd once worked with Clarence, pretending to be on the Penemue team. And considering it was Penemue who'd ended up with the prophetical champion—me—on his team, I think my hypothesis had a lot of weight. Especially when you add to the equation the fact that Johnson had done most of the dirty work to get me here.

It was Lucas who'd taunted my sister until I couldn't stand it any longer. And it was Lucas who had smiled at me, oh so victoriously, when I'd pulled the trigger and slammed a bullet through his heart.

Johnson hadn't sought out Rose because he was a pedophile and she's pretty.

He'd sought her out because of me. Because they needed me. Because I was the one who had to die.

Why me, though?

Had I done something? Had my mother, my father?

I honestly had no idea, and the idea that it might simply be the cosmic luck of the draw didn't sit well with me. I wanted a *reason* that I'd been thrust into this horror. Someone to blame. Something concrete.

And the reality that I might never know why ate at me.

"Pie," Kiera said, the moment the waitress came over to refill our coffees. "And ice cream. I need sugar. You got apple?" The waitress nodded, and Kiera looked across the table at me. "You chowing, too?"

"Can I have a hamburger and a milk shake and onion rings?" Rose said, reminding me that I'd fed her nothing except candy from the motel vending machine since I'd yanked her away from the demonic ceremony early that morning. Save her, then starve her. So much for my amazing skill at nurturing. Wouldn't Mom be proud?

Since I'd been living off Kit Kat bars, too, I ordered

the same thing Rose was having, then leaned back and sipped my coffee, trying to decide what to make of my new partner. She slid over until her back was against the wall, then kicked her feet up, her boots landing with a *thunk* on the tabletop. From two tables over, the wait-ress glared, but Kiera lazily lifted her hand, then shot her the finger. Then she rolled her head over and looked at me. "I really do try to be good, you know? I mean, my boy Clarence handed me this whole big chance to get my shit together, and you'd think I'd be a little more prissy sweet girl about the whole thing. But that's just not me."

A burly cook started to walk in our direction, and she exhaled loudly, then swung her feet to the ground and sat up straight. "Sometimes I wonder if with what we do, redemption's even really possible."

I licked my lips, wary. "What do you mean?"

She eyed Rose, and I nodded. "It's okay. She knows." Not entirely true. I had yet to have *the talk* with Rose. But under the circumstances, I think Rose had picked up on the salient details.

"Just all the killing," Kiera said. "I mean, shit, yeah, we're whacking demons, but it's still heavy-duty, you know?"

"Yeah," I said, because I knew exactly what she was talking about. At the same time, I didn't believe a word she was saying. I mean, sure. Maybe Clarence had paired me with a partner who'd been duped just like I'd been— who thought she was out there fighting bad guys so that

St. Peter would open those pearly gates up wide. Maybe Clarence would do that, but I didn't believe it.

I hooked an arm around Rose and pulled her close, pretending to focus on comforting my sister. Mostly, though, I just wanted the chance to check Kiera out. She looked human enough, but I knew better than to assume anything. The second demon I'd killed had not only looked human, she'd had Rose's big, innocent eyes. And although that had thrown me for a loop, there hadn't been a single speck of humanity in her.

I wondered if there was any in Kiera. I thought of my hands—of my visions. I could figure it out, I knew. All I had to do was touch, and look. But she'd know I was in there, poking around. I couldn't sneak into minds like a thief in the night. Instead, my entrances were like home invasions, rousting the mind's owner and making my presence very well-known.

There had to be a way to fix that. Because if I could figure out a way to sneak in, I'd be in that much better position to protect Rose, not to mention myself.

And, I thought, I could finally learn the truth about Deacon.

I frowned, then looked down at the tabletop, fearful my thoughts would reflect on my face. The truth was, I felt bad—even disloyal—to still keep Deacon at arm's length. After all, he was the reason I knew the truth about Clarence, about everything, and the old Lily would have hopped on the Deacon train, no questions asked.

The new Lily was more cautious, though. The new

Lily had been seriously burned and wasn't inclined to be scorched again.

"So what's your story?" I asked, figuring that at least some bit of truth would filter through the bullshit.

She grabbed the saltshaker and spun it on the table, making a pattern of salt on the Formica. "Typical, I guess. I was arrogant and angry and messed up in the head. Did a lot of drugs. Fucked for money. A lot of breaking and entering—I'm great at B-and-E—and I'd fence whatever shit I stole. One night, I'd been out drinking, you know? Ended up on the road. Some jerk cut me off. Got pissed. Gunned it. The next thing I knew, both our cars were going over and over, then I felt this pop in my neck."

I realized I was holding my breath. "You died."

"So they tell me. And it wasn't pretty. Where I ended up, I mean." She shivered a little, her eyes cutting away from mine. Then she shoved the saltshaker away and drew her hands through her short hair. "Anyway, when I woke up, I was in the hospital, and Clarence was there. He said I was getting a second chance."

"Wait a sec," I said. "You woke up in your own body?"

She looked at me like I was from Mars. "Uh, yeah."

"What about your parents? Your friends?"

She lifted a shoulder. "Haven't seen my parents since I was fifteen, so going on ten years now. Still see my friends sometimes, but we have a different groove going on now, you know?"

"Yeah," I said, thinking of all the friends I'd left behind. "I know."

"Pretty fucked-up, huh? But you know what they say about mysterious ways. And here I am now, ready to whup some demon ass." She reached her arms out, clasped her hands, and cracked her knuckles. "Gotta say, I thought you'd be a little more badass."

I lifted my brows. "Excuse me?"

"Oh, come on! That demon was about to whup your pretty little hide. If I hadn't showed up when I did, you and Little Bit would be nothing but a stain on the concrete."

I couldn't deny she had a point. "You didn't catch me at my best."

"Guess not." She nodded at Rose, who had looked up with interest. Not at me or Kiera, but at the waitress, who was now delivering our food. "What's the story with the kid? The demons want her. I got that. But what are you doing with her? Just protecting her, or is there more going on?"

The waitress's eyes went wide, at least until Kiera tilted her head up and stared the girl down. Then she spun around and hurried off, glancing once back over her shoulder before sidling up near the burly cook who'd started coming our way earlier.

I eyed them for a moment, then decided that neither appeared to be about to kick us out, call the cops, or contact the local psychiatric ward. "She's my sister," I said. Since Clarence already knew the scoop, I didn't figure there was any harm in telling Kiera.

"No shit?" She shot another glance toward Rose, then frowned. "So, what? You drag her around on missions and stuff?"

"Not as a general rule, no."

"But today's an exception because?"

"Because it's national Bring Your Sister to Work Day," I snapped. "What's the deal with all the questions?"

She leaned back, hands up, eyes wide. "Shit, chill. Sorry." She took another bite of pie, chewed, swallowed, and pointed her fork at me. "So what do you say? Let's go see what you've got going on."

"You want to go kill demons?"

"No, I wanna go kick puppies," she retorted. "Hell, yeah."

"Oh." I considered that. "So, where exactly does one go to find a demon?"

She shook her head, as if baffled by my very existence.

"Damn, you are green. I thought I was getting paired with some big-shot superchick. What were they doing, hiding you under a log?"

"Something like that," I admitted. "I started out with a mission. Very top secret. Not a lot of opportunity to go out looking for demons on my own."

"Right," she said, with a knowing nod. "You were out there keeping those sons of bitches from opening the Ninth Gate. You're like a legend now among us soldiers."

"Really?" I couldn't help the quick swell of pride. Pride, then guilt. Because I hadn't really done a good thing. I'd done a crap thing, and from the way Kiera was looking at me, she didn't know it. To her, I was some sort of hero.

Except even that probably wasn't true, was it? More likely, she was in on the whole big thing. And to her, I was the biggest sort of fool.

ELEVEN

"This probably isn't the best time to go demon-baiting," I said, casting a significant look toward Rose as we climbed back into Kiera's Pontiac.

"The hell it's not. The beasties have been buzzing lately. The convergence is coming up, and they can feel it, and they're all rooting for their buddies to find the *Oris Clef* and open the gates up wide. Fortunately, we're not going to let that happen." She raised a hand and waited for me to meet it with a high five, which I did. Why not? That was my plan, too, after all.

"I'm all for the killing demons and stopping the convergence plan," I admitted. "But that wasn't actually my point." I cocked my head toward the backseat and Rose, remembering what I'd promised my mom and thinking that rabble-rousing the demon population wasn't high on the Keep Your Sister Safe list.

Then again, neither was getting her infected with a demon's essence.

Kiera dug the keys out of her pocket and started the engine. "Oh, please. What? You think seeing a demon turn to goo is going to scar her for life? From what you've said, she's seen worse. Probably be damned cathartic for her."

When she put it that way, I had to agree.

"Besides," she continued, "we're fighting the good fight here. I mean, hell. Forget shielding the kid. You should be training her."

And, once again, she had a point.

Still, every decision I'd made since I'd gone out to kill Lucas Johnson had somehow been tied to me watching out for Rose. How could I justify all my efforts to protect her if I was going to turn around and thrust her into the middle of the fray?

I couldn't—which meant I needed to say no-go to the demon-hunting thing. I needed to be the responsible big sis. And I needed to get my kid sister (and her hitchhiking demon companion) home and into bed.

I knew it, but somehow I couldn't do it. Because once the idea had been planted in my head—once I was thinking about the kill and the dark and that somber, sensual rush that came right after my blade cut them down to goo—well, by then I couldn't seem to do anything else.

I needed the kill. I craved the dark. And I hated myself for what I'd become.

I should go home. I should march through the door, plunk myself down on the couch, and tune the television to the Disney Channel. I needed saccharin to counteract the tug of the demonic inside me. Because it was there, that dark, and it wanted to be fed.

And damned if I didn't want to feed it.

We drove back the way we'd come, all three of us in the car so tense, I'm surprised the windows didn't fog up. But we saw no sign of the warrior demon.

"Looks like our demon friend is long gone," I said.

In the backseat, Rose drew her legs up onto the seat and hugged her knees to her chest. She looked at me, the whites of her eyes eerie in the reflected light of the dashboard. She didn't have to speak; I knew what she was thinking. That demon might be gone, but there was still another right there with us, alive inside of her.

I reached back, wanting to take her hand and offer some sort of comfort, but she shifted away, turning on the seat so that my fingertips only brushed her knee. I pulled back, rebuffed and uncertain.

I was distracted from my own self-loathing by the sight of my bike, splayed out at the side of the road, wounded but apparently untouched.

"Later," Kiera said, watching me eyeing it. "We'll catch it on the flip side."

"I'm tired," Rose said. "Can't we just go?"

I wanted to say yes, to be responsible. So help me, I

wanted to tell Kiera to pull over, then plunk Rose on the back of the bike and speed off toward Boarhurst. But I didn't, because I was hard up by then. I'd gotten the idea of a hit in my system, and I wasn't backing away. Not then. Not even for Rose.

"Soon," I said. "This is important." And it was. Every kill made me stronger, right? And if warrior dude was any indication of the kind of demons that were in store for me now, I needed all the strength I could get.

All true . . . and at the same time, all utter bullshit. Because right then, it wasn't strength I was craving. Not by a long shot.

I had Kiera stop just long enough to retrieve Rose's duffel, then we were on our way again. It wasn't even ten when Kiera eased the car into a slot in front of the gray façade of a club that had no visible signage. But despite the early hour, I saw a couple of junkies finalizing a deal in the shadows near the front door, and a drunk couple getting so down and dirty with copping a feel that even I was about to get embarrassed. And, honestly, considering all I've done in my twenty-six years—and Alice's twenty-two—it takes a lot to get me embarrassed.

"I love this place," Kiera said, killing the engine and opening her door. "It's got atmosphere."

In the backseat, Rose's eyes were wide. "Don't look at anything," I said, channeling a responsible sister for a few seconds. "And anything you do see, I want you to forget by morning."

Either my words or my tone broke the spell, and she rolled her eyes and sighed. "I'm fourteen, Lil. I'm not a baby."

"I'm just trying to make sure you're fourteen going on fifteen, and not thirty."

"A little late for that," she said, and I had to silently concede the point. She'd been through hell, and she'd grown up fast. And maybe I couldn't turn back the clock, but I was damn sure going to try.

The door was manned by a beefy guy with arms so thick he couldn't actually put his hands down by his side. He gave Rose the evil eye, then shook his head. "ID. And it better not be fake."

I eyed Kiera, who was clearly thinking that he would be a good subject on whom to practice her knife skills. Rather than deal with the inconvenience of a homicide investigation, I sidled up close and turned on the charm. Or I tried to. The truth is that despite having absorbed the essence of an incubus, I hadn't yet mastered the control aspect of my newfound sexual prowess.

My lack of skill, however, was not an issue. Either enough sex-goddess aura oozed out without me trying, or the guy was too damn horny to care. But when I put my hand on his shoulder and whispered in his ear that I would be really, really, *really* grateful if he let the girl in with me, he complied without complaint. True, he squeezed my ass, but he didn't complain, and he let us pass. Kiera gave me a questioning look, but I just lifted a shoulder, shook my ass, and led the parade inside. Some tricks it was better not to share.

The club was the kind of place that can only be described as seedy. Actually, that's not true. It could also be described as dark, dangerous, smelly, and loud. In other words, exactly the kind of place responsible caretakers did not take fourteen-year-old girls. And although that twinge of guilt once again settled over me, I shoved it down with brutish finality. I'd made the decision, we were there, and that was that.

I led our little group to a booth in the back that smelled of sex and alcohol, and we slid in, risking half a dozen communicable diseases as we did. I took a quick look at Rose, mostly to assuage my guilt, though I wasn't sure what I was going to do if she looked completely freaked-out. As far as I was concerned, we were there to stay.

Fortunately, guilt wasn't an issue. Rose didn't look freaked; on the contrary, she looked fascinated. And, yeah, there was a little bit of guilt associated with that— this was a world I'd never wanted Rose to glimpse— but at least she wasn't cowering in fear and disgust.

More than that, she seemed truly to be Rose. Her eyes were clear, her body not shaking, and when she looked at me with that soft little smile I knew so well, my heart almost melted. Johnson was nowhere in sight, and even as I celebrated that little tidbit, I also couldn't help but feel a little uneasy. Because he'd be back. And I figured it would be sooner rather than later.

I reached out and squeezed her hand. Her life was in a complete shambles, and a lot of the blame fell on me. But right then, I was just glad to have my sister back.

"We're never gonna get a waitress," Kiera said, sliding back out of the booth. "Tequila for me. Coke for the kid. What do you want?"

"Tequila," I said. "And thanks."

She sauntered over to the bar, then squeezed in next to a tall blonde desperately in need of a bra.

I edged sideways and regarded my sister. "You never asked," I said.

Her head tilted to the side. "Asked what?"

"How come I'm in another body." I looked over at Kiera to make sure she wasn't on her way back. "You were screaming, and Johnson was inside you, and you called me Lily. You *knew*, Rose. How did you know?"

When she frowned, a little crease appeared over her eyes. She shook her head slowly. "I don't know. I just . . . I just knew."

"What else do you know?"

She pressed her lips together, and I saw her eyes begin to glisten. "I know a lot of stuff," she said, her voice drawing down to a whisper. "Stuff I don't think he wants me to know."

I fought the urge to hug myself against a sudden chill. "Like what?"

She leaned forward. "He called. That night you died. He called a man named Egan and told him it was time. Told him to go fetch Alice."

I made a muffled sound and realized my hand was up over my mouth. *I was right.* Lucas had been playing both sides, helping to fulfill the prophecy so that in the end his boss could use me to find the *Oris Clef.* I was still a pawn in some massive celestial game, but at least now I knew the score.

"What else?" I asked, but her eyes were wide and she shook her head. "Can't talk," she said, then pressed a finger over her lips even as her other hand pressed flat against her chest. "He's always listening."

I forced my face to stay bland, refusing to let her see the depth of my disgust that a creature as vile as Johnson was inside her. It didn't matter, though. That same disgust ate at her already, and when she blinked, two fat tears spilled out. I held out my arms, and she slid into them, then her head pressed against my shoulder.

"Why is this happening to us?" she asked, but I could only shake my head.

"I don't know."

"It's because we're dirty," she said, in a voice not her own. A voice that sent chills up my spine. "Dirty, filthy, little bitch-whore girls."

I pushed away, and when her face tilted up to meet mine, it wasn't my sister I saw behind scared, weary eyes. I was suddenly lost, wanting to lash out against the thing inside her even as I wanted to pull her close and comfort her. "Dirty girls," Johnson said. "But worthy. So very, very worthy."

"Kiera's coming back," I said, speaking through gritted teeth and forcing my voice to stay calm and harsh. My words were a ploy, but the trick worked. I could practically see the demon skitter away behind her eyes, and Rose return, ever so tentatively, to the world.

"I don't like that," she said, scooting over to the corner of the booth and lifting her thumb to her mouth. She gnawed on her cuticle, her knees tucked up near her chest, and at that moment she looked closer to four than fourteen.

"Rosie," I said, reaching for her. She turned away, though, tightening her arms around herself. Deep inside me, I felt my heart break, even as the dark bubbled up, wanting release. Wanting satisfaction.

Across the room, Kiera still stood at the bar, chatting up the girl next to her. I saw her slam back a tequila, then order another. Just as well. I wanted time for Rose to get her bearings.

After fifteen minutes, Rose's feet were back down on the floor. "Rose?"

"I'm cool," she said. She lifted a shoulder. "Honest."

I didn't believe her, of course, but I could hardly argue. Especially not since Kiera had finally decided to join us again. "Drink up, campers," she said, sliding a Coke toward Rose and a tequila shot toward me. "Plenty more where that came from," she added, after I slammed the shot back without even taking a breath.

"Glad to hear it," I said. Right then, five or six more sounded like just the ticket.

"So what are we doing with Little Bit here?" Kiera

asked, looking pointedly at Rose. "You gonna be okay sitting while we go hunting?"

Rose gnawed on her thumb, then nodded. "I'll be okay."

She would be, I knew. Because even if some badass demons wandered in and tried to get it on with her, Johnson was close to the surface, and he'd fight the bastards off.

Kiera cocked her head, then took off into the crowd. I eased out of the booth and followed her to the bar. She ordered another round of tequila shots for both of us, and while we waited, I scoped out the crowd. Definitely not a Harvard hangout—that was for sure. And while I had a feeling that no one in the crowded club had a rap sheet less than an inch thick, that didn't make any of them demonic.

"This isn't going to work," I said. "There's no way to tell the demons from the rest of them."

She watched as the bartender filled up the shot glasses, and she slammed one back. "I can tell," she said, tapping her nose and reminding me of the way she'd earlier smelled Johnson on Rose. "They gave me two gifts when they brought me back. I'm strong, but I guess everyone gets that one. And they gave me the magic sniffer."

I'll admit to a little flutter of envy. How come *I* couldn't sniff out the bad guys? The answer, though, was obvious. Even if a supersniffer was a standard trait

for your average brought-back-to-life-soldier girl, that
was one trait they would have kept off the checklist when
they were making me. After all, if I could sniff out demons, Clarence's game would have been over before it
started.

"Want me to prove it?" she asked, then sidled close
to me. I stiffened as she pressed one hand on my waist,
then eased up my body, leading with her nose until her
breath brushed my ear. "I smell them in you," she said
in a whisper, and that was all it took to have the black
edge of my temper flaring. I whipped her around until
her back was to the bar and the point of my knife was
right over her kidneys, my body shielding the blade
from the view of those around us.

"You're going to want to be very, very careful," I
said.

I saw a quick flash of fear on her face, replaced almost instantaneously with the cool calm of someone
who faced death every single day. "Chill out, Lily. I get
the way you work. Kill 'em and suck 'em in. I was
briefed, okay. Clarence briefed me."

I stared at her for one long moment, searching for
the truth, wishing I could tell if she knew the whole
story. Then I backed away, sliding my knife back into
the thigh holster that was hidden beneath my duster.

"I didn't mean anything," she said, and this time I
was certain I saw compassion in her eyes. "I mean, it
must be a bitch to have all that crap floating around in

you. But you have to admire the irony. You get to use their essence to go out and kill their buddies. It's beautiful."

"Trust me," I said. "There's nothing beautiful about it." But I wasn't inclined to slit her throat anymore, so I thought that was a good thing. I cocked my head toward the dance floor. "Okay," I said. "Let's find us one."

With Kiera leading the way, we shimmied onto the dance floor, squeezing close to strangers, getting pulled into arms we'd never touched before, and grinding down in a hard, sexy beat that had all the juice I'd tried to turn on for the bouncer bubbling up inside me. A few yards away, Kiera had her arms around an Aryan-looking blond, with a jawline that would have made a New York modeling agency orgasm and just enough beard stubble to shift the androgynous beauty over the line toward masculine.

She was pressed close, her crotch rubbing up against him, and his erection straining in his jeans, announcing the state of his arousal to anyone who cared to look.

Dammit, I was looking.

She turned her head and sent me a significant look and, yeah, I balked. *Him?* But I had no reason to doubt. Deacon, after all, was a demon, and though he wasn't as pretty as this guy, Deacon was one hell of a lot sexier, with his sultry heat and piercing black eyes.

I shoved Deacon out of my mind and concentrated on my new mark, cutting in as Kiera backed away, laughing, to pass me off.

"Whoa," the guy said. "What the fuck?"

She patted his cheek. "Not my type," she said, then eased off into the morass of bodies.

"Is it so bad with me?" I asked, sliding my arms around his neck, and grinding against him with the music. He really didn't have to answer my question. The answer was right there in his jeans. It was heady, the desire rolling off him, and the truth is, I was finding it hard to remember that he was the bad guy.

Was he the bad guy?

Kiera said so, but could I trust her? After all, she worked for Clarence. And what if she was setting me up to kill someone good? Someone human?

What if the whole smelling-demons thing was bull-shit?

But why would it be? If Kiera'd been duped like I'd been, then she'd have no reason to lie. And even if she were playing a role like Clarence, she wouldn't want me to figure out the game, right? She needed to build trust. And she couldn't do that unless the supposed demon she pointed me to really did dissolve in a puddle of goo when I got it with my knife.

And, yeah, that would mean she was targeting her own allies, but Clarence and company didn't want me absorbing good. They wanted me absorbing bad. Becoming bad.

Bad to the bone. That was me. Or it would be soon.

I raked my gaze over the crowd, finally finding Kiera in a clench with a pencil-thin brunette in hip-hugger jeans and a tight white T-shirt, damp with sweat and clinging to every curve of her breasts. I watched as they moved, every once in a while catching a glimpse of Kiera's knife stuck in between her belt and her jeans and hidden by the short denim jacket she wore.

She must have felt my eyes on her because she turned to me, and I saw the tiniest of grins. Then she cupped her partner's face, kissed her hard, and slowly eased her free hand down over the blade of her knife.

I turned away, my eyes going automatically for Rose. I found her, sitting at the booth just where she was supposed to be. And I found something else, too, only a few yards away. Watching her. Watching me. *Deacon.*

I felt the familiar tug in my gut, that tightness, that awareness, that I'd come to associate with him. I wanted to go to him, but I could hardly look like I was best buds with the boy. Not in front of Kiera. Still, I was thinking of him, and considering the way my dance partner was suddenly behaving—his hands skimming my ass, pulling me in tight, grinding hard against me— I think my inner incubus was showing.

"With me," I said, leaning in close to whisper, and at the same time knotting my fist in the collar of his shirt. With one quick glance toward Kiera, who was still involved with femme-fatale demon, I eased my prey toward the door and out into the parking lot.

I had no idea what kind of demon he was, and I knew I shouldn't wait. Shouldn't wonder. Shouldn't do anything but take him out. But I was curious, and I was turned on, and damned if I didn't want to make the moment—the hunt—last as long as I could.

"What do you want?" I asked, brushing my lips over his ear.

"You." His hand slid down to cup my crotch, the contact sending shivers through me despite the vileness of the hand that was touching me. I imagined it was Deacon, and shifted my stance, opening my legs wider, and moaning when he closed his hand over the hot denim of my jeans. "Give us a kiss," he said, and I could hear it now, that voice that seemed to echo through my head. A voice that came not from the man but straight from hell.

He leaned in, his mouth open, and I leaned forward to meet him, battling his kiss with one of my own—fighting, hard, as he tried to draw out my soul. He jerked back, eyes open with fear. "What the fuck?"

"Sorry, buddy," I said. "I like this body. I think I'm going to stay."

"Bitch," he said, his hands going for his back pocket and the knife he undoubtedly had hidden there.

He didn't make it. I got to him first, drawing my blade in seconds and thrusting it forward even as he lunged. I got him in the gut, my blade piercing flesh and muscle to stab him deep in his liver before I sliced up, gutting his belly like a fish.

Death oozed out of him. Not blood, but the black goo that was the life force of demons. He fell backward, and as he melted into a puddle, I fell to my knees, overwhelmed by the flood of strength I'd gained from the kill, and the dark, sensual heat I'd absorbed from the demon. He was death. He was destruction. And that essence was in me, a low, needy buzz, desperate for satisfaction. For release. For the kill.

I heard the crunch of gravel behind me, and I whipped around and up onto my feet in one motion. *Deacon.* Before I could speak, he had me pressed back against a nearby car, his mouth hot on mine, his hands on my breasts, and damned if I didn't want him right then, right there. I'd been primed on the dance floor, and I hadn't come close to being satisfied. And now, with this darkness inside me, I just wanted it. Wanted him. Wanted the release.

"I didn't like seeing you with him."

"He's dead," I said, arching back as he cupped my breasts, trying to keep a hold on thought and reason, then wondering why I was bothering. "He was a demon. That's what I do."

"Kill them," he said. "Don't fuck them."

I arched up, then met his eyes, and for the briefest of seconds the marks on my arm seemed to burn. Then there was a *snap* as the vision took hold, but he jerked away, and the moment was lost and, honestly, I wasn't disappointed. I didn't want to know any more. Not then. Right then, I knew all that I could handle. "You're a demon," I said.

"I'm an exception," he murmured, then closed his mouth hard over mine. I moaned, wanting nothing more than to ease into the kiss and lose myself in the touch of this man who was danger and mystery and delight all rolled into one.

I fought to keep my senses, though, and through the haze in my brain, I saw the back door open, and I saw Kiera step outside.

I shoved Deacon—hard.

His eyes flashed. "What the—"

"Kiera," I said. "Fight."

He did, making it look damn good, but I wanted no questions. Nothing that Kiera could take back to Clarence that raised suspicions. And with his back blocking her view, I thrust my knife into his hand. "Kill me," I said.

"What?"

"Kill me, goddammit, and make it look good."

"Lily," he said, and though I saw the pain in his eyes, he did what I asked. He shoved my knife deep into my heart.

And then, dammit, I died.

TWELVE

The convenient thing about being me is that death no longer sticks. So I came back, and when I did, I found Kiera crouched over me with Rose beside her, and both their expressions frantic.

"Holy crap," Kiera said, as I blinked the world back into focus. "You were dead. Fucking A, you were absolutely, completely dead."

Beside her, Rose's mouth hung open, tears streaming down her face. I reached for her, and she crouched down, her arms around me, her sobs shaking us both. "It's okay, hon," I said. "I'm fine. Swear. See?" I pointed to the hole Deacon had left in my shirt, then at the unmarred flesh beneath. "I'm okay."

She backed up and sniffed. "How?"

"Perk of the job," I said.

"Fucking A," Kiera repeated.

"Just one of my many party tricks," I said, managing to draw a smile from both of them.

"Who?" Kiera asked.

"Deacon Camphire," I said, and Rose sucked in air. I met her eyes, shaking my head ever so slightly, afraid she'd say something stupid. Like, oh, mention that she and I and Deacon had all been happily hanging together just last night.

"I thought that was him," Kiera said, apparently not noticing my silent exchange with my sister. "I saw someone running away. I was going to go after him, but Rose came out, and you were here, and—"

"It's okay," I said. "He's strong. You don't want to screw with him."

"I know. He's on Clarence's Do Not Disturb list."

"Right," I said. When I'd first become Prophecy Girl, Clarence had made it clear that I shouldn't try to kill Deacon, what with him being superstrong-demon dude. But then all that changed, and Clarence told me that Deacon had been the one who murdered Alice. A big fat lie that I'm certain he spun so that I'd take the bastard out. He did it, we assume, because he'd learned that Deacon was trying to close the Ninth Gate. But that didn't explain why Deacon was suddenly back on the Don't Kill list. Clarence had to know Deacon was still trying to lock the gates up tight. So why would he want Kiera steering clear?

These, however, were not issues that I had time to

ponder. Instead, I sat up, wincing a little, and held out my arm for Rose, who pressed her head onto my shoulder. "It's okay," I said. "I'm fine. Just stiff." I drew in a breath, wanting to change the topic before this one got too dangerous. "I got that other demon, though," I said to Kiera. "How about you?"

"Nailed her," she said with a wide grin, and I realized I didn't have any way of knowing if she really had. Right then, though, I had to admit I didn't care. The darkness was still surging through me, even more intense now that the dead demon's essence had been sucked in and was filling me up, shooting down into my fingers and toes like a drug. I'd gotten a hit—that was for sure—but I still craved another. "Let's go," I said.

Kiera frowned. "Where?"

"There are more, right? There must be more?"

She grinned, slow and wide. "Look at you, all dressed up with somewhere to go."

I shrugged, then climbed to my feet. "This was your idea. I'm just trying to get into a rhythm with my new partner."

She looked me up and down, then stepped close, her gaze warm and appraising. "I wasn't sure at first," she said. "Thought maybe you were all hype. But you'll do. Man, oh, man. You'll seriously do."

"I missed that last one," I said. "Missed him and ended up dead."

She shrugged it off. "Apparently, being dead didn't

take. And like I said, you don't want to take Deacon Camphire out. Too risky."

I thought about that some more as we headed back inside, frowning as a new thought hit me. Maybe it wasn't me and Kiera that Clarence's Don't Kill order was protecting. Maybe it was Deacon.

I shook it off, because no matter how much I wanted the truth about Deacon, just then there was something I wanted a whole lot more. "Come on," I said to Kiera. "Find me another."

"You got it, girl."

I looked sideways at Rosc, who stood straight and silent. I needed to get her home. Needed to take care of her.

But I couldn't think about that. Couldn't think about anything but the need for the slow, cold burn of the kill.

"We're staying just a little bit longer," I said. She tilted her face up to meet my eyes, hers clear and more focused than I'd seen in a year.

"Good," she said, the harshness in her voice like a knife to my heart. "Kill more of them. Kill them all, and this time let me watch. Because I don't think I'll be happy until they're all dead."

My mouth was dry, but Kiera let loose with a guffaw. "Listen to the kid. She's got balls."

Except I didn't want her to have balls. "No, I—"

"There," Kiera said, pointing at a lanky man who was stumbling out of the club, a bottle of beer tight in one hand.

"No. Forget it. I changed my mind."

I shook my head, but Rose grabbed my arm. "Please," she said, her voice plaintive. "It's like you're killing him."

And though Kiera might not have understood, I knew Rose was talking straight to me. Talking about Johnson. And, yeah, I understood. I hated it, but I understood.

Except Rose didn't get what she wanted. Because as I took my first step toward my new quarry, a sharp stab of pain doubled me over.

"Lily!" Both Kiera and Rose gathered around me. "What is it?"

"My arm," I whispered, barely able to force the words out. "Oh, God, oh, God, I think it's on fire." I scrambled to shove up the sleeve of my duster to reveal my forearm, the first image now red and raw, as if someone had taken a branding iron to my skin.

"Oh, wow," Kiera said. "He told me about that. He's trying to find the bridge, right? Trying to conjure a bridge despite the protections?"

I nodded, trying not to grit my teeth. "That's what he said. Maybe this means he found it." I clenched my fist, trying desperately to block out a pain that was so intense I was seeing the world in shades of gray and red.

"So what now?" Kiera asked.

"Now I go," I said, realizing that as much as I hated the fact that I was a walking cliché of Beam Me Up, Scotty, this was actually going to work out pretty handily. Being a double agent stuck with a partner was damned inconvenient, but I couldn't pull her into my own skin, and that meant I couldn't take her across the bridge with me. Whatever I had to do on the other side, I could do it in secret.

For at least a little bit, I could drop my cover. Color me supremely happy.

"You're going to have to hold on to me until I'm through," I said. "That's how I find my way back."

She looked mildly concerned about that, and I'll admit that I was petty enough that her discomfiture gave me a small thrill. After all, so far she'd definitely come across as the cooler one in our dynamic duo. Now it was my turn to show just how über my über-girl-superchick routine could be.

She held my hand, and Rose held tight to the back of my shirt. "It'll be okay," I said.

"It better," she retorted, and though I listened for a warning from Johnson, I heard none. Just my sister, wanting me to come back. I smiled. "I swear," I said. "I'll be back before you know it."

Actually, that wasn't entirely accurate. The bridge crossed space, not time, and if it took me a while to find the relic once I crossed over, they'd be standing in the middle of the parking lot, babysitting a glowing, spinning vortex.

Probably better to find someplace more private.

"Ladies' room," I said, and we all bustled in that direction, then squeezed into the handicapped stall, ignoring the curious looks from the girls gathered in front of the mirror adjusting dresses and skirts.

"So go," Kiera said, though I wasn't sure if she was anxious to see me do my stuff, or because she wanted out of the cramped little stall.

I pressed my hand to the still-aching mark, drew in a breath, and waited for that sharp tug around my middle, then the sensation of being jerked by the umbilical cord into another world.

It didn't come.

"Nothing," I said, slapping my palm down and trying again. "Dammit, there's nothing."

Kiera sighed. "Come on," she said, her tone suggesting that she'd been partnered with a complete and total loser. "Let's go see Clarence."

THIRTEEN

Zane's basement looked just like it always did. The training ring in the middle. The gray cabinets that I knew were filled with a variety of unusual and lethal weapons. The man himself, standing dark and tall, with catlike grace and commanding sensuality.

The only thing different—other than the presence of Rose and Kiera—was the large red circle that had been painted on the floor.

"That's only paint, right?" I asked, eyeing it suspiciously. Actually, it was a dumb question. If it were blood, I would have smelled it. If it were blood, I'd be craving it.

I looked over at Clarence, who was walking beside it, mumbling something to himself. "So, what exactly is that?"

"The bridge, *ma chère*," Zane said. "It is the path to your destination."

Behind him, Rose was curled up on a bench, her head on her knees. At his words, though, she lifted her head and her expression was sharp. It reminded me of a wolf. A predator. And the wolf had something in its sights.

"I thought I was the bridge," I said. "I thought I traveled through the portal on the tattoos."

"The protections," Clarence said. "Can't get there through you anymore. Now you're the navigational system, not the train."

"But I went once," I complained. "I dove through my arm, and I saw those funky cave buildings. Why couldn't I go again?"

Clarence looked at me, his expression stern. "You went once. You saw too much. Do you think the magic will willingly let you return?"

"Enough with the fricking metaphors," Kiera said, stepping up behind me, her hand on my shoulder. "What are you talking about?"

"As a rule, Lily's gift allows her to both find objects and travel through the locator tattoo to the object's location. The image becomes a portal," he said, and I provided the visual aid to his little speech by holding my arm out. "But whoever hid away these relics was clever. Nefarious. And very, very careful."

"She can't get there," Kiera said. "That was what you were trying to do in the bathroom."

I nodded. "Didn't work."

"*Couldn't* work," Clarence said. "The protections are too strong."

"Can't you fight them?" Kiera asked. "Find some sort of mystical mumbo jumbo to take them down?"

"Probably," Clarence said. "With enough time. But we don't have time." He looked back over his shoulder to one of Zane's gray weapons cabinets. Zane had taped a calendar there, the kind with a photograph on one page and the month displayed below it. On this one, the photo was the famous poster of a cat struggling not to fall from a bar, along with the caption: *Hang in there, baby*.

But it wasn't the cute cat that had us all suddenly somber. It was the date circled in red—the next full moon, and it was fast approaching.

I nodded at the circle on the floor. "So this isn't about removing the protections?"

"This is about sneaking in around them," Clarence said. He looked from me to Kiera. "You two ready?"

"Wait," I said. "She can come, too?"

"That's the beauty of my solution," he said with a smile that turned almost immediately into a frown. "It's also the curse."

"Explain," I said, sharply.

"I'm using your arm to aim the bridge in the right direction, but it's an open doorway now, not a private portal through the map on your arm."

"So?"

"So you may not be the only ones who use it to travel."

I held up a hand. "Wait. *What?*"

He had the grace to look sheepish. "If they're paying attention, other demons might recognize the energy. They might follow you. And they might try to get to the relic before you do."

"Are you kidding me?" I gestured between me and Kiera. "You're not sending only us, right? I mean, we're going with a team, right? An army? You do have another group to go in with us, right? I mean, have you seen what's out there?"

He looked from me to Kiera, his forehead creased.

"We ran into a little trouble," Kiera said, then pulled out her knife and started to clean under her fingernails with the blade.

"A little?" I countered. "Guy was seven feet tall if he was an inch, had a face covered with warrior-style tattoos. He wielded a blade taller than I am without even popping a sweat. Oh, and he had superhero hands."

"He had what?"

I held my hands out, demonstrating. "That's all he did. And Kiera's car started backing up toward him."

Clarence's face went tight, and he turned around, his shoulders hunched as he paced, his chin cupped in his palm.

"So we're getting someone else, right? Because I don't want to meet him again in a dark alley, much less on a dark bridge."

"Sorry, girls. You're the dream team."

"But—"

"My hands are tied," he said, shooting both of us a significant look. I wanted to argue, really I did, but I knew better than to think it would do any good. The bigger question was *why*. If finding these relics was so damned important, then why only send me and my sidekick?

Not a question I had time to ponder. Because Clarence had effectively cut off any more discussion of the subject. By then, he was walking the circle, dropping a fine yellow powder on the red line. "I need your arm," he said, fixing me with a stern expression.

"Right," I said, absolutely certain that this was not going to be fun. "Hang on." Before he could protest, I hurried across the room to Rose's side. I tilted my head sideways to face Zane. "You'll stay with her?"

"She is important to you?"

"She's my sister."

He cut a quick look toward Clarence. "And that is not a problem?"

I drew in a breath. "We came to an agreement."

He nodded, and I wondered if he was thinking about his own deal with the devil. The one that kept him stuck down here in the basement, training warriors until the day when the job was finished and the Powers That Be would grant him the thing that he so craved: mortality. "I will watch the child," he said.

I hesitated, wondering if I should tell him that she

was more than a child. Because I couldn't help but wonder: Was he really aligned with Clarence, or was he just getting by to get by, wanting to be released from his cell? Wanting to die?

I couldn't say a word, though. Everything I suspected about Zane was just that—suspicions. For all I knew, he was as vile as Clarence or Johnson or Penemue. Reveal the truth, and I risked both my neck and Rose's.

So instead, I simply said, "Thanks." Then I turned to Rose. "Give me a hug," I said, and she melted into my arms, hers tight around my neck. "I'll be back," I said, whispering in her ear.

"You feel almost as good as your sister," came the soft reply, and I froze, then drew upon all the strength that had been crammed into my body not to bolt.

Instead, I whispered back, calmly and coolly. "You get the fuck back inside and you stay there. Because if you even think about peeking out in front of Zane, he will kill you without hesitation. And I swear, I will hunt down that freakish body of yours, and I will make it my mission in life to finish the job. Do we understand each other?" Silence. *"Do we understand each other?"*

"Lily?"

I sagged, holding on tight to her, because *that* was Rose. That was my sister. And she was back in the forefront, and that bastard was under again. "I'll be back," I said. "Zane's gonna take care of you."

"I'm scared."

"Yeah," I said, leaning back to look at the bridge of her nose, avoiding her eyes just in case. "I'm scared, too."

I stepped away, then held out her hand for Zane. He took it, with a quick nod to me, and I suppressed a wave of gratitude. I didn't know whose side he was on—not really. But I was certain I could trust him to protect Rose.

"Okay," I said, turning back to find Clarence impatiently tapping his foot. "Where do I go?"

"Right here," he said, pointing to the center of the circle. His finger shot out toward Kiera. "Ah, ah," he said. "None of that sarcasm. Not today. Not with so much riding on this."

She shrugged, then mumbled an apology, and for a moment I was completely lost. Then I realized what had happened—Clarence had gotten into her head, exactly the way he used to get into mine. As with Zane, I didn't know if Kiera was really on my side or not, but right then, she had my full sympathy.

"Kiera, you're here, just left of center. Lily, take a step back and hold out your arm. I want the mark over the center point, just the mark. That's it," he said, as I moved into position. "Perfect." He scurried backward until he was out of the circle.

"Uh, what now?" I asked.

"It's your blood, Lily," he said, which I probably should have known. These days, pretty much everything was about my blood.

"Kiera," Clarence said, tossing her a knife. "Cut her across the image, then throw me the knife."

"You?"

"I'll need your blood to call you back."

"Oh." I supposed that made sense. Next time, though, I'd be sure to bring my passport along. Just in case I got stuck going home the more traditional commercial-jetliner way. "How will you know when to open it?"

"I'll know," he said, though his expression did not fill me with confidence.

"Ready?" Kiera asked. "It's either going to work, or it isn't."

She had a point, and even though I was far from ready, I nodded. Rose was behind me, but I swear I could feel her eyes upon me. And then, when Kiera slashed the blade fast and sharp against my skin, I heard my sister's sharp intake of breath.

"The knife!" Clarence said, as Kiera tossed it. "Now clasp hands. Quickly! Quickly!"

We did, and not a moment too soon, because almost simultaneously with my blood dripping onto the symbol drawn onto the floor, the concrete beneath us seemed to fall away. The colored outline that had been drawn around us began to spin and rise, as if pulling up a thin, misty curtain, and leaving us encased in a writhing, moving tube. It stretched and pulled, and as everything outside the tube went black, I held on tight to Kiera's hand, for the first time grateful I had company on this freakish journey.

At first, it didn't seem like we were going anywhere, then the tug came, that hard yank at the gut. Kiera yelped, so I knew she felt it, too, and, all of a sudden, we were hurtling through space, hands clenched tight and nothingness all around us.

Except it wasn't nothing. There were sounds. And bits of light. And strange mists. And the overwhelming sense that we were not alone.

The ground had disappeared from beneath us, and the only purchase I had on any sort of reality was my death grip on Kiera's hand. Her fingers were tight in mine, too, fingernails cutting into flesh, drawing blood, and the pain was grounding me, because I was starting to feel like if we didn't end up somewhere soon, I was going to scream and scream and scream and—

"Holy shit!" Kiera's voice cut through the darkness of the room we'd just landed in.

"Shhhh." I had my hand over her mouth without thinking. "Someone was with us," I whispered, my mouth by her ear, my voice low.

I felt her nod. I couldn't see her, though. Wherever we were, it was pitch-black, and I was beginning to fear that Clarence's bridging skills needed some work.

A slight breeze stirred my hair, and I twisted my head, finding the direction from which the air was coming. I tapped Kiera, then crawled slowly in that direction, small rocks digging into my palms and knees as I inched my way through the chamber. After what seemed like an eternity but was probably only fifteen minutes, I found the far wall. I didn't know whether we were alone in the room, and if we weren't, I didn't want to reveal ourselves to our companion. I didn't really see an alternative, though. If there was a way out of this chamber, it was there by the draft. But I couldn't feel the exit point, and I was out of ideas.

I reached into the interior pocket of my duster and pulled out my cell phone, silently berating Clarence for not loading us up on all sorts of survival-type goodies. Like, say, some C-4 and a detonator.

Barring that, I flipped open my phone and let the light shine back into the chamber, illuminating Kiera's face in the strange blue light. Hers, thank goodness, was the only face I saw, and I immediately felt a dozen pounds lighter. Maybe nothing had come with us through the bridge. Maybe we were there on our own, and we'd get the key and get out without any trouble.

I mean, hey. A girl can dream, right?

Kiera scrambled up beside me, adding the light from her phone to mine. "Where are we, anyway?" she asked.

"Dunno. Do you have a signal?" My phone was flashing *No service*, and it was clear hers was, too. Hundreds of dollars of technology between us, and the most we had were expensive flashlights. "Right here," I said, pointing at a seam in the stone. "I think if we just push—"

I pushed as I spoke, and, sure enough, the stone wriggled loose. "Help me." She got up close, and the two of us pushed and shoved until finally the stone gave way and we had a nice, girl-sized hole in the wall. I looked over my shoulder at Kiera and shrugged. "Here goes nothing," I said, then wriggled through the hole. It was tight—my shoulders scraped the sides—but it wasn't as if I had far to go. I emerged on the other side of the wall in a cavernous room, the walls of which were decorated with images that looked like something from Pier One. And, no, I'm not history, science, geography girl, so "from Asia somewhere" was the best that I could do.

I remembered the rooftops on the buildings I'd seen protruding from the hills. Like pagodas, I'd said, and the memory made me feel a bit better. If we were somewhere in Asia, maybe we were in the right place after all.

"What now?" Kiera asked, squeezing out of the hole behind me.

"I don't know." There was no neon arrow pointing the way. No sign saying *Push Here to Retrieve Relic*. Nothing at all to help us find the thing we were looking for. I didn't even know if the thing was bigger than a bread box, and right then I felt a spurt of dark, sour anger. A low fury that I'd been thrust into this job—by both Johnson and Clarence, no less—and neither one of them had given me a clue what I was supposed to do once I got in the general vicinity of the thing.

"I don't like this," Kiera whispered. "I can fight demons. They trained me to do that. But I'm not freaking Indiana Jones."

I felt the same way, but there wasn't a lot we could do about it at the moment. Complain to the management, and management might just decide to leave us there. Somehow, the idea didn't appeal.

"Listen," I said. "Do you hear that?" It was faint, but I was pretty sure I'd picked up on the sound of running water.

"A stream?"

"Where?" I don't know why, but I was certain the stream was important.

She pointed to the far side of the cavern. "There. Look."

She was right. From where we were standing, it was almost impossible to see, but there was a small stream running alongside the far wall of the cavern, snaking around past the stone wall and into the connecting chamber.

"Come on," I said, unsheathing my knife. "We're following it."

I knew the moment we followed the stream around the wall and into the next chamber that we'd made the right decision. Not only had the pictograms on the walls changed—the new ones depicting hellish, demonic images fighting bright, shining beings in a pitched battle staged across all four of the chamber's walls—but my arm was burning like a son of a bitch again.

"This is the way," I said. "My arm's burning."

"Like that hot-or-cold game," Kiera said. "Guess we're getting hot."

The stream widened in this room, moving away from the wall to divide the room into two distinct sections. The side we were on had nothing of interest. Floor. Walls. Us.

The side across the river seemed much more promising. Not only was the climax of the pictograph story being played out over there—the shining creatures were beating back the snarling beasts—but there was a stone table covered with Chinese characters. Four statues of warriors, each holding a sword, stood beside the table. On top of the table there was a mirror positioned to reflect off another mirror on the roof. One that looked straight down at an ornate jade box sitting on the bed of the river, surrounded by and covered with water.

Bingo.

I wasn't entirely sure how the general public would access this chamber—as far as I could tell, the only way into this entire area was the way we came—but whoever had designed it had obviously wanted visitors to understand, and clearly, that whatever was in that jade box was Important Shit.

And considering the way my arm was burning, I'd bet money it was the Important Shit I'd come for.

"Let's go," Kiera said, taking a step toward the stream.

"Wait." I put a hand on her shoulder, but she shrugged me off.

"Dammit, Lily. Let's get the thing and get out of here." She hurried toward the stream, prepared to jump over it. I saw her bend—

—and then I saw her fall, laid flat in the blink of an eye.

What the fuck?

I whipped around, my heart pounding, my knife ready, and faced her attacker.

I turned around and faced Deacon.

FOURTEEN

"No!" I yelled. "You can*not* be here. You can't."

"I can't let you do this."

"You're still singing the same song, Deacon."

"I don't want to fight you."

"Then don't," I said. I took I step backward toward the stream. It didn't look deep. If I could get across it, and somehow get my hands on that jade box before Deacon got to me . . .

I didn't know if that was possible. In fact, about the only thing I did know was that Deacon meant business. If I wanted this first piece of the *Oris Clef*, I was going to have to fight for it. And, dammit, that meant I had to trust that Clarence would get the bridge to me when I needed it.

Deacon was watching me warily, his gaze shifting from the mirror to the stream and to me. "Work with me," he said. "We're running out of time, and you know damn well I'm not your enemy."

"Tell that to Kiera," I said, glancing toward my partner, who I *really* hoped was only laid out and not dead.

"Paralytic," Deacon said. "I'm surprised you don't remember. It's the same one I used on you."

"I didn't pass out," I countered.

He shrugged. "Combined it with a sleeping agent. She'll have one hell of a headache, but she'll be fine."

"Gee, that was considerate of you. But you shouldn't have wasted it on her. I'm the one getting the relic. That means I'm the one you need to stop."

"I intend to," he said, and this time there was no conversational tone to his voice. No banter between two people who'd been skirting around the edges of a building tension. No small nod to whatever tenuous trust had developed between the two of us. No, this time there was nothing but sharp edges and the promise of danger.

This time, I saw the Deacon under the surface.

I told myself not to be scared. Of all the people in the world, Deacon wouldn't hurt me. After all, I was at the center of his belief system, wasn't I? I was the girl who was going to lock the gate to hell with him.

Which meant he wouldn't do anything to put me truly out of commission.

But knock me out, take me far away, destroy the

relic that I needed to save my sister? Any of those options was still highly plausible. Even probable.

"Enough with the talking," I said, then turned and made a break for it. As I did, I heard him cry out, *"No—the water,"* and then I felt something hard and fast grab my legs. I barely had time to process the fact that he'd leaped forward and grabbed my ankles, pulling me backward toward him.

I went sprawling forward, smashing the side of my face on the stone floor. My cheekbone felt like it exploded, and white-hot pain radiated out like the sun, filling my face with liquid pain and turning the entire room a sickly red color.

"Acid," he said, as I climbed to my feet. "The water's acid."

"What?"

He pulled a coin from his pocket. He tossed it in the stream, and it immediately dissolved, leaving nothing but a bit of smoke fizzing on the surface of the water. "Holy shit," I said.

I took another look at the altar and the setup of mirrors. Then I crawled to the edge of the stream and peered down. Sure enough, the jade box was down there, somehow unaffected by the acid. And inside it, I was certain, was my prize. The piece of the relic that was making my arm ache and burn.

"It's impossible to retrieve," Deacon said.

"And you know this how?"

He ignored me, turning away, moving to bend down next to Kiera. "Her pulse is steady."

"Yay," I said. "Wasn't really worried. Focus, dammit. Because I'm going to get that thing."

"No," he said. "You're not. It's down there. In acid. And it's not coming out."

"If it's acid, why isn't the box burned up?"

He lifted a brow. "It's magic acid," he said, his tone dripping with such sarcasm that I had to laugh. Especially since that was clearly the truth. It *was* magic acid. And if there was one thing that the magic didn't affect, then I had to assume there was something else as well.

"Jade," I said. "Maybe there's more jade in here. We can dam up the acid water around the box, and when it's dry, we can reach in and get the relic."

"Brilliant," he said. "But the jade will disintegrate."

I looked pointedly at the obviously intact box that lay within the flowing water. He shrugged, then nodded toward the murals on the walls. "The gemstones on the swords in the pictures," he said. "They're made of jade."

"You're helping me?" I asked. But I wasn't foolish enough to argue about it. Instead, I went to the wall and used my knife to pry out one of the jade pieces. Then I hurried back to the stream and dropped it in.

Seconds later, it had dissolved.

"Like I told you," Deacon said. "It's impossible."

"I don't believe that." At the moment, however, I had nothing to back me up. Just a deep sense of righteousness. After all, a fricking map had appeared on my skin. So what was the point of having a map to lead you to something that no one in the entire world could get their hands on? And I wasn't in the mood to believe it was a cosmic joke. When your arm has been slashed and diced, and your blood smeared and drained as much as mine had, the idea that you did it all so that the cosmos could have a big laugh really didn't go over well.

Even then, my arm was aching. Deep, steady throbs, like some damned coded message I was too dense to understand, too stupid to get.

Except . . .

I cocked my head to the side. Surely it couldn't be that simple.

Could it?

"Lily?"

I pulled my knife back out, and as Deacon watched, I sliced my palm, wincing only slightly as the blade cut through flesh. Then I crawled to the edge of the acid stream, held my hand over the churning water, and let the drops flow from my hand into the acid.

I flinched when the first drop hit, expecting a flurry of smoke and the fizz as my blood burned in the acid water. But there was nothing. Just a red stain that slowly dissipated as the acid diluted my blood.

I met Deacon's eyes, suddenly smug. "My blood," I said. "It's wicked cool."

Not that this newfound knowledge about my blood

did me a lot of good right off the bat. Because I had a feeling it wasn't *me*, but rather my blood, that was the magic elixir, and to test that theory, I plucked a strand of hair, then watched it fizzle and pop as the acid consumed it.

Damn.

Carefully, I used my knife to slice a thin strip of skin from the pad of my thumb. I dropped it into the acid water, too, and it was consumed even before my palm started to heal. Damn, damn, and double damn! How the heck was I supposed to get to the box if the acid-proof blood was hidden away inside my skin?

"Am I supposed to let it burn off my skin? My muscle? All the way down to the bone?" I looked up at Deacon, certain he could see both the disgust and the fear in my eyes. "I heal, so—"

"Give it up, Lily," Deacon said. "It isn't meant to be." As he spoke, a low buzzing seemed to fill the chamber, and across the stream, the stone guards shifted, moving their swords into attack positions.

"Deacon," I said, warily. "Did you see that?"

"We're running out of time. We need to get out of here."

"Screw that. You heard Johnson. Rose's life depends on me."

"You really think Johnson's going to let her live? You rely on a bargain with Johnson, and your sister is already dead."

"I am *not* leaving without the relic."

He shot a significant look at the stone warriors, all four of which had taken a step toward the stream. "Then you may not be leaving at all."

"Then help me, dammit."

He frowned at me, then turned and looked back over his shoulder, at the source of that loud humming, almost like the thrum of an electric generator. When he turned back to me, I could see harsh resignation in his eyes. "This isn't over," he said. "I help you now, you have to help me. I want to find the key. The key to lock the gates, not open them."

I licked my lips, then nodded. "I don't know how I'd have any more luck searching than you, but I'll help. I'm not taking any risks with Rose's life, but I'll help you look."

He glanced at the stream. "Give me your arm."

"What are you—"

"Hurry!"

I complied, and he sliced my forearm as I cried out in pain and surprise. *"What the fuck?"*

"Wait," he said, squeezing my flesh, drawing blood to the surface.

"Oh, shit," I said, realizing what he was doing. "That's brilliant."

"I hope so," he said, as he began smearing my hand and arm, painting me in a protective armor of my own blood. "Now," he cried, and I plunged my arm into the water, my teeth clenched as I expected the worst.

The worst, however, didn't come, and my hand closed

around the jade box. I lifted it, drew it out, then opened the lid to reveal what looked like a sparkling gold chain necklace.

Across the stream, the warriors sprang fully to life. Beside me, Deacon rose, his weapon at the ready. "Take it," he said, "and let's go."

Going, however, wasn't an option. Because even though I drew out the chain and slipped it over my head, there was no portal to take us back. We were stuck. And that meant that we had to fight.

"Clarence!" I screamed uselessly, pressing my hand over the tattoo. "Dammit, Clarence, I have it!"

I thrust my arm up into the air and saw that the tattoo of the second location was now raised and burning like the first. Even the third tattoo felt prickly, burning even more than the second one did at that moment.

We were ready to move on, but we couldn't, and I really wasn't keen on being stuck down there forever. Especially since for me, forever was a literal thing.

Even as I was pondering how those soldiers' swords could easily slice me into a bunch of small, eternal pieces, the soldiers themselves leaped over the stream, swords ready. I rolled to the side as one came straight at me, then turned around to stab it in the back with my knife.

Nothing happened.

The statues had started out stone, and apparently they still were.

Honestly, this didn't bode well.

"We need Kiera!" I shouted to Deacon, who was dodging and parrying two warriors, each of whom appeared ready to remove his body parts.

"At least another hour," he shouted back, and since my only response to that would have been a very loud curse, I stayed quiet and focused on fighting. My blows were amounting to nothing, as there really is no effective way to fight a rock. With an iron mallet, maybe I could have smashed their heads to smithereens, but I was all out of mallets at the moment. It was just Deacon and me and our knives in an empty chamber with nothing but a stone table, four walls, some murals, and a damned dangerous stream.

A damned dangerous stream.

I was, I realized as another of the stone beasts leaped on me, a complete idiot. Rather than attack, I ran, this time heading for the stream. What I planned to do was dangerous, but right then I didn't see another option. The stream was wide, and if I lost my footing at all, I'd be living out the rest of my immortal existence as microscopic bits of fried Lily. *Not* my idea of a good time.

The warrior thundered after me, so close I could almost feel the point of his blade at my back. I reached the edge, I launched—

—and I landed on the far side, falling into a roll and twisting back around to face my oncoming attacker.

As I'd expected, the warrior followed in my footsteps, but as it was about to land, I kicked out, catching it across the face with a solid crescent kick and throwing off its trajectory. It tumbled to the ground, right at the edge of the stream, and for a moment I feared it would claw its way free. To offset that possibility, I raced forward and kicked it once, hard, in the face. That was all it took. The warrior slid backward, its tenuous grip lost, and fell into the stream with a sickly, hissing *splat*.

Two seconds later, the warrior was no more.

Not that I had time to congratulate myself. My melted warrior's buddy was already launching himself over to my side of the stream. But these dudes weren't too bright, and I was able to get him with the same maneuver. And as I watched the stone body fizzle away in the acid, I saw that downstream, Deacon had followed my lead and taken his two attackers out the exact same way.

I stepped back, took a running start, and leaped over the stream, then hurried to crouch beside Kiera. "I don't know how to leave," I admitted to Deacon. "Clarence conjured the bridge, and he was supposed to send another one. But . . ." I trailed off with a shrug. "We need to get out of here, but I don't even know where here is."

"China," he said. "The Buddhist grottoes." He looked around. "Somehow, I don't think the Chinese have excavated this far back."

China. Great. Now I really was wishing I'd brought my passport. "Can you conjure a bridge?" I asked, hopefully.

He shook his head. "I piggybacked."

I frowned, then nodded toward Kiera. "You knocked her out; you get to carry her. And let's go."

Once he had her up and in his arms, I realized that even though the stone warriors were destroyed, that odd, low thrum still filled the chamber. "What is that? Is that the bridge? Is it about to appear?"

Deacon shook his head, and I caught the wary expression in his eyes. "No. I think that's something different." He shot me a sharp glance. "Come on. And hurry."

He didn't have to ask me twice. The sound was getting louder and louder, and I'd seen enough adventure movies to guess what was going to happen next—now that we'd stolen the treasure, the chamber was going to collapse around our ears.

Except it didn't.

No, what happened was much, much worse. Because while the walls stayed high and strong, our path was immediately blocked by a whirling, swirling mass of air and energy, and right in the center of it all was my hulking, tattooed, warrior-demon friend. And he looked seriously pissed.

"Fuck," Deacon yelled, which summed up my feelings nicely.

"Come on!" I have absolutely no idea what I expected to do. I'd already learned that fighting this behemoth was a risky proposition, so the flight part of the fight-or-flight response had kicked into high gear. Except I wasn't going anywhere. Whatever power the warrior had used to grab the car had a hold of me, and I couldn't run, I couldn't hide, I couldn't do anything except slide backward, my feet suddenly not my own, and though I fell forward and tried to grip the rock with my hands, all I accomplished was ripping my fingernails to shreds as the force field dragged me back, back, back toward the behemoth.

"Deacon!"

"The bridge! Lily, the bridge!"

He was right. Across the stream—less than five feet away—the bridge had appeared, an orangish cylinder of mist and light, and I needed to be inside there. Needed to be whisked to safety, but it wasn't happening because I was being sucked into the hell beast's arms.

Deacon was at my side, Kiera at my feet, and I grabbed on to her lifeless body as Deacon took his knife and slashed my arm. "What the fuck?" I yowled, but he wasn't listening. Instead, he was smearing his arm with blood, and then, as I watched, he took the jade box I'd retrieved from the stream and, using his bloody hand and arm, thrust it into the water and filled it up. Then he ran toward the warrior, drops of acid burning holes in the rock as it sloshed out over the sides of the container.

He hurled the acid toward the warrior's face, and though I'd expected his flesh to melt away, in fact, all it did was make him howl, a thunderous roar that shook the very walls of the cavern.

But it was enough. Because it also shook off his hold on me, and before he could reach out with his mind and grab me once again, Deacon grabbed up Kiera, and he and I lunged forward, jumping over the stream, and thrusting ourselves through the mist and into the bridge that led back home.

The darkness consumed us once again, and I could see nothing. Could hear nothing. And then I felt the press of Deacon against me, his body hard against mine, his lips firm and demanding, and then his low whisper. "Remember your promise."

And then my hand was closed not around Deacon's hand, but around Kiera's.

Deacon was gone, and it was just me and Kiera and a job well-done.

FIFTEEN

"Paralytic," I said, as I put Kiera gently onto the floor in Zane's office. "She'll be okay."

"How?" Zane asked, and since I wasn't sure what, if anything, Kiera had seen, I had to answer truthfully.

"Deacon Camphire." I met Clarence's eyes. "I almost took him out," I lied, intrigued by the way he winced when I said that. "But I lost the opportunity."

As I'd expected, relief flashed on his face, so brief that I wouldn't have seen it had I not been looking for it. But it was there, and I didn't understand why he wanted Deacon alive.

I was, however, going to figure that out.

"We got away, though," I said, because I didn't want to linger and give Clarence the chance to realize how very interested I was in the subject. "There was another demon—huge—and he and Deacon got at it. And in the midst of all the scrapping, I got the relic."

"And this other demon?"

"The dude we met before." I smiled wryly. "I don't think he likes me much. And he's got power, Clarence. Just like we told you. Serious power. He shows up again, there's no guarantee I can beat him." And that was an assessment I really didn't like to make.

What I also didn't like was what I was going to say next. Except that a part of me *did* like it. Because I liked the hit. Liked the power. And I needed more power and more strength if I was going to win. "I need more," I said, looking hard at Zane. "I need to train, and I need to train hard and fast and often. I want to be as strong as I can be. If I'm not, Tattoo Boy may end up getting it all in the end, and that's not going to make anybody happy."

Zane inclined his head. "Very well. We shall train, and we shall train hard."

I nodded, trying not to look too excited by the possibility, by the knowledge that soon I would feel the kill inside me, and it would fill me up and make me strong.

I shivered, hating myself for those thoughts but realizing that they were coming more and more often. I was changing. I knew it. I could see it.

And I didn't know how to stop it.

I ran my fingers through my hair. "At any rate, on the whole, a successful mission."

"Where is it?" Clarence said, moving toward me, his hand outstretched.

I hesitated, knowing that in the end Johnson wanted the thing, but when I looked over at Rose, now curled up on the bench and watching me impassively, there was no sign from Lucas that I shouldn't cooperate. I didn't know what plan he had for getting the key back from Clarence and Penemue, but apparently it wasn't thwarted by handing the necklace off to Clarence.

Not that I intended to let him follow through on whatever plan he was hatching. My priority might be getting Johnson out of Rose, but that didn't mean I was keen on Penemue getting his hands on the *Oris Clef*. And since I was finding the key in pieces, I was beginning to think that the best thing to do was use the third piece to bargain for Rose, then somehow turn the tables on Lucas and Penemue and prevent them from getting the *Oris Clef* altogether.

How exactly I'd do that, though, was another question. What I *did* know was that if Clarence had the pieces, my plan would be more difficult. So I hated to hand them off.

Not that I had much choice.

"There's more," I said, as I reluctantly passed the thing to Clarence. "My arm popped on the next location."

"Did it?" Clarence asked. "Well, let's see."

I begrudgingly held out my arm and discovered that

the second tattoo was no longer raised. "But it was," I protested. "It started burning right after I got the necklace."

"After you *obtained* the necklace?" Zane asked, leaving Kiera's side to join us. "Or after you put it on?"

I tried to remember. "On," I said. "I remember I slipped it on, and my arm began to burn again."

He turned his attention to Clarence, and damned if he didn't look a little smug. "I'm afraid your time with the relic is up, *mon ami*. If you wish to find the second hiding place, the relic belongs in Lily's hands."

Clarence hesitated, then peeled off the necklace and passed it to me. "All right, then. Let's see it."

I slipped it back on and felt my flesh begin to scar.

"They're connected," Zane said. "Each one untraceable until the previous one has been found. And none discoverable except by the one who holds them all."

"Lucky me," I said, but though I'd added sarcasm to my voice, in truth, I was secretly pleased. This new turn of events gave me another level of control. And so far, in this crazy world, control had been seriously lacking in my life.

"What are you waiting for?" Clarence asked. "See if you can get there."

"Now?" The idea was really not appealing.

"The convergence comes, Lily," Clarence said. "There is no time to waste."

And since that was a point I really couldn't argue with, I let out a loud, annoyed breath and held out my hand for Clarence. "Don't let go," I said. Then, on the count of three, I pressed my palm over the tattoo and let the portal suck me in.

Once again, I encountered the same protections, and I couldn't get close. The bridge didn't work, and my mission was going to be aborted until Clarence could manufacture another spell to conjure another bridge and get me close to the relic.

This time, however, it wouldn't be a mystery where I was going. Because this time, even I knew the landmark.

"Stonehenge?" Clarence said, when I'd returned and told him.

"That's what I saw. But how a piece of the key could be hidden around a bunch of big rocks is completely beyond me."

Kiera was sitting up by then, still weak, but alive and alert. "Another dimension?" she said, the words clearly costing her. "Maybe Stonehenge really is a doorway to another dimension, like in all those stories you hear."

I moved to sit beside her, momentarily forgetting that I didn't trust her. I'd been paralyzed like that before, though I hadn't been put to sleep as well, and I still vividly remembered the sense of helplessness and fear that had overcome me in that vulnerable state.

"It's a good idea," I said. "Except my mystical magical map powers don't work if the doohickey is in another dimension. It's there," I said. "It's just hidden."

"And now we build the bridge," Clarence said, standing and beginning to move around the room. Now that he knew what to do, I assumed it didn't take a whole lot of prep to put the thing together.

"Hold it," I said. "We're wiped. And I told you about warrior dude. I want to get stronger. And Kiera and I both need to rest." I also needed time to figure out if there was a way to force Johnson out of Rose. If this whole thing moved at lightning speed, there was no way I'd keep up.

For a moment, I thought Clarence would argue. Then he nodded, apparently realizing a rested hunter is a happy hunter. "Very well." He held out his hand. "The relic, Lily."

"But—"

"You don't need it at the moment, and it needs to stay safe."

I'm not sure why, but I twisted around to find Zane's eyes. He nodded, and I took the chain off again. "Don't lose it," I said dryly, earning me a smile from Clarence that was utterly lacking in humor.

Kiera turned down Zane's offer to train, claiming she still felt ripped from the paralytic. I, however, was eager for the kill. And though I knew I should get Rose home—though I knew that the last thing she needed to see was her sister impaling demons—I stayed and took them on. Demon after demon, letting Zane release them, then toying with them until I grew bored and stabbed them hard with my knife, then stood there, head back, as the power of the kill filled me and flowed through me. *Glorious.*

"It is enough, I think, *chérie*," Zane said, when I ordered him to send out one more. My count at that point totaled ten, and I was hot and bothered and itching for a real fight, not this pansy-ass shit, where the demons were so easy to kill I could practically do it in my sleep.

"More," I said, stepping gingerly out of the training arena to get right in his face.

His hands pressed gently on my shoulders, and his eyes were infinitely sad. I looked away, both fearful of getting sucked into a vision, and also oddly ashamed. "Lily. You do not want more."

"Don't I?" I asked. "Don't you want me to have more. Suck more in. Make me a badass warrior?"

"No," he said, and that one simple word did me in. I released a small sob and clung to him. "I hate it," I whispered. "I hate the dark." Except I didn't. I wanted to—so help me, I wanted to despise it—and yet it called to me. Enticed me. And lured me in with sweet, whispered promises.

He said nothing, merely stroked my hair, but his body was tense. Tight. And I couldn't help but believe that he hated it, too. I wanted so badly to break down and ask him if he knew who he really worked for. Or if he did know, if he did it because he wanted to, or because he craved the mortality that they'd promised him. Death for a man who'd lived forever, and would otherwise continue on.

But I couldn't. I wasn't sure if I was afraid of the answer or of blowing my cover. All I know is that I was afraid, and that I kept silent.

"Take the girl home," he said. "Rest. Eat ice cream." He tilted my chin up. "Be Lily for a night."

I managed a smile and didn't tell him that I wasn't sure I remembered how. More than that, being Lily wasn't my biggest concern anymore. That had shifted to Rose being Rose, and with that problem in mind, I thought of someplace—and someone—who actually might be able to help me.

By the time we'd taken a taxi and retrieved my bike, it was already almost two in the morning. Rose was staggered, the exhaustion so thick in her body it practically leaked out of her. I couldn't take her home, though. I needed to do this errand. I didn't know how much downtime Clarence would give me, and I needed all my ducks in their proper order.

"Where are we going?"

"To mark you," I said, the words surprising me when I realized they were true. I'd had my name—Lily—tattooed on the small of my back not long after I'd found myself hanging out in Alice's body. And now, yeah, I intended to mark Rose with her own name, despite the interloper inside her.

I had a particular tattoo shop in mind, and when we arrived, I was grateful to see that the *Madame Parrish, Psychic* sign was still lit. *She* was the real reason I'd come. But if I could put Rose on the table with John working his magic on her skin, then I could talk with the strange woman myself and not risk being overheard, by either Rose or the demon who lived inside her.

"Well, look who's back," John said, as we walked in. He was doing something in his work area, and I saw Rose go a little pale when she saw the table on which she'd lie.

"Do you want to?" I asked Rose.

For a moment, I thought she'd say no, the thought distressing me more than it should. My mom might not approve, but I wanted her marked. Wanted her *named*.

"My name?"

"That's right."

She drew in a breath. "Does it hurt?"

"A little."

Her lips disappeared, she'd pressed them so tight together. "Let me see yours."

I shrugged out of my coat and pulled up the back of my shirt, revealing the intricate lily tattoo, along with my name spelled out above.

"I get a rose, right? And my name."

"Sure thing. Whatever you want."

She looked at John, whose easy smile calmed her. Then she nodded.

"Come on, then," John said, holding out his hand. "Let's get you set up."

From the shadows near the window, Madame Parrish stood. "And you have come to see me."

I cocked my head. "How did you know that?" I'd

killed a Secret Keeper and absorbed his essence. She shouldn't be able to get into my head.

She laughed. "A guess. Don't worry. Your secrets are now safe." She held out her hands. "It is good to see you, Lily."

"How do you know about me?" Because I was certain that she did—that she knew even more than what she'd seen in my head during my previous visit. And though I knew I should be wary of her, I wasn't. I was also certain she was on my side, and if I was wrong, I didn't want to know it. Having an ally, even one who looked to be ninety and hid in a tattoo parlor, made me feel safe and warm.

"I know many things," she said, and I knew better than to press. Press, and she might leave, and I'd be stuck there watching Rose get a tattoo. "She is your sister?"

I nodded, watching as Rose climbed onto the table. "She's why I'm here. Most of it, anyway."

"I see." Madame Parrish stood. "It is a lovely night, and there is a bench in front of the shop. Shall we step out and watch the sky?"

I followed her out, grateful she'd understood my need for privacy. I was a little concerned Johnson would peek out and scare the artist, but since I couldn't think why he would bother, the fear was little more than a paranoid niggle. And even that faded as we reached the door. Rose, I saw, had fallen asleep on the table.

"There's a demon inside her," I said once we were settled on the bench. "I need to know how to get it out."

Madame Parrish put her hand on my knee. "I'm am so sorry. For you and for the child. And I'm sorrier still for what I must tell you."

"What?" I asked, tamping down on fear.

"There is no removing a demon who does not wish to be removed. Another demon could move in and perhaps engage the first in battle, but your sister's soul . . ." She trailed off with a shake of her head. "It would surely be a casualty of such a hard-fought war."

"Oh." I drew in a breath, determined not to cry. "Then that's it. There's nothing I can do except what Johnson asks. And hope that he'll keep his promise."

"I would not put much stock in the word of a demon," she said.

"I don't. But it doesn't sound like I have a choice."

"You cannot get the demon out of your sister, but there may be another way."

I turned to her, confused, curious, and definitely hopeful. "How?"

She held out a hand, indicating me.

I recoiled, realizing what she was suggesting. "Another body for Rose? But—" Even if I knew how, that would mean killing someone. Forcing another soul out as Rose moved in. "I couldn't. I—"

"I'm only telling you the possibilities, child. You cannot fight unless you understand all the rules."

"I couldn't do that," I said. "I couldn't take someone else's life. Not even for Rose."

Her smile bloomed bright. "The darkness that consumes you," she said. "The darkness that you fear . . . I think that it has not yet tarnished your heart."

"Thank you," I whispered, and though her words lightened me, there was grief there, too. Because I'd come hoping to find a way to save Rose, and I realized now that I would be leaving with no answers, only the certainty that I had to keep playing Johnson's game.

"That is not all you came for," she said, watching my face.

"No. I wanted help. For me. For my visions." I waited for her response, but she said nothing, and so I continued on. "They're shared. I don't want them to be."

"You wish to move in stealth through another's mind."

"I do. Is there a way?"

"There is."

"How?"

The quick quirk of her lips reminded me of my mother's easy smile. "Practice."

I leaned back, sagging against the bench. "That's it? No demon I can kill and absorb his essence? No secret magic formula?"

She laughed. "Lily, sometimes things must be accomplished the old-fashioned way." She pressed a hand to my cheek. "Practice. Eventually, your efforts will pay off."

"Right. Great. Will do."

She stood. "Let's go see how your sister is coming along."

I followed her inside, and we watched as John finished the tattoo on Rose's back. Once he was done, I woke Rose up and helped her, staggering and groggy, back to my bike.

The fast ride in the cold wind woke her, and her eyes were bright and wide by the time we reached my apartment.

"So who are you?" I said, as I helped her off the bike.

"Mostly me," Rose said. "But I can feel him in there. He's moving around, you know? Like he's trying to take root."

Her words chilled me. "Don't let him."

Rose's expression was pure sass—and pure vintage Rose. "I'll do my best."

I gave her a quick hug, that tiny glimpse into the Rose I remembered refueling my resolve to protect her. To save her. "Let's get you in bed," I said, trying on my responsible-sister hat. "And tomorrow, we're buying you a helmet."

Despite the tattoo, despite the nightclub, I was doing my best, and I hoped my mom would be proud. I hadn't abandoned my sister. I was keeping her safe, or trying to.

And I figured that had to count for something.

SIXTEEN

Not even a full day had passed since I'd met Clarence at Alice's—I mean, *my*—apartment, but it felt like it had been a hundred years. The place even seemed to smell musty, as if someone had died there, and the landlord had locked the place up for a year before rerenting.

And how nice a thought was that?

I opened the windows, letting the chilly October air blast in and shove out all the bad stuff, wishing I could just open a window in Rose and shove Lucas Johnson out as well. Didn't work that way, though. The way it did work was both dark and dangerous.

"I live for danger," I muttered.

"What?"

I turned to find Rose staring at me. She'd stripped down, and was now wearing only a T-shirt and thick socks.

"Hey, honey. It's almost four. Go crawl into bed." Even I, who no longer actually needed sleep, was down with that plan. At the moment, I wished I could sleep for days.

That, however, wasn't possible. In just a few hours, I needed to go open the pub. Egan's pub. And now that he was dead, it belonged to me and Rachel, Alice's sister.

I frowned, wondering if Rachel even knew that Egan was dead yet. For that matter, wondering if the police were after me. I'd been running around doing so much killing, but most of the time, my victims dissolved in a puddle of goo. Not so Egan. He'd been human, and I'd killed him. Killed him in retribution for what he'd done to Alice.

And I didn't regret it for a second.

At the same time, I wasn't terribly keen on getting arrested, and I found the lack of police attention odd. It wasn't, however, the kind of thing I could investigate without drawing attention to where there might otherwise be none. And so I was just going to have to wait for the other shoe to drop.

I noticed the light flashing on Alice's answering machine and had to wonder if maybe that other shoe hadn't decided to contact me by phone. A bit unprecedented, maybe, but not unheard of, and it was with a bit of trepidation that I pressed the button to play the messages.

Nothing from the police. But I did have at least a dozen messages, including a number of frantic phone calls from Gracie, two invitations to go out from Brian, an irritated message from Rachel, followed almost immediately by one that sounded extremely worried, then a third one that managed to hit the mark between worried and frustrated, and which told me that the pub would be opening for lunch that day per usual.

I didn't return any of them. Not then. Not with Rose in the other room and me wanting, right then, to slough off Alice and just be Lily, even if it was for only a few short minutes.

Short being the operative word because although I curled up on the couch and fell asleep, I was immediately awakened by someone pounding at my door. I groaned, and glanced at the clock, and realized it was eight in the morning, and I'd been asleep for four hours.

I shook off the fogginess of sleep and dragged myself into the hallway. I peered through the peephole, realizing only after the fact that my visitor could have been Mr. Tattooed Demon himself, and there was really nothing to stop him from jamming a big stick through the peephole and into my eye.

But it was only Gracie, and when I let her in, she threw herself into my arms with such relief that I found myself not worrying about the apocalypse or demons or bizarre missing keys. I was just happy to have a friend.

Then she pulled away from me and smacked me hard on the arm, and I had to start rethinking that friend thing. "I saw your bike out front," she said. "Where the *hell* have you been? I've been worried sick. My uncle was one of the cops called in to the pub, and Egan was stabbed, and no one could find you, and—" She cut herself off, wrapping her arms tight around me once more and mumbling something that sounded like, "Damn you."

"I'm sorry! I'm sorry! I'm okay. Really."

Once again she pulled away. "Uncle Tito wouldn't tell me what happened. What you told the police, I mean. Can you tell me now? Or are you supposed to keep it a secret?"

What I told the police? It occurred to me suddenly that Clarence had been a busy boy after discovering the state of the pub and Egan's body and me gone from the premises. It also occurred to me for the first time to realize that demons and their helpers had probably infiltrated the police department. That made sense, right? And that also explained why no one was waiting on my doorstep to arrest me or question me. If I'd already supposedly been questioned, what would be the need?

Of course, since I didn't have a clue as to what I supposedly said, best to keep the details to a minimum.

"They told me not to say anything," I said. "But I guess there's been some stuff going on for a while. Big-picture crime, you know," I added, hoping her mind would leap to drugs. "And Egan got caught in the cross fire."

"Wow," Gracie said.

"I know. Wow."

"So you're really opening back up today? Rachel said she was going to open up for business again."

"Yeah," I said. "I guess so."

"I'll be there," she said.

"Great. I'll buy you a pint."

"No," she said. "I mean I'll come back to work."

"No way." I shook my head. "No. Thanks for the offer, but no."

She managed to look both hurt and confused at the same time, and so help me, I felt bad. Because I wanted her there. I wanted a friend. And even though Gracie hadn't started out as my friend, I'd claimed her anyway.

"It's not—" I sighed. "Well, why on earth do you want to come back? I thought you liked your new job." Alice had arranged for Gracie to interview for a receptionist job, and it had been that job that had taken Gracie out of town the night that Rose was almost sacrificed. Had she been there, it would have been Gracie on that stone tablet and not Rose.

"I do like it," she said, but she started picking at her cuticles and didn't look me in the eye.

"But?"

She shrugged. "It's just paperwork, you know? Paperwork and phones and all the buttons on the phone confuse me, and I don't like talking on the phone anyway, and it's not like you go home with tip money, and—"

"Okay, okay," I said, then realized I was laughing. When, I wondered, was the last time I'd done that? "Okay, but on one condition."

"Sure. What?"

"Remember that day when we were at lunch? When you saw one of my visions?" That had been a total accident, and thank God Alice had told Gracie about her visions as a kid; otherwise, Gracie probably would have bolted. The vision I'd seen had been enough to make me almost bolt—a girl strapped to a stone table, the victim of a demonic sacrifice. But I hadn't been able to see the girl. Now I realized I'd been seeing Gracie in a possible future. At the time, I thought I was seeing Alice. Some latent memory in my own mind or something. I hadn't fully understood how visions worked, and so I hadn't been vigilant. And because I hadn't been completely on guard, the demons had taken another sacrifice—they'd taken Rose.

I wasn't going to let it happen again. Anything hinky in that girl's head, and she was staying far, far away.

"I want to try it again," I said.

"What? You want me to see one of your visions?"

"Something like that," I said.

She dragged her teeth along her lower lip. "You sure?"

"You wanna get hired back at my pub, that's my condition."

"It's kind of a freaky condition."

"I'm kind of a freaky girl," I countered, making her laugh.

"Yeah, all right. Whatever." She held out her hands. "Not any weirder than getting my palm read, right?"

Actually, I thought it was quite a bit weirder, but I didn't mention that. I just took her hands, looked into her eyes, and waited for the world to pop from color, to red, to gray.

It only took a second. One second before I was fast-forwarding through her head, wishing I'd practiced this trick so that I'd have more control, because right now all I was seeing was Gracie waiting tables and laughing. Gracie flirting with her new boyfriend, Aaron. Gracie dancing. Gracie standing in the rain, her head tilted back, as she laughed and laughed and laughed.

I pulled away, and realized that I was smiling, too. *She was safe.* I'd known that the future could change—after all, Deacon had seen a vision of me locking the Ninth Gate, and we know how well *that* vision turned out—but now I knew for certain that for Gracie, at least, it had changed for the better.

"Wow," she said. "That wasn't freaky at all."

"Nope," I said, happily. "Not freaky at all." I tilted my head to the side, considering her. "Actually, are you willing to let me try again?"

Her eyes narrowed. "Why?"

"I want to see if I can go in without you noticing."

"Yeah? Why?"

I shrugged. "Might be handy." I didn't explain about how if I could be Stealth Girl, it would open up a whole new world of possibilities. Like Kiera. And Zane.

And even Deacon.

I leaned back, considering. If he found out, there would be some serious hell to pay. But the idea of being able to get back inside his head—to see the secrets he was working so hard to keep—I couldn't deny that was seriously tempting.

"Will you?"

"Um, okay."

I didn't give her time to change her mind. I tried again. And again. And on the third time, although she still felt me, she said the image was fuzzier. As if my efforts to shield myself really were working.

I leaned back, smiling smugly. "We can practice more later, right?"

"Sure."

"Thanks. And if you really want to come back to waiting tables, I'd love to have you."

"Yay!" She leaned forward and tossed her arms around me, giving me a big hug. "After we close tonight, we totally have to go out. Me, you, Brian, and Aaron. Nothing major. Just a drink and friends. At Thirsty. Okay? You should get out. I know you, Alice, and you can't sit in here and brood, or go off and hide wherever you were hiding."

"I wasn't hiding."

"And no avoiding the subject."

"I'm just not sure it's a great idea."

"Why not?"

"The last time we went to Thirsty," I said, "I got

jumped in the alleyway and technically died." The paramedics had been called, and everything. Turned out they hadn't been necessary, what with me being immortal and all. But at the time, no one knew that. Least of all me.

She frowned. "Well, yeah. But isn't that all the more reason to go back?"

I couldn't help it; I laughed. The question was so very Gracie.

Her cheeks flushed. "No, I mean it. You'll be fine. Because lightning doesn't strike twice in the same place, right?"

"I really shouldn't," I said, thinking of Rose and the fact that I'd entered the ranks of single parents who required babysitters. *Or demon sitters,* I thought with a frown.

"Alice, come on. You have got to be running out of excuses by now."

My current excuse stepped into the hallway, her hair mussed, a fluffy pink robe tied at her waist. "Who's she?" Rose asked.

"A friend," I said. "Gracie."

Rose took a step forward. "Oh. Hi. I'm Lily's sister."

Gracie's forehead scrunched up. "Whose?"

"A friend of mine," I said. "She died recently." I held out my hand for Rose, who walked slowly over and took it. "This is Lily's sister, Rose, and her dad is having a hard time of it, so Rose is staying with me for a while, and—"

"Oh, God, Alice. I'm so sorry. Your friend dying, then Egan, and here I am trying to push a night out on you, and—"

"No," I said, "I like the idea. I think it's a good idea." For that matter, the more I thought about it, the more I wanted it. That pocket of normalcy to balance out the doom. That moment of laughter to make me remember why it was important to fight the dark that was building up inside of me and threatening to take over. "I want to go," I said, meaning it. "But I can't leave Rose alone."

"Of course you can't," she said. "I guess she could come . . ."

I shook my head. "Actually, I have an idea." Zane. He'd already watched her once, and I knew that Johnson would behave around the immortal. More than that, though, I wanted a reason to speak to him again, and I was more than happy to grasp my sister as an excuse. "After work," I said. "We'll go out for drinks after work."

"He won't like it," Rose said darkly, after Gracie left, and I didn't need Clarence's mind-reading powers to know that she wasn't talking about Zane but about Johnson.

"Yeah? Well, that's too bad for him. I'm doing his damned dirty work, but I'm not on the job twenty-four/seven. He'll get his little bits of key, but that's all he's getting. Not my life. Not my time. And he's damn sure not getting you."

She licked her lips. "He already has me."

I let out a breath, realizing I'd gotten too worked up.

"Yeah," I said. "I know." I took her hand. "But I'm not going to let him keep you."

Rose nodded, her face pale, her eyes huge against her sunken cheeks and sallow skin. "I want to hurt him," she said. "Even though he's inside me and can hear me, I have to say it. I have to say it out loud, you know? I want to hurt him. I want to kill him."

"I know you do," I said, my stomach clenching with the knowledge that my sister—my sweet, innocent sister—now had murder in her heart. "I know you do," I repeated, "but you're going to leave that part to me." I might not have been able to save her from this horror, but I could damn well do that much for her. And I would. So help me, I couldn't freaking wait.

SEVENTEEN

"You don't mind?" I asked Zane, as we stood near the weapons cabinet. I cast a look back toward Rose, who was watching videos in Zane's office.

I remembered what Clarence had once told me about possession. About how human bodies were frail and couldn't take it for long. And I was afraid, desperately afraid, that by the time I got the relics and dangled them in front of Johnson in exchange for my sister, it would be too late, and the sister I would get back would be irreparably injured.

If I got her back at all.

"You're sure?" I repeated, since Zane hadn't yet answered me.

"You are off to hunt this night?"

I shook my head. "The pub," I said. "And then I'm going out with Gracie." I looked down at my feet, suddenly embarrassed, as if it were foolish for an über-assassin-chick to care about such things. Clarence, I was certain, would think so.

Zane, however . . .

Zane only smiled, then moved toward me, making the air between us fizzle and pop. He took my hand, and I almost looked into his head, wanting to go deeper than I had once before.

When I'd peeked in before, I'd seen only sadness, but I'd broken away quickly, afraid he would feel me poking around in there. I knew now that the sadness was the weight of eternity bearing down upon him. A weight that I would eventually come to know, but which right then didn't feel real to me.

To Zane, though, it was beyond real. Alive forever, and yet confined to this small basement. He'd made a deal, he'd once told me. Train the warriors, and his mortality would be restored. Train, and eventually he would be allowed to die.

The real hell for him, though, was that after so long being alive, the reality of death now terrified him. And he was trapped between a desire to end his tenure on earth, and his fear of what he would face once gone.

As for me, my fears about immortality were more practical. I was terrified of being alive forever and yet trapped like Zane was. Maybe I could survive in a pimped-out basement with television and the Internet, but what I really feared was being dismembered and left in small pine box. My arms removed. My legs taken. And only me and my thoughts for all eternity.

I shivered.

If Zane noticed my discomfiture, he didn't say so. "It is good that you are going with your friends, *ma chère*." He stroked my cheek, the simple touch making my senses fire. Zane was sexuality personified, an immortal incubus, whose essence I'd absorbed, and the call of like to like was making me tingle. Making me burn. I wanted him. Wanted his kiss, his touch.

And yet I didn't, because I knew it wasn't real. It was the thrall of the incubus, that heady sensual cloud that I cast over the men I squeezed up against at dance clubs. A fake lust, a pretend infatuation.

I didn't want pretend. I wanted the real thing, and my mind was filled then not with Zane, but with Deacon. A man I still didn't trust but who set my body to melt even so. I was, perhaps, a fool to crave him so desperately, but I was powerless to escape my own emotions.

"Zane . . ."

"I know, *ma petite*. He calls to you still, this other man. This one you will not name."

I licked my lips. Wanting to tell him. Wanting to tell him everything and learn if what I was slowly coming to believe about this man was true—that he had no more loyalty for Clarence than I did. That if he knew my true battle, he would help me even more.

Those weren't words I could say, though, and so I simply smiled. "I'm not going with him tonight. Just Gracie. Just friends."

"And again, I say that is good." He twirled a strand of my hair between his fingers, and the sadness I saw in his face about broke my heart.

"I wish you could come, too," I said.

"Ah, *chérie*, so do I. So do I, indeed."

I left him to his melancholy, knowing that he would watch over Rose, and confident that Johnson would stay well buried in Zane's presence. But as I moved through the hallway toward the door that led to the dank alley that accessed Zane's basement, I realized I wasn't much in the mood to go out with friends. Instead, I was in the mood to go kill something. To feed the darkness and the sadness growing inside me.

I couldn't even do that, though, because I had to go to the pub. Had to go be Alice and put together the pieces of the real life I'd adopted when I'd slipped into her skin.

The Bloody Tongue was somber when I arrived, Egan's death hanging over the place. The demons were frustrated that their source for innocent girls had been so soundly removed, and the human patrons were merely expressing their condolences for a family that had lost its patriarch.

I tried to look upset that Egan was gone, but despite the fact that I'd become a method actor by default, I'm not entirely sure I managed.

Rachel was behind the bar, and when she caught my attention, I headed that way, passing by two round, bald men nursing Guinnesses in one of the booths.

"That her?" Tweedledee asked.

"That's the one," Tweedledum answered.

I started to turn back to them. To ask them ever so politely to step outside. But before I could do that, Rachel called, instructing me to get my butt over there, pronto.

"About damn time," she said, as I sidled up. "We need to talk."

She signaled for Trish, who stepped in to take over. Gracie was there, too, and she sent me a supportive smile as I followed Alice's big sister into the back, then down the stairs to the small stockroom, a place that would, at least, give us some semblance of privacy.

"We're selling the pub," she said without preamble, the moment I shut the door behind us.

"What? No." I didn't know what the future held, but I did know that the pub was a demon magnet. And that meant that I wanted to keep a hand in it. I didn't have Kiera's nose for demon scent, but if they gathered here, I could surely weed them out from the humans. And then, I thought, I could kill them. Get a nice little hit of strength for me and eradicate another demon from the world.

And, yeah, the thought of letting that dark curtain fall over me for just a moment held some pretty significant appeal, too.

All in all, a win-win situation.

But not if Rachel wanted to sell the pub.

"You can't," I said. "We own it together. We have to sell it together, and I don't want to."

"I'll ask the court to partition," she said. "Sell the pub under court order, split the proceeds. I've already talked to a lawyer, Alice. It's what I'm going to do. So get used to it."

"But why?" I could hear the whine in my voice and took a mental step backward. "Why not just go back to your life and let me deal with the pub? I mean, why are you even here?" She'd never worked there before. For that matter, I'd only actually met Rachel once before, when she'd burst in at Alice's apartment and asked me to watch her dogs. Then she'd bopped off to London for some work thing. "You have your life," I pushed. "Let me have mine."

She drew in a breath. "I gave it up."

"What?" I had no idea what she was talking about.

"My jewelry business. I signed all the assets over to a charity."

"You what?" None of this was computing.

"You heard me, dammit. I should never have had the business in the first place." She turned away from me, then drew her arms in tight to her chest. "Uncle Egan's murder just drove that home."

"But—"

She rounded on me. "Go to Harvard, Alice. Call them and tell them you'll start up in January. Get out of this life. For once, do what Mom wanted you to." She sucked in air. "I'm going to try. I'm really, really going to."

There was a whole conversation going on under the surface, and I was pretty certain I understood the gist of it. Pretty sure, but not positive. And I needed to know. I really, desperately needed to know if Rachel was walking away from the dark arts.

I took a step toward her and held out my hands. "Rachel," I said, and when I did, she looked in my eyes. That was all it took, and this time, when the pull came, I didn't rip away. On the contrary, I held on tighter, even when I heard her gasp. Even when I got sucked into the black. Even when I saw the rituals and the candles and the dark symbols. When I learned how she'd started her business with blood money, and how just days ago she'd screamed and ranted and destroyed the inside of her apartment, wishing all the while she could destroy the inside of herself.

She'd given it up, just like she'd said. She'd given it up, but she still felt trapped. Trapped, and afraid, and lost.

And now she wanted to run.

With a *pop*, the connection between us broke, and I stepped back, only to feel the sharp sting of her palm against my cheek. "Dammit, Alice. You do *not* do that. Ever. Do you understand me?"

I nodded, not planning to say anything else. But the words that came out surprised me as much as they surprised her. "I'm not Alice," I said. "I'm not really your sister."

EIGHTEEN

"What the hell are you talking about?" Rachel asked, staring at me as if I'd gone completely out of my mind, a reaction that didn't much surprise me.

"They killed her," I said. "Egan sold her to the demons, and they killed her."

"'Her,'" Rachel repeated, and I could imagine her dialing 911 and asking the operator to send the men in white coats to come pick up her sister.

"I'm not Alice," I said again, and even as I spoke, I wondered why I was bothering. Except that this was Alice's sister. The woman who'd loved her, and who wanted Alice to be free of the dark. Who was, in her own way, fighting the demons, too.

Or maybe that was just a bunch of random justification. Maybe I just wanted someone to know the truth.

She took a step backward. "This isn't funny, Alice. If you think that pulling this sort of bullshit prank on me is going to keep me from selling the pub—"

"No. It's not about the pub. Rachel, please. It's true. My name's Lily Carlyle." I paused. "And they killed me, too."

She stared at me, and for a moment—one brief, sparkling moment—I thought she believed me. Then her face tightened, and she pointed a finger straight at my face. "You have to stop this, Alice. I don't know what kind of sick bullshit you've gotten sucked into, but you have got to stop this."

She yanked off the apron she'd been wearing, and threw it on the floor. Then she spun on her heel and stormed out of the stockroom. I took a deep breath. So much for my maiden voyage into the land of bitter honesty.

"What's up with Rachel?" Gracie asked, when I returned upstairs. I just shook my head, too disheartened to come up with even a plausible lie. Gracie cocked her head, picking up on my melancholy. "Brian's looking forward to seeing you again."

I managed a smile. "Great. Can't wait." But I know she could tell I was lying. So much so that I could see the disappointment on her face when it was time to lock up, and I told her to go ahead and I'd meet her there.

"Dammit, Alice—"

"I just have to finish up here," I said. "I swear, I'm only five minutes behind you."

"Really?"

"Promise. I need a night out," I said. And it was true. It really was. I wanted a night of trying to be normal. A night of not craving the fight, the kill.

Of not hoping for a demon so that I could suck in its essence and get a nice little hit of the dark.

Yeah. I was totally down for the night-out plan.

Of course, that five-minute estimate turned out to be a little off because when I returned from taking out the trash, I found that not everyone had left the pub. Tweedledum and Tweedledee were still there, standing side by side in front of the bar.

"We're closed, boys."

"Glad to hear it," Tweedledum said, and before I could even react, he'd whipped out a knife and had lobbed it straight at me. I rolled to the side, but it didn't matter. It sliced my arm, bare because I was wearing a Bloody Tongue tank top. The scent of my own blood filled my senses, riling me, and I was up on my feet even as Tweedledee joined in the fun, coming at me with a knife of his own. *Screw that.*

I didn't have my own knife on me—it didn't go with the pub-girl outfit—but that didn't mean I couldn't find another weapon, and I dove over the bar and smashed the butt end off a bottle of tequila. One of our house brands. Not the top-shelf stuff.

"Foolish girl," Dum said.

"Indeed," Dee agreed.

"We will cut you," Dum said, opening a duffel they'd shoved under their table. "We'll break you. We'll slice you up good."

Dee's eyes narrowed. "We know your secret, little girl. And we'll lock you up and keep you forever and ever and ever."

"No!" I shouted, knowing that I shouldn't let fear and anger get the better of me and knowing I should stay behind the bar and hunker down.

I knew all that, and yet I lunged, leaping over the bar to land a solid kick in Dum's face, sending him reeling. He was back up in seconds, agile despite his girth, and he smashed and flashed and twirled and pummeled, and I met each of his attacks dead on, desperate to knock him back long enough so that I could race to the kitchen and retrieve my knife from the pocket of my coat. I could kill with any old knife, but only if I killed with an owned knife would the demons be reduced to goo.

And only with an owned kill would I gain the strength and absorb the essence—something I damn sure wanted.

The two of them attacked from opposite sides, and I dove, finding myself in front of the knife that Tweedledum had first thrown my way. A knife that had drawn my blood.

Shit. That blade was mine now, and I snatched at it, kicking as the two demons tried to pull me back by the legs. My fingers brushed the hilt and then, *yes*, I had it.

I twisted at the waist and thrust myself up, leading with the blade. And not a moment too soon. Tweedledum had been only inches away, his own blade falling harmlessly to the ground as my knife sliced through his neck, and the demon dissolved into disgusting black goo.

There was no celebration for me, though, because as my blade was outstretched, Tweedledee had come up from behind, and now he had his knife at my throat. "Headless," he said. "I think it's fucking beautiful."

To my complete mortification, I actually whimpered, then closed my eyes, trapped, and knowing that I'd lost. For the world, for myself, and for Rose.

I waited for the pain, then for the awareness that came from being broken but alive.

It didn't come. Instead, the knife jerked sharply, cutting me, but not killing me. And then I felt the demon behind me turn to goo, and the slime dribble down my back to puddle on the floor behind me.

I whipped around to find Deacon standing in the kitchen doorway. He'd thrown his knife, and he'd thrown it true.

"Deacon," I said. And I rushed him. My body was humming from the kill as much as from fear. From the knowledge that I'd almost fallen into my worst nightmare, and by the need—desperate and demanding—to hold on right then to the man who embodied my most ardent fantasy.

He met me halfway, understanding what I craved, what I needed. His mouth was hot against mine, and I drew him in, our tongues doing battle as our bodies slammed together. He was all heat and muscle, all danger and dark, and I had to have him. So help me, I had to let the dark take me. Had to let desire rule me, and I pressed him back, farther and farther until there was nowhere else to go.

"More," I demanded, and he complied without complaint, his mouth deepening the kiss, his hands hard on me. On my hips, on my waist. On my breasts.

The tank top was flimsy, and he yanked it up, then shoved my bra down, giving him access to my breasts. I arched my back and moaned, the pleasure that shot through me absolutely exhilarating, and completely overshadowing the slow, burning ache that had begun in my arm. I had no idea why my arm had decided to go on active duty, and right then I didn't care. I was content to ignore it.

I wasn't about pain right then; I was about pleasure. Pleasure and heat and complete satisfaction, and the way that Deacon was touching me wasn't enough. I needed more. I needed *all*.

Desperate, I fumbled with the button on his jeans, and when I couldn't manage that, I fumbled with my own, then wriggled out of them until I was standing there in the lacy pink panties that Alice favored and I hadn't had time to replace.

Deacon's hand dipped down, his fingers following smooth skin, then easing slowly, so slowly under the waistband of the panties. He teased me, his finger dipping down, finding me wet, then making me whimper as he refused to touch me the way he knew that I wanted.

I grabbed the belt loops of his pants and urged his hips forward. "Dammit, Deacon," I said. "Now."

And this time, when I fumbled with his button, I actually managed to make progress, and before I knew it, our jeans were on the floor, and we were on the couch in front of the fireplace. The leather couch with cloven feet.

"Lily," he said, as though my name were both a prayer and a curse.

"Don't wait," I begged. "Don't wait; don't stop."

I was breathing hard, my body on fire, lust running through me like a wild beast. And when Deacon thrust inside me, I rose up, desperate to meet him, to match him. To take him over the edge with me.

We moved together, hard and demanding, as if we'd both just discovered something we couldn't get enough of. And as the pressure built and built, I clung to him, pulling him closer, this man who I had come to need so desperately. This man I barely knew.

His body shuddered against mine, and he cried out in pleasure, sending me right over the edge with him. I collapsed against him, sated, and breathed in deep of the musky scent of sweat and sex. Of *us*.

He had claimed me and, so help me, I'd claimed him, too.

When I could breathe again, I rolled over, trying to shift to a more comfortable position. I had my hand pressed to his chest, and I smiled at his face.

He smiled back, and our eyes locked.

And, yeah, that was a big mistake.

The vision snapped, and I jerked as it sucked me in. I had a glimpse of the darkness. A sensation of fear, then the cold press of the pub floor against my cheek.

I sat up, rubbing the side of my face, realizing as I did that Deacon had actually thrown me off him rather than let me look deep inside.

Shit.

I crossed the pub to grab my jeans and started stuffing my legs back into them. Suddenly I didn't feel nearly as warm and languid. Now I felt irritated. And not even at Deacon. At myself.

"Lily."

"Don't." I held up a hand. "I shouldn't have done that."

"Unless my memory is faulty, I think we both did that."

I rounded on him. "Dammit, Deacon, I don't need this. This thing," I said, gesturing between us. "I can't fight it—I don't even want to fight it—but I'm goddamned terrified of it."

"Why?"

I stared at him. "You know why."

"You can trust me, Lily."

"No," I said. "How about this—*you* can trust *me*. Let me in, Deacon. You think your reality can be any worse than my imagination? Or is there something in there you really don't want me to know?" I took a step closer, and the heat between us arced like electricity. "Like the reason no one seems to want you dead."

"They don't want me dead? Or they don't want to risk trying to kill me?" He cupped the back of my neck with his head. "I've destroyed more than you ever will, Lily. I could destroy you right now if I wanted to. No, don't argue. You know I'm right."

I did know, and the knowledge scared me. But, dammit, it also excited me.

"Do you think the other demons will take me on lightly?" I shook my head, not knowing what to believe anymore.

"I want you, Lily. I want you, and I need you." He tilted my chin up. "You know what we can accomplish together. Work with me."

"I'm not sacrificing Rose."

"I know." He stepped away, his back to me. "There's a way to save her."

"Move her soul out into another body?"

He turned around, and I shrugged.

"I have sources, too. And I don't like that solution. I'm not killing so that Rose can live. Not, unless I'm sure I have to." It was, I realized, the first time I'd voiced the truth about the matter. And while a part of me hated that I could do that—that I could take an innocent life to use as a shell for my sister—another part of me was relieved to know that possibility was out there. A solution, dangling out for me to take if I was desperate enough.

Whether I would ever be desperate enough to do to an innocent what Clarence and company did to me . . . That, I didn't know.

"There may be another way," Deacon said, gaining my instant attention. "It's risky, but . . ."

"What?"

"The Vessel of the Keeper."

"The what?"

"It has a fancier name," Deacon said, "but the translation describes it best."

"What is it?"

"A vessel," he said. "Like a pot or a jar. I don't know exactly. I've never seen it."

"And?" I prompted, though I really didn't need to prompt. I had a feeling I knew what this vessel did. It held souls. And Deacon was going to suggest that it hold Rose's.

"Only until we can find a suitable body," he said, after he'd explained exactly that.

I shook my head. "No. No way."

"Why not? It's a perfect solution. Move her out. Destroy her body. And with any luck, destroy Johnson along with her."

"How? How do you move her out?"

He turned away from me. "I can handle that."

"Explain."

I watched his shoulders straighten before he turned back around. "I can send my essence into the body. I can push Rose out."

"And Johnson? He's just going to put up with that?"

"He may fight to stay. He may jump out."

"Out?" I repeated. "Where would he go?" A horrible thought occurred to me. "Oh, God. What if he went into your body?"

A small smiled danced at Deacon's mouth. "I'm glad to see the possibility mortifies you as much as me. But no. I have ways of protecting my body when I'm not in it."

"Oh." I pondered the idea some more, thinking about what would happen to Rose. "So she lives in a pot like some creature out of an old *Star Trek* episode?" That really wasn't sounding appealing to me.

"We find a body," Deacon said patiently.

"I'm not killing an innocent to provide for my sister."

He pointed to the oily stains on the floor. "What would have happened if you'd killed with a different knife?"

"The bodies would still be there," I said slowly. "Empty. Just, dead."

"Exactly."

I shook my head, the idea creeping me out. "She wouldn't be herself anymore."

"Are you still yourself?"

I frowned, because I honestly wasn't sure of the answer.

He cupped my chin. "Lily, he's killing her body anyway. She's running out of time. And so is the world. I need you with me, looking for the key. And you need Rose free of Johnson. This is the way, Lily. It's the only way."

"But a demon body . . ." I protested.

"It's not about the body. It's about the essence. You know that, Lily. You of all people know that."

He was right. I did. I didn't like it, but I knew it.

"All right," I finally said. "Where is it?"

He frowned. "Well, that's the problem. I don't know. I've been doing research, but I haven't located it yet."

It was my turn to frown. "Not exactly helpful."

He traced his fingers lazily up and down my arm. "Too bad we don't have access to a map that can find lost objects."

I lifted my brow. "Great idea. I'll just ask Clarence to tell me how to figure out the incantation for conjuring a portal."

He aimed a significant look at me. "You don't have to ask."

I took an involuntary step backward. "No way. You want me in his head? I don't have any control. He'd know I was in there. Shit, Deacon. I'd have to kill him."

"If it gets Rose free, isn't it worth it? And if you kill him, you'll have his essence. *You'll* be an Incantor, Lily."

I bit my lower lip, weighing my options. Weighing the risk. Because as tempting as the plan was, unless I was certain it would work, I couldn't risk my sister.

On the floor, the stains from the two demons seemed to call out to me, reminding me of the danger of the world I lived in. I toed them, looking up at Deacon and deliberately changing the subject. "Why do they want me dead? All these demons. If they know I'm looking for the *Oris Clef*, shouldn't they be cheering me on from the sidelines?"

"Depends on the demon," he said casually. "The portal's open, so Armageddon is coming, and most of the demons are happy with the status quo. They don't want any one demon to have the *Oris Clef*. They don't want a demon king in the ranks."

I nodded. I hadn't considered that before.

"Others do want the power. They're not trying to kill you, but to capture you."

"But I'm no good without Clarence's incantations."

Deacon shrugged. "Maybe they don't know that."

"At least that explains the tattoo-faced demon. The one we ran into in China," I said, in response to Deacon's questioning look. "That was the second time I've met up with him, and I'm still alive."

Deacon was looking at me with the strangest expression.

"What?"

"You don't know who he is?"

"Why would I?" I asked, completely baffled. "He didn't stop to introduce himself."

"That was Gabriel, Lily. The archangel."

NINETEEN

"Wait," I said, completely freaking out. "An *angel* wants me dead?" I was doing all this fighting for good, and a freaking *angel* wanted me dead? What was wrong with that picture?

"I'm sorry, Lily," Deacon said, after I'd kicked one of the barstools so hard it went careening across the room.

"Was Johnson right?" I asked, my voice barely a whisper. "Have I really sworn fealty to the demon side?"

"You haven't," Deacon said, putting his arms around me. "No more than I have."

I twisted back to look at him, because once upon a time, that was where his loyalty had lain.

"I renounced," he said, his voice harsh. "Believe me or don't, but I swear it's the truth. I renounced the dark, and still I was pushed away from the light."

I believed him. For better or for worse, I trusted Deacon. I could admit that finally, as he held me tight in his arms. I *did* trust him. But I still wanted inside his head. I wanted proof that my trust wasn't once again misplaced.

"I know angels aren't all white gowns and halos and harps," I said, "but warrior tats really weren't what I was expecting."

"But that's what he is," Deacon said. "A warrior."

"Then why does he want me? He could have killed me a half dozen times over—I'm certain of it. But I'm alive. And yet he still keeps coming. So what does he want with me?"

Deacon shook his head. "I don't know."

"I mean, I'm trying to do good. Doesn't God know that I'm trying to do good? Didn't he tell his angels?"

Deacon's mouth twitched. "I'm not sure heaven is run on a memo system."

"Well, why doesn't he just freaking ask me what I'm up to?"

"Lily," Deacon said, squeezing my hand, "I don't know. But I don't think that a sit-down is Gabriel's typical modus operandi."

I sighed and drew my knees up to my chest. "I have to fix this. Rose. The gate. The whole freaking Apocalypse. I have to make it better."

He pressed a kiss to the top of my head. "You will."

I could only hope that he was right.

I drew in a shaky breath. "They know who I am now.

All of them. Demons. Angels." I twisted around to look at him directly. "Why haven't they come to my apartment? They come here to the pub, but never there."

"Protections," Deacon said. "Penemue had Clarence endow Alice's apartment with protections. Make sure the demons couldn't get in without being invited."

I nodded. That made sense. Though I supposed I needed to be even more on my guard from then on. Since the memo about my secret identity had apparently circulated, and there was nothing to keep them off my street. I frowned, not worried about myself so much as I was about Rose.

"You can stay with me," Deacon said. "I assure you my place is safe. And secret."

I almost took him up on that but ended up shaking my head. "You don't want Johnson in your house," I said.

He nodded. "True enough. But for you, I'll take the risk."

"I don't know."

"It's a good idea," he said, then bent low and whispered his cell phone number into my ear, his voice holding so much heat I was certain I would either melt or change my mind and go home with him right then.

After all that drama, I really wasn't in the mood to go to Thirsty, but Gracie was expecting me, and I wasn't going to disappoint the one non-demon-related friend I now had in this world. I invited Deacon to join me, but he declined, his expression amused. Apparently whatever the parameters of our fledgling relationship were, they did not include the traditional, old-fashioned date.

Probably just as well. Because although I was not interested in Brian, he was interested in Alice. And even in my darkest funk, I knew that it would be beyond rude to show up at Thirsty with a date in tow.

"There you are!" Gracie said, as I pushed my way through the crowd to their booth. More restaurant than club, Thirsty still had a great dance floor, and tonight the patrons were making full use of the live band that management had brought in.

Brian scooted over, and I slid in next to him, the incubus in me picking up on his attraction. And, yeah, I felt the desire in me ratchet up. Felt the sensuality flare. And I felt the darkness in me murmuring that I could have this boy. Could do whatever I wanted, wherever I wanted. And all the while, I would be thinking of Deacon.

I snatched up a menu and clutched it tight, determined to back those thoughts down. To fight the darkness that not only threatened to explode, but which threatened to make me hurt an innocent guy.

"We were beginning to wonder if you were going to stand us up," Brian said, leaning in close so that I could hear him over the music. His breath tickled my ear, and despite myself, I felt that tug of heat. I glanced away, torn between wanting the heat to dissipate and wanting to stoke it, and I found myself looking at the doorway—and right at Deacon.

The burn I'd been trying to push back erupted, and I knew then that I'd lost the battle. I hadn't yet learned to control my incubus side, and that was only too apparent with the way Brian now put his hand on my thigh. "So, um, Alice, do you want to dance?"

Gracie's eyes were narrow, but she didn't say anything. I left my coat on the seat, and Brian and I slid out of the booth, then eased onto the dance floor. "Do you want to do a movie sometime?" Brian asked, as I raised my arms above my head and let my hips move with the music. I'd been looking over his shoulder, watching Deacon, the way he stood straight and tall. The way a muscle twitched in his cheek.

I moved closer to Brian.

And, yeah, one part of me felt like a shit for doing it. For smiling at him when he slipped his hands around my waist. For arching my back so that our bodies brushed when my hips gyrated. I was driving both of us a little crazy—and Deacon, too.

That, of course, was what I'd wanted, what I craved. That sexual spark. And if the dark part in me wanted to use Brian to get there . . .

Well, I'm ashamed to admit that the part of me that knew better had been soundly subjugated.

"Alice?" Brian pressed, moving his arms up to hook around my neck. "The movie?"

I slid my fingers through his hair and spun around on the floor, giving Deacon my back, and then closing my eyes and letting myself pretend that it was his arms

I was in, not Brian's. "Maybe," I whispered. "Right now
let's just dance." I wanted to do nothing more than move
to the music. To be the old Lily, who danced and drank
and bummed smokes off her friends. A Lily who didn't
hunt demons and didn't care about the dark.

I could feel Brian's pulse increase, and I pressed
closer, enjoying the fantasy. We moved together for a
while, lost in lust and the music.

Then I felt Brian's erection and caught the intense
thrum of his desire. I eased back, the bubble bursting. I
wasn't the old Lily. Not by a long shot. And I wanted
out of there. Wanted to make amends to this nice guy
for the games I was playing. Games he probably didn't
even realize were going on.

Someone tapped at my shoulder, and I whipped
around, expecting to find Deacon.

Instead, my eyes met Gracie's, hers wide and disturbed.

"Gracie," I said, the buzz fizzling. "I'm sorry. I—"

"It's about Rachel," she said, thrusting my phone toward me. "It rang, and I couldn't catch your attention,
and—"

I wasn't listening anymore. I had the phone up to
my ear, and the man on the other line was telling me
that he was from Carney Hospital and that Rachel had
been assaulted.

I didn't hang around to hear the rest of it. With the
phone plastered to my ear, I grabbed up my coat, signaled to a worried-looking Gracie and a dazed Brian

that I was leaving, then raced out of Thirsty and gunned the bike to the hospital.

"Rachel Purdue," I said to the first person I saw with a name tag. "Where do I find her?"

"I'm sorry—"

"Patient. Emergency room. Assault victim."

"Right." The woman's voice was soft and calming, and she walked me to a set of double doors and pointed me down the proper hallway. "It'll be okay, honey," she said with a soft pat on my back.

I wasn't at all sure about that, but I jogged down the corridor until I reached the emergency room, then accosted yet another employee.

"She's doing well," the lanky redhead said. Her hair had been pulled back into a severe ponytail, and she moved with an efficient step to one of the small cubicles set up for ER patients. I followed her in, then exhaled in relief when I saw Rachel sitting up in bed, her face a black-and-blue mess, but her eyes bright and alert.

"What happened?" I ran forward and took her hands.

"Some of my old acquaintances weren't exactly thrilled that I decided to change the way I'm living my life."

I winced, understanding perfectly who the old friends were. "What did they do?"

"Jumped me. By my apartment." She twisted her head to look at me. "They said I ought to follow your example. You wanna tell me what they meant by that?"

I didn't, of course. And at the same time, I wanted her to know. I didn't want her to believe her sister had fallen in with the very thing that Rachel herself was trying to escape. And, yes, I realized that this could be one big, huge, honking trap. Use Alice's sister to bait me into revealing my true allegiance.

But do that, and they either had to kill me, or I'd have to run. Either way, they couldn't use my arm to find the rest of the relics.

So I figured I was safe.

Or maybe I was just rationalizing. Bottom line, I wanted Rachel to know the truth. I felt like I owed it to her. She'd lost a sister, after all.

"Alice," she pressed. "Do you know what they meant?"

I sat up straighter. "It means I'm doing something right," I said. "It means they think I'm working for the demons. And Rachel," I added, "my name really isn't Alice. I told you. I'm Lily."

"All right, Lily," she said in an exasperated tone. "Tell me. Tell me everything."

And I did. All of it. Or most of it. I left out a few bits. Like sex on the floor of the Bloody Tongue. I figured we could skip those details.

When I was finished, she was no longer looking at me like I was crazy. Instead, she closed her eyes and sank back into the thin hospital pillow. "My uncle Egan killed my sister."

"Yes."

"And a demon is trapped in your sister."

"Yes," I said. And this time my voice broke.

She rolled her head and opened her eyes to look at me. "And now you're killing demons."

"That's my plan. It's complicated. I have this whole double-agent thing going, and they—"

"I need to sleep."

I jerked back, almost as if her words were a physical blow. "What?"

"I need to sleep now," she said. She turned away from me, but I saw the way her shoulders hitched as she held back tears.

"I—okay." I stood up, wishing I could comfort her. I couldn't, though. She'd lost her sister, had her world shattered, and looking at me only reminded her of the horrible truth.

"So, I'll see you at the pub, okay?" But she didn't answer, and I slid out the door, feeling like this was all my fault. I don't know. Maybe it was.

I was still in a funk when I reached Zane's, then felt even more guilty because I had actually considered simply leaving my sister there with him. But she was my responsibility, demon warts and all, and even on a day when I wanted nothing more than to curl into a ball and moan about the sorry state of my life, I had to at least put on a responsible face.

A lesson in parenting that my stepfather had never understood.

It was late when I arrived, and I found Zane up, doing some sort of slow martial arts moves on the mat in the middle of the basement. He saw me, and even as he balanced on one foot, he held his finger to his lips, warning me that she was asleep. I nodded, then stood to the side, waiting for him to finish. When he did, he came toward me, glistening with sweat.

"Where's Kiera?"

"She is well," he said. "I sent her home."

"Oh." I actually hadn't thought of her as having a home and felt a little bit foolish.

"What has happened, *ma fleur*?"

"Rachel," I said. I dragged my fingers through my hair, then sat on the floor, my back to the gray weapons cabinet. I licked my lips, choosing my words carefully, but needing to say what was on my mind. "She chose a side, Zane, and she was punished for it."

"I see. And which side did she choose?"

"The right one." I watched his face, searching for a clue as to his true allegiance.

"It is hard sometimes," he said. "To choose. There is always a price to pay."

"Did you make a choice?" I asked, softly.

He stood, then moved away from me. "I did not," he said. "Perhaps I should have."

I swallowed, the import of what he'd just revealed to me striking home. He hadn't chosen. Not right. Not wrong. "And now?"

He turned back to face me. "Now I think only of myself." He lifted his head to look at me directly. "I've told you my story, Lily, and it's a selfish one."

"What about Kiera?" I asked, blurting out the question before I had considered my words. "Do you think she's . . ." I trailed off, wanting to ask out loud, but I couldn't. Instead I backtracked. "Do you think she's a good partner for me?"

He met my eyes, his expression shuttered. "I think she has your back."

"That's not really what I meant."

He stood up. "Yes," he said. "I think she is a fine partner."

"Good." I stood up, knowing I should just take Rose and go. But I was still antsy. "Rachel's going to be okay, but she was beaten pretty badly. And all because she wanted to get free."

He looked at me, his eyes seeing more than I wanted. "It can be hard to give up the dark once it gets inside you. Once it starts to fill those spaces."

I felt the tears flood my eyes and wanted to sink into the floor, the weight of his words pressing me down. I'd never be able to give up the dark, no matter how much I wanted to pretend otherwise. I wasn't a normal girl anymore, and even the most fervent wishes wouldn't bring back my old life.

"Rachel will survive, Lily," he said, pulling me close. "And so will you. Survival," he added. "I fear it is what we do best."

TWENTY

"Just fold and roll," I said to Rose, putting a knife and fork in a napkin and demonstrating how to wrap the silverware service. "If you can do all of these, that'll be a huge help."

She nodded and started in on it, looking like nothing more than a kid working in the family business. Nothing to suggest she was a kid with a demon inside her. Nothing, that was, except for the pallor of her skin and the way her pupils stayed overly dilated. And, of course, the haunted way she looked at me when I'd asked that morning if Johnson was still there.

"He's here to stay, Lily," she'd said in that slow, singsong voice. "I thought you knew that."

"Not to stay," I'd said, a note of panic rising. "He's not staying."

But she hadn't answered. She'd just turned back into the bathroom and lost herself in the shower.

Now, though, even that dreamy interchange seemed like history. She was awake. She was alert.

She was Rose.

I fingered the locket I wore around my neck, a souvenir of my life as Lily, with pictures of both me and Rose. And as I touched it, I couldn't help but wonder how long before the other shoe dropped.

The hour was still early, so we had only a smattering of patrons in the pub. Just the few diehards who came in for a prelunch half-pint to warm them up for their lunchtime pint. Rachel had been here when I'd arrived, but she'd managed to avoid me all morning, moving to the kitchen or the stockroom or the walk-in whenever I got within five feet of her.

Now, though, she came up behind me as I polished the bar with some Brasso and an old rag.

"She's your little sister?"

I didn't turn around, but I could see her reflected in the brass I'd just polished. "She is."

"I didn't even know I'd lost Alice," she said, her voice hitching.

"I know. I'm sorry."

"I wasn't a very good sister to her."

Her words, so familiar to me, hung heavy on my heart. I looked across the pub, my eyes finding Rose. "You did the best you could."

She took a bar rag and started drying the already dry glassware. "Do you know how to find them? The demons? Do you know how to tell them apart from the humans?"

I turned, wanting to see her face, and when I did, all I saw was controlled anger. "No," I said, thinking of Kiera and her demon-sniffing schnoz. "I don't."

"I do." She licked her lips. "I want to help you. Will you let me?"

"Every demon I kill makes me stronger," I said, then looked up and met her eyes dead on. "I need to be pretty damn strong if I'm going to win in the end."

"I get it," she said. "Those two, for starters." She nodded to two burly guys nursing beers and a basket of cheddar fries. Both were wearing Red Sox caps, and both were making it a point not to look in our direction. "Egan used to supply them with herbs and stuff for their ceremonies."

"And stuff?"

Her eyes went hard. "I didn't know," she said, referring to the fact that I'd told her Egan had also been in the business of supplying the demons with sacrificial girls. "And now that I do, I don't have any compunction about you taking them out. I'll even hold them down if it'll help."

"It wouldn't," I said, "but thanks for the support." I checked on Rose, who had put her head down on the table and gone to sleep. A quick shiver of worry ran up my spine. Johnson might not be popping out to shoot off his mouth much, but he was making his presence known in other ways. Like the fact that he was slowly killing my sister. Stealing her energy. Snuffing out her soul.

I needed him out. And soon.

And as much as it terrified me, I was beginning to think I was going to have to risk killing Clarence so that we could find the vessel and set Deacon's plan in motion. I'd bring the wrath of hell down upon us, but if it meant saving Rose, then maybe hellfire was worth it.

Except I wouldn't really be saving her, would I? I'd be trapping her inside a vessel. Trapped, just the way I feared I would end up if the demons got their claws in me.

Could I do that to her?

I looked at her, and drew in a breath. Dammit, I just didn't know.

I shook off the melancholy and forced myself to go back to polishing as Rachel went back to checking the inventory behind the bar. We were both engrossed when the door opened, sending a flood of sunlight across the dimly lit pub. I looked up and saw Kiera silhouetted in the doorway.

She stood for a moment, getting her bearings, then moved across the room toward me in long, confident strides. "Nice place," she said. "Need another waitress?"

"Excuse me?" I was doing a bad job of hiding my

amusement. And, yeah, now that I had Zane's seal of approval, I admit I was warming up to my partner even more.

She rolled one shoulder. "Not like our regular gig pays that well," she said. "Or, like, pays at all. I need a job. Figured you could use me." She flashed a wicked grin. "I'm strong. Bet you don't have anyone who can carry a pub tray like me."

I figured I could give her a run for her money but didn't say so. After all, I was now management. And management didn't play who's-got-the-bigger-dick with the staff.

I glanced over my shoulder at Rachel, who was listening with unabashed interest to our conversation.

"My partner in crime," I said, by way of explanation, glancing quickly at the burly Red Sox fans in the corner. "Kiera, my sister, Rachel. Alice's sister," I clarified, in a much lower tone.

"Then give the girl a job," Rachel said, tossing Kiera a tank top from behind the bar and telling her to go get changed.

"I like this," Kiera said with a grin. "Honest employment. Who knew?"

"So we're not selling the pub?" I asked once Kiera was out of earshot.

Rachel glanced toward the demons, then shook her head. "Not if keeping it helps you and her."

"It does," I promised her. The pub was demon central. A lot like those roach motels, the vermin just seemed to be attracted to the place.

"Then that's your answer."

Kiera came back in, her red bra visible under the white material of the tank top. I met Rachel's eyes, but she only laughed and shook her head. "Okay," I said, sliding a laminated sheet with all the tables sketched in toward her. "You take this half, and I'll take the rest, then we can mix it up again when Gracie comes on shift."

"Got it," Kiera said, turning to walk away.

I winced as my arm started to burn. "Wait."

She turned back, her brow furrowing, then immediately clearing. "Now?"

I nodded, doubling over and clutching my arm to my chest.

"What?" Rachel was right beside me, her expression concerned. "What's going on?"

"My arm," I said, looking over toward Rose. "We have to go."

Rachel bit her lip, then nodded. "Then go," she said. "I'll watch Rose."

"I'm not sure that's a good—"

"I can handle it," she said severely, and it occurred to me that considering her family history, she probably could. So long as the demons didn't try to express their displeasure with her again.

"Come *on*," Kiera said, as I stood there debating.

"Go," Rachel said.

In the end, it was Rachel that decided it for me. I ran to the back to get my coat and knife, then whispered a quick good-bye in Rose's ear. And I told Johnson in no uncertain terms that if anything happened to Rachel while I was gone, he would face the brunt of my wrath. Somehow, someway, I would make him pay.

I didn't know if he heard.

I didn't know if he heeded.

But I did know that my speech made me feel better, and I walked a little bit lighter as I followed Kiera out the front door, having succumbed to her insistence that we take her car and not my bike.

We were at the car and Kiera was unlocking the driver's-side door when I saw them—the Red Sox demons from the pub.

"Kiera," I said, keeping my voice low and even. "Toss me the keys." The downside of a classic car—no automated door locks.

She didn't question. Just did as I asked in a perfect-partner rhythm that was a joy to behold.

Unfortunately, the joy came to a screeching halt, because both demons had decided they wanted to party and were barreling toward us. Worse than that, apparently they had friends. Little demon friends who didn't care that it was daylight and that attacking two seemingly frail girls on the street was a really stupid plan.

Or not so stupid since nobody rushed from the nearby

buildings to give us assistance as the demons rushed in for the attack. For that matter, the street seemed deserted, and I had to wonder if regular humans could sense the danger and had locked themselves up behind closed doors.

Not that I wondered much. I was too busy using the car to get leverage as I kicked my legs out and tried to knock some demon heads together. The demons all appeared human, and at least none of them had Gabriel's sort of hyped-up powers, but there were ten of them, and those odds really weren't good.

I tightened my grip on my knife and vowed to make the odds a little better.

"Kiera! You alive over there?"

"I've got the bastard," she said, and I heard the wet *schlurp* as her knife struck home. "You?"

"I'm good," I said, whipping myself into a frenzy. I kicked out, and got one hard in the gut, sending him tumbling backward. I leaped on him, my hand on his throat and my knife ready to slice through him like butter.

And then I caught his eye, and damned if I didn't snap to a vision.

Deacon.

Surrounded. Deferring.

Fearing his wrath.

And then blackness, and he's searching. Looking.

For the Oris Clef?

For something. Something lost. Something important.

And they say he knows. He knows where it is. Deacon Camphire has secrets. And he knows . . .

And the demons whisper among themselves, and the word travels on the wind—be wary of Deacon Camphire, for he will one day rule us all.

TWENTY-ONE

I broke the connection, my heart pounding, my mind spinning. Beneath me, the demon quaked, and I barely paid it any attention, just sliced its throat and shoved it back onto the street, darkness swirling within me even as dark thoughts about Deacon flooded my mind.

Deacon, seeking the allegiance of the demons.

Deacon, searching for the *Oris Clef*.

I didn't want to believe it, and yet I'd seen it, and if the images in the dead demon's head were true, then I'd once again stuck my trust in where it didn't belong.

Dammit. You'd really think I would have learned by then.

Not that I had a chance to think about that, because the rest of the demons were moving in, and I was kicking, fighting, stabbing, and thrusting. I was in a mental funk, my thoughts getting darker and darker with each kill.

I was in such a funk that I barely noticed when Kiera came by, her color high, her breathing hard, and I saw that we were fresh out of demons; together we'd wasted them all, and right then that didn't make me happy. I wanted more. More kills. More dark. And damned if I couldn't have it.

I'd managed to shake off a bit of the darkness by the time we arrived at the basement, but not the terrible sense of betrayal. Clarence had already prepared the bridge, and he returned the necklace to me. Because we'd already determined that the relics of the *Oris Clef* were interconnected, it made sense that the game of hot-or-cold I played with my arm worked better if I had all the pieces to work with.

This time, he also loaded us down with a few more tools, though not many. Apparently the best way to travel through a portal is naked. The more stuff you carry, the more likely you are to get tossed off course.

Kiera was down with the naked plan. Me, not so much.

We ended up wearing our regular clothes—jeans, our Bloody Tongue tank tops—our weapons, and flashlights. Still nothing spectacular as far as blasting our way out of a rough spot, but when I suggested C-4, Clarence told me about a theoretical risk of detonation while we were on the bridge. That pretty much ended that conversation as far as I was concerned.

Finally equipped, we stepped into the portal, did the

whole blood-on-the-symbol thing, and then the world was spinning, and we were on our way to the British underground. But not, as I would have preferred, the London Underground.

"You know what sucks?" Kiera whispered, as we crouched in a dimly lit passageway, breathing deep the scent of fresh earth. "I've always wanted to go to Britain. Always wanted to see Stonehenge. I mean, druids, right? How cool is that? And now here we are, as close to Stonehenge as I'm likely to ever get, and *this* is the view I have?"

We were, at the moment, somewhere underneath the famous stones. At least, I assumed we were. Since Clarence's bridge had dumped us out in this underground tunnel, I really couldn't be sure of anything.

By then, I was wondering if having a bit of plastic explosive wouldn't have been worth the risk. "Look," I said, shining my light in front of us. "The tunnel's caved in."

The beam from my flashlight played over a pile of rocks that reached from the floor all the way up to the top of the corridor. Through a few cracks and crevices, a hint of light shone. "Can you get up there?"

She climbed up, me lighting the way. "Can't see anything," she said. "And I can't move these damn boulders."

I sighed. "Come back down. Maybe there's another way."

With our narrow beams of light leading us, we headed in the opposite direction. We hadn't gone that way in the first place because my arm burned as we approached the pile of rocks, and the pain eased up when we backed away. Now, though, I was hoping we could circle back around and find the pain again.

And didn't that sound like a country-and-western song?

For that matter, I was feeling a bit like my entire life was a country-and-western song. The kind that's sad, and bemoans losing love and trust and all that mushy stuff. I was also on edge, expecting to see Deacon any second. Because from what I'd seen in that demon's head, Deacon Camphire was more interested in finding these relics than he was letting on.

More than that, the demon seemed to believe that Deacon knew where the third piece was. And if that was the case, then it explained why Clarence didn't want him dead. If something happened to me, Deacon might be the only source of information.

What I didn't get, though, was why Deacon would let me keep the first relic. If he really was intent on collecting them, then wouldn't he have done everything in his power to get the necklace from me while we were in China?

I reached up to touch the necklace, realizing that Deacon had actually played it smart. If he didn't know where the second piece was, then he needed me to find it. And that meant that as soon as I located piece number two, it was a good bet that Deacon was going to jump out and try to take the relics from me.

Damn his rotten soul. And damn me for falling for him.

Not that I had much time to curse either myself or Deacon, because Kiera had come to a dead stop in front of me.

"Here," she said, her voice low. She'd found a fissure in the stone, about the shape of a keyhole but the height of a rather short person.

"Does it cut through?" I asked, shining my own light into the dark.

"I think so. Look." She wiggled her light, and the beam seemed to reflect off something, giving the impression of an open space and not merely more caves closing in.

"Here goes nothing," I said, then eased inside. At first it was pitch-black, and because of the tight quarters, I couldn't get my flashlight arm to move in front of me, which meant I was heading in blind. After a few minutes of that, though, the space opened up into an actual cave, and I was free to move more easily. Kiera was right behind me, and we slowly inched forward.

Soon I realized that I could see beyond the beam of my flashlight. "Turn your light off," I said, doing exactly that.

She did, then gasped. I did, too. We were standing in

a crystal cave, and some unknown light source was illuminating the quartz that covered the walls and ceiling, making the place glow like something out of a storybook about heaven.

"I take it back," she said. "Forget some stupid old rocks. This is amazing."

I silently agreed. And, since my arm had begun to burn again, I also figured we'd arrived at the appropriate place. "It's here," I said.

She looked at me. "You're sure?"

I held out my arm. "Major ouch. I'm sure."

"Well, where?" She turned in a circle, taking in the place, as did I. She was right. There really wasn't anything there that looked relic-y. "Maybe you should walk around some more? See if your arm *really* starts to hurt somewhere?"

Considering the size of the room, I wasn't thrilled with that plan, but since I didn't have another one, I did what she suggested—and realized right away what we'd missed at first glance.

"Kiera," I said. "Come here."

She hurried to my side. "Oh," she said, her voice filled with awe. "There we go."

I'd found a symbol carved into the floor. A geometric pattern that perfectly matched the design burned into the middle spot on my arm.

"Now what?" she asked.

"I don't know," I said truthfully. "But I can guess."

I moved to the center, then pulled out my knife. In one quick motion, I sliced through the symbol on my arm, wincing as I did, and then tilted my arm so that my blood dripped onto the floor, and onto the duplicate symbol carved into the ground.

For a moment, nothing happened, and I was afraid I'd been too quick to assume that once again my blood was the key. Then the floor started to shake, and the symbol started to rise. I jumped to the side, then stood by Kiera, our weapons out and ready, as the stone lifted like a dumbwaiter, revealing a staircase beneath. We looked at each other, then cautiously proceeded downward.

We found ourselves in a smaller chamber, also crystal.

And this time, we weren't alone.

An old man with a beard as long as his arm and rheumy eyes peered at us through a dancing flame. *"You are not the one they said would come."* He spoke not out loud but directly into my head. And, considering the way Kiera straightened, then eyed me, he must have been speaking directly into her head, too.

The words, though, were meant for me and not Kiera. Of that, I was certain. His focus on me was intent, and I was certain his words referred to the prophecy.

"The champion," he continued. *"The champion turned from righteousness."*

I glanced over at Kiera, who looked utterly confused.

As for me, I thought of the darkness I'd consumed. The darkness I couldn't keep boxed up inside me, that kept leaking out around the edges no matter how much I tried to shove it inside.

Yeah, I'd say the description fit better than I would have liked.

"That's me," I said.

Beside me, Kiera's eyes narrowed, and I wondered what she was thinking. More than that, I wondered about what Zane had told me. Then again, Zane hadn't said she was *good*. Only that she was a good partner for me.

Fuck.

I didn't even know who I was, much less who she was. All I knew was that if I went back to the beginning, I fit this guardian's description to a T.

"I'm the champion," I said. "And I once set out to kill a man only to find myself at the edge of hell. Does that satisfy you, old man?"

He blinked slowly. *"You seal your own doom by the path you take."*

"So I've been told. But I'm doing my damnedest to unseal it."

"Drink."

I realized then that a goblet had appeared in his outstretched hand. I took it and peered inside. It was filled with clear liquid, and at the bottom of the goblet was a crystal with a small metal loop on the end. A charm, I thought. Designed to fit on the chain around my neck.

"Drink," he repeated.

"Why can't I just reach inside?"

He inclined his head, as if offering to let me try. I did, and when my fingers reached the bottom of the cup, nothing was there.

"Drink."

"Yeah," I said, testily. "I get it. What is it?"

"It will either kill you or help you."

Beside me, Kiera shifted.

"And I won't know until I drink?"

"I shall give you reassurance," the guardian said. *"What you seek—I do not wish it released. From that, extrapolate my nature and determine if I would kill to protect my treasure."*

"Great. Logic." It's times like this—trapped in a cavern with a goblet full of possible poison—that I really regret dropping out of high school.

I looked to Kiera, but she just shrugged. Apparently, this one was up to me.

"Okay," I said, thinking it through. "The gemstone is part of the *Oris Clef*, and we know that it will lock hell wide-open. You're hiding it, so you're one of the good guys. Good doesn't kill. Except I don't believe that. I think good will kill to protect. I think good has. And I think good should."

"You are wise."

"But that means it's poison," I said, and waited for confirmation. I got none, so I continued. "Or you could be a demon who wants to keep the *Oris Clef* yourself.

And you would kill to ensure it doesn't fall into the wrong hands."

"You are astute. Will you drink?"

"You just said that either scenario means poison," Kiera said.

"Yeah," I said, lifting the goblet to my lips and looking hard at Kiera, willing her to remember what she'd seen that night outside the dance club. "That's what I said."

"Ohhhh." I saw her slow smile as she remembered. "I really do have one hell of a cool partner."

But I didn't hear any more. Because I drank. And, once again, I died.

The first time I'd died and come back, I'd felt the serpents of hell twisting themselves around me as the EMTs worked me over. The last few times—and I did seem to be making a habit of dying—there was only blackness. A dark, lonely emptiness that seemed almost more frightening than hellfire because it truly meant what I suspected: I was tainted. And lost. And utterly alone in a cold, dark place. The kind of place where demons dwelled. The kind of place that had the demons inside me waking up and moaning, keening for release into the cold, dank dark.

Whether I would be ultimately redeemed or lost remained to be seen, but as the demons within writhed and clattered and begged for release, I knew that at the very least, right then, the dark inside was winning.

And then, with a jerk, I was alive again, the dark

vanquished, and the lights of the crystal cave so bright it was blinding.

I wanted to soak it up, to revel in it, but there wasn't time. Kiera had taken the gemstone from the goblet and was slapping my face, trying to hurry my revival.

"He disappeared," she said. "You drank, and he poofed. Man," she continued, rambling on. "That not-dying thing comes in pretty damn handy."

"It has its uses," I agreed, still a little freaked-out by the fact that I'd been dead, but conscious enough to think deep thoughts about the state of my soul. "Let's get out of here." In truth, the whole place was giving me the willies.

I slapped my hand over the symbol, hoping to call Clarence, but nothing happened.

"Maybe the portal's back on the other side?" Kiera suggested.

"Let's go." I hesitated only long enough to slip the gemstone onto the necklace and replace the whole thing over my head. Then I looked down at my arm, expecting to see and feel the third symbol lighting up.

"Weird," I said, as we squeezed out from the keyhole-shaped doorway and back into our original corridor.

"What?"

"Last time the second symbol lit up when we got the first piece. But now that we have the second, the third symbol's not doing a thing."

She peered at my outstretched arm and frowned. "Maybe because we're so deep underground?"

I shrugged, doubting that. I didn't think my arm operated on the same theory as cell phone service.

What I was really wondering was if Deacon hadn't already found the third relic. Because if he had—and if he'd hidden it in another dimension—then my arm wouldn't burn. I could only find things in *this* world, after all.

"Is that the portal?" she asked, peering at the stone wall.

I looked but didn't see anything, and said so.

"No, I feel it," she said, pressing her hand to the stone wall. "Don't you?"

I stood still and realized that, yeah, I felt it, too. Like the rumble of an approaching train. The portal? Or something more sinister?

Like Deacon, come to collect the two relics he needed to complete his collection.

I should be so lucky . . .

Because it wasn't Deacon. It was Gabriel. And he exploded through the wall with such force that the tunnel began to collapse around us. "Run!" I shouted to Kiera, who really didn't need the encouragement.

Neither did I, for that matter, and we raced together toward the opposite end of the tunnel, with Gabriel coming up fast on our heels, the rock walls imploding as he moved, as if sucked in by the magnetic force of him.

"Through here," Kiera said, diving through a person-sized hole that had opened up in the wall.

I followed her, and I was almost through when the whole world seemed to shake.

I tried to shift away, but it was no use—the rocks came tumbling down, and I was trapped.

And somewhere behind me, a pissed-off archangel was fast approaching.

TWENTY-TWO

"My leg!" I cried. "It's stuck. Dammit." With my free foot, I smashed hard against the boulder, trying to shift it. Even with my über-girl strength, however, I couldn't manage it.

"On three," Kiera said, positioning herself beside me. Behind the wall of boulders, I could hear Gabriel coming, picking the rocks up and tossing them away as easily as if they were cotton balls. "One, two, *three*."

She shoved, and I pushed, and it took our combined hyped-up strength to move the damn thing, but we managed, getting it to shift just enough for me to pull my leg free. "Can you walk?"

"I damn well better be able to run," I said. "Where's the portal? Where's the damn portal?"

"I don't know," she said, hooking an arm around my waist. "Clarence!" she called, uselessly. "Where's our damned portal!"

"I don't think it works that way," I said, wincing as I tried to run. I might heal faster now, but not instantaneously, and I was pretty sure some bone was seriously crushed.

"Shit," Kiera said, turning back to look behind us. "He's coming through."

Sure enough, I could see a bright light shining through a small hole in the wall of boulders. Then fingers in the hole, and then he was pushing the boulders aside, and the hole was growing bigger and bigger and—

"There!" Kiera said, and I turned and saw the portal opening up on the stone floor in front of us.

She had my hand, and she raced forward, pulling me along with her. I was slower, but still managing to eat up the distance. Even so, I wasn't fast enough, and I could hear Gabriel behind me. Could feel the tug of his energy on my back. "Kiera," I called. "Your hand."

She slowed, her fingers outstretched, and I latched on. "Jump!" I said, and she did. We hung in space for a moment, trapped between the whirlpool-like suction of the portal and the magnetic pull of Gabriel's fingers. And then I heard a *schlurp*, and we were in the portal, and the tug from the angel was gone, and we were sliding down, down, down into the sweet abyss.

Never have I enjoyed nothingness so much, and when

we emerged with a *thump* onto Zane's training mat, I just lay there, my arms akimbo, reveling in the fact that we got away.

"Qu'est que c'est?" Zane asked, hurrying to us. "What is it, *mes fleurs*?"

"Demon," Kiera said, though she looked at me when she spoke, her expression queer. "Really powerful."

"Did you get the relic?" Clarence asked.

"Got it," I said. "And we're fine, thanks for asking. Kiera saved us."

"She died," Kiera said. "All in a day's work for Lily."

"Let me see the relic," Clarence said, completely uninterested in jokes.

"That's what she died for," Kiera said. "It was like a test. I don't think he expected she'd pass it."

"It's just a jewel," I said, pulling it out of my collar and holding it out for him to see. "Hard to believe it has such power."

"And the third piece?" he asked. "Has your arm lit up now?"

I shook my head, then pulled up my sleeve. "Nothing."

He grabbed my arm and peered close, then muttered the incantation over it again.

"Jeez, Clarence, get a grip. It'll pop when it's ready." In truth, though, I was thrilled the damn thing hadn't popped. I needed to get Clarence alone. Because I realized now that we were getting so close to the end that there was no time to waste. As much as the prospect terrified me, I needed to kill him and take his essence so that I could figure out how to find the Vessel of the Keeper. And I needed to do that before my arm popped again.

And, of course, there was that other issue about the third piece. The issue that focused on Deacon and the fact that I didn't trust him and feared he was playing both sides against the middle, looking for the relic as well so that he could wield the *Oris Clef*.

Antsy, I shifted my weight. "So I keep it, right? I mean, we know it won't pop if I'm not wearing it . . ."

"You keep it," he said reluctantly. "Do not take it off your neck." He pointed to each of us in turn. "Tomorrow. Training. Time is drawing short."

"Sure. No problem."

As Clarence slouched out of there, I glanced down and wiggled my toes, intending only to hide my victorious smile, but at the same time pleased to find that they were all functioning again. This superhealing thing really was cool.

"You are well?" Zane asked.

I nodded, then reached over and squeezed Kiera's fingers. "You really earned your keep this time."

She rolled her eyes. "Yeah, yeah. Just doing the job." She climbed to her feet. "And now I'm ravenous. Zane, we're gonna grab a bite. With us?"

His eyes cut to mine, and he shook his head. "No, thank you, *chérie*. I am content to stay here."

"Tomorrow," I said, my heart twisting a little. I stood, then brushed my fingertips along his jaw, catching the stubble of his chin, and offered him a small smile.

"Indeed, *ma chérie*."

"So we can eat, right?" Kiera asked, as the elevator climbed. "I'm totally starving."

"I need to check on Rose," I said. More specifically, I needed to make sure that Lucas hadn't decided to peek out at Rachel. "I'll just grab something at the pub. You want to go there?"

She shook her head. "And have Rachel put me to work? Nope. I'll find something."

"So who is that guy?" Kiera asked as we headed toward the pub. "The one who keeps trying to kill us?"

I looked at her sideways. "I thought you said he was a demon."

"Nope. Got a whiff of him this time. No demon there."

"Really?" I hoped I looked astounded. "Well, he's not human—that's for sure." She was eyeing me suspiciously, and I didn't much like it. "He was pretty impressive. Maybe he's so high up on the demon hierarchy that he doesn't register for you."

She shook her head. "I don't think so."

"What do you think?"

"I don't know."

"Well, when you figure it out, tell me."

"Don't worry," she said. "I will."

Fortunately, she let the matter drop, though she was still looking disturbed when she pulled up in the alley.

Since I wasn't keen on working either, I had her drop me at the back door. My vague plan was to signal to Rose, have her tell Rachel I was there, tired, and was heading home, then ease back into the alley and onto the bike.

It didn't work that way. Primarily because I didn't even get the back door open before I was jumped by a demon who'd been hiding out in the Dumpster. And not only did he smell disgusting, he looked it, too.

In other words, this wasn't a human-looking demon. This was a beast of the straight-from-hell variety, and he was coming toward me full speed. Wings flapping, claws slashing.

And as if that weren't the worst of it, five other demons raced into the alley only moments after Kiera's car pulled out.

Wasn't that just lovely?

I pulled out my knife and prepared to get into it again, though I have to admit I didn't much like the odds.

As the winged demon swooped in for an attack, the other demons lurched toward me, blocking my exit.

I was trapped. And that, frankly, sucked.

Figuring I had no choice but to blow through, I climbed onto my bike, and only then realized that I'd managed to lose my key somewhere. I was debating whether it would be better to search for the key or run for it when I saw Deacon on the fire escape of the opposite building.

At first, a wall of anger rose within me as I remembered the thoughts I'd snatched from my demonic opponent. Had Deacon come to betray me? Had he set up this ambush so he could get the first two relics of the *Oris Clef* from me?

I didn't know, and I didn't want to hang around to find out.

About that, though, I appeared to have little choice.

And every second, the demons got closer. Soon, I was going to have to dismount and fight.

"Lily!" Deacon called.

Something small and silver rose up from the ground and floated toward him. He snatched it out of the air, then turned it around and winged it back at me. I caught it, then opened my hand.

My key.

I glanced up at Deacon, more than a little astounded by this levitation thing. "Go," he said. "Just go."

I didn't hesitate. I fired the engine, kicked the bike into gear, and took off down the alley.

The demons rushed in, but so did Deacon, and he was enough of a badass that he cleared a path for me.

I gunned it forward and realized that Kiera was racing toward me in her car.

"Get out," I yelled to her, waving my arms to signal her to reverse the hell out of there. "Just back off, now!"

She did, her eyes going wide with surprise. I raced

past her, squeezing the bike in between the wall and her car, then careening around the corner and racing on toward freedom.

Rose, I figured, could stay with Rachel just a little while longer.

TWENTY-THREE

I circled the block, tempting fate and speeding tickets, then parked in front of the pub. I didn't think the demons would go inside. For one, I didn't think Deacon would let them. For another, I was pretty certain Lucas Johnson would defend his turf.

I couldn't be certain, though, and that was my sister in there. And I wasn't leaving her alone with a demon battle going on in the alley behind her.

I burst through the double doors so violently that all heads in the bar turned to look at me, Rachel and Rose included. I signaled to them to follow me, and they rushed to my side at a secluded table near the kitchen.

"Demons," I said, keeping my voice low enough that the few late-afternoon patrons didn't hear me. "In the alley."

"Are they still out there?" Rachel asked, sidling closer to me.

"No." The answer came from behind us, and I turned to find Deacon standing in the door to the kitchen. "It's safe."

Rachel looked between me and Deacon.

"Where's Kiera?"

I shot Deacon a significant look, afraid that Kiera had seen Deacon, whom she knew only as a badass demon, toss me my key, and had drawn the wrong—or, technically, the right—conclusion. "I don't know," I said, my voice dark.

"Right," Rachel said briskly. "You know what? I'm shutting the bar down early tonight anyway. I can take Rose home with me."

I hesitated, then nodded. "Sure. Thanks. I just need to have a little chat with Deacon before you close up."

She nodded stiffly. "Sure. No problem."

Beside her, I saw Rose blink back tears. I wanted to rage and to scream and to beat Lucas Johnson to a bloody pulp. That, however, was nothing new. Instead, I pressed a kiss to the top of Rose's head. "We're going to be okay," I said. "I promise."

And my sister—my sweet, trusting sister—nodded. And didn't say one word about all the promises I'd already broken.

I couldn't think about that now. I'd made a promise to keep Rose safe, and I'd blown it in a big way. But maybe, just maybe, I could somehow make it all come out right in the end.

To do that, though, I needed to know who my allies were. And right then, I feared I'd messed up on that one big-time.

I pointed a finger at Deacon. "You. Outside. Now."

I followed him back out to the alley. Not only did I want privacy, but I wanted to see for myself that the demon hordes had disappeared. They had. All I saw when we went out back was the dank filth of a dark alleyway, the afternoon light filtering through the dust like a curtain.

"They're getting more aggressive," Deacon said. "Stay with me, Lily. You and Rose. We need to make sure you're safe."

"Safe?" I repeated, my temper snapping. "Is that what you call it?"

He wore the dark glasses still, but he cocked his head, as if I were a curious animal in a zoo.

"Dammit, Deacon," I said. "Do *not* fuck with me."

"What the hell are you talking about?"

"You," I said, slamming him against a brick wall and getting right in his face. Heat arced between us, and I hated myself for noticing it. For letting it weaken me. Because right then I needed to be strong. "You son of a bitch," I said, my voice a low, vicious hum. "*You* want the *Oris Clef*. You've been looking for it all along. And I'm pretty sure you have the third relic, too."

I realized then that my arm was burning, and glanced

down, hoping to see that the tattoo was lit up, wishing that I could whip through the portal right then, right there, and retrieve the damn thing from wherever Deacon had hidden it.

The tat wasn't lit, though, and I had no explanation why my arm was doing its skin-on-fire routine.

"I search only for the key to *lock* the gates, Lily. And you damn well know it."

"I don't," I said as the air cracked between us. "I wish I did, but I've seen things, Deacon."

"What things?"

"Dangerous things," I whispered, pitching my voice low and bringing my body in close. I wanted him—so help me, I did—but right then I wanted the truth more. "Why doesn't Clarence want you dead? Why did the demon I killed earlier believe that you're on a quest for the *Oris Clef*? How did you know that we were in China?" My lips brushed over his ear, and I heard a low growl rise in his throat. "You've been playing me, Deacon, and I don't much like it."

The growl turned into a roar, and he grabbed my shoulders, whipping us around and slamming my back to the wall. "Playing you?" he asked, his hand skimming down my thigh, then gliding back up to cup my crotch. "Have I been?" His mouth closed over mine, and my knees went weak. I was held up only by his kiss and his intimate touch, and dammit—*dammit*—the man had me losing my head.

"Maybe I have been playing you," he continued as

soon as he broke the kiss. This time it was his voice that was low, edgy. "But only because I want you. Because I need you. And not to find the *Oris Clef*. If I wanted to, I could find that key all on my own."

My heart was pounding in my chest. "What do you mean?"

He slid his hands up my body, bringing his hips in close. I could feel his erection, and I wanted him. Wanted him so desperately, and I hated myself for craving him. For needing him. He was darkness. He was danger. And yet somehow, when he touched me, the darkness inside seemed to fade, and the demons I'd absorbed backed off.

I needed that.

I needed *him*.

Right then, however, was not the time.

I needed answers, not lust, and I was determined to get them.

Before he could react, I reached up and ripped his glasses off. His eyes met mine, and I held on, my hands on either side of his face, holding him still. I felt the *snap*, had one moment of regret that I'd yet to learn stealth, and I let myself get sucked inside even as Deacon's guttural curse echoed in my ears.

*D*arkness.
       Darkness and blood and the scent of rotting, moldering flesh.
  Tentacles, long and deadly.

And an open mouth, saliva dripping, teeth gleaming.

All searching. All looking. Trying to find the one who betrayed.

Huge wings spread wide. Flapping as they moved through the night. Searching . . . Searching . . .

Finding.

He's there. Deacon Camphire, and the beast swoops down and gathers him up.

"You will give it back. You will return what you took."

And then the darkness. And screams. And the pain, the pain, the unyielding pain. Hot needles to the flesh. Poison in the veins. A hammer to the head. And worse, worse, so much worse.

Until it fades.

A respite.

A gift.

A woman.

Alice.

No, me. Lily.

And I'm touching him. Touching the pain, soothing the pain.

Taking the pain in and changing it. Making it bearable. Making it fade.

I save him.

But I don't understand from what.

S*nap.*

I was out, and Deacon had backed off, his breath

coming fast, his expression furious. "Goddamn it, Lily."

"You don't want it," I said, the pieces I'd seen finally coming together. "You weren't trying to find the *Oris Clef*. You were trying to hide it."

"I worked for Penemue," he said, his voice dark. "When he realized I was no longer loyal, he tossed me into the pit."

I licked my lips. "That's how you became a Tri-Jal."

He met my eyes. "I deserve the mark of the Tri-Jal, Lily. The things I have done—"

"—you tried to rectify." I took his hand. "Deacon. Do you know where the third piece is?"

He shook his head. "I've already told you, Lily. It's too dangerous. The key restored is too dangerous to be in the hands of Penemue or Kokbiel."

"I would never let them get it."

"It is too dangerous even for you."

"But—"

"I destroyed it," he said flatly.

"I thought it couldn't be destroyed."

He looked me dead in the eye. "I managed."

"I—"

But I didn't get the chance to speak. Because at the end of the alley, I saw Kiera, her eyes wide, her expression one of utter betrayal.

I realized my clothes were askew, and that she'd seen me clinging to Deacon. Not the vision. But the wildness of our bodies. Of our touch.

She'd seen.

And she'd assume I was cavorting with the enemy.

"Kiera!" I called, but it was too late. She was gone.

I turned to Deacon. "She's going to go to Clarence, dammit. She may not understand completely, but he will. He'll know exactly what game I've been playing."

"Where? Where will she go to meet him?"

I didn't know. "We never have a planned meeting place. Zane's. Sometimes he shows up at my apartment."

"No matter where Kiera meets Clarence, the question is, where will Clarence want to meet you? If he believes that you are a traitor, would he assume that Zane would be his ally? Or his enemy?"

I wasn't certain what Clarence would think. For that matter, I wasn't certain what Zane would do. He had no allegiance to the dark. Of *that*, I'd become certain. But he wanted his reward, and if he helped me, they would certainly take away the promise of mortality.

"I don't know."

Deacon nodded, and I could see that he was thinking. "Your apartment," he said finally. "I could be wrong, but I think Clarence would want to confront you there, where he first met you. Back when he was in control. In Zane's basement, you're stronger."

"I'm stronger in my apartment, too."

"And that's why you're going to win." He took my hand. "I'm coming with you."

"No. I need you watch out for Rachel and Rose. If Clarence is onto me, that's how he'll try to hurt me."

He hesitated, then agreed. I think he knew better than to argue with me where Rose was concerned.

My apartment isn't that far from the Bloody Tongue, and I made the trip in record time, barely even paying attention to where I was going. Only driving. And imagining what I would do when I saw Clarence. Because everything hinged on him now. Everything.

Deacon had destroyed the third relic. I had no idea how he'd managed that, but it didn't matter. All that mattered was that it didn't exist, and apparently no one realized that, a fact that gave me the tiniest bit of bargaining power. Because, hey, I was Map Girl. And if you were still in the process of searching for treasure, you didn't destroy the map, right?

Except I wasn't so much worried about being destroyed as I was about being tortured. Which was why I had to win this round.

More than that, I had a plan. A simple, brilliant plan, and one I had yet to share with Deacon. But I was certain it would work. It would, because it had to. I was running out of options here, and I figured it was my turn to have some luck, if not for me, then for Rose.

If Penemue and Clarence and Kokbiel all still thought the third key existed, then Johnson did, too. And once I got the incantation out of Clarence's head for the Vessel of the Keeper, then what was to stop me from telling Johnson that I was going after the third relic?

Nothing, right?

And he'd insist on coming along for the ride, planning on ambushing me for the full *Oris Clef*. But it wouldn't matter. Because we'd pull Rose out of Johnson, hide her in the vessel, and get the hell out of there, my sister disembodied but safe and Johnson stuck with his thumb up his ass.

I'll admit I was still fuzzy on the details—like how long she could stay in the vessel before we found her a suitable body—but on the whole, the plan worked for me.

Best of all, it got Rose free of Johnson and me free of Clarence. There were still almost two weeks left until the convergence, and with Rose safe, I'd happily spend that time searching for this lost legendary key that Deacon seemed to be so convinced existed.

On the whole, my plan put me in a happy place, the only downer the fact that for it to work, I had to kill Clarence.

In theory, that didn't bother me.

In practice, I had to wonder what kind of tricks the wily beast had up his sleeve. Because I had a feeling there was a lot more to Clarence than met the eye.

I expected to see them both outside my apartment when I got off the elevator. But there was no one. And since Clarence wasn't allowed in my apartment without permission—and I now realized that must be part of the protections—I almost turned around and headed back to the pub and Deacon.

But I didn't. For all I knew, the revelation of me as

a traitor to the dark cause destroyed the protections. At the very least, I had to look.

I pulled my knife out and held it ready as I unlocked the front door, then pushed it open.

And there he was.

Clarence stood in my living room, his squat body in front of the window, and a beer in his hand. Beside him, Kiera was stretched out in a chair, her feet kicked up on my coffee table.

She turned to look at me, her eyes dark and anger rolling off her in waves. "You fucking bitch," she said, which was Clarence's cue to turn around and face me with big, sad eyes.

"How did you guys get in?" I asked, keeping my voice light, deciding to play this as if I were completely innocent.

Kiera cocked her head. "Duh. You think your crappy lock would keep me out?"

"I'll have to remember to upgrade," I said. I kept my knife in my hand—which probably destroyed the whole "innocent" thing—and headed toward them.

"What were you doing?" Kiera asked. "Why the *hell* were you up close and personal with Deacon Camphire?"

"Oh, for fuck's sake," I said, shooting for an annoyed, yet casual, tone. "That's what this is about? What do you think I was doing? Trying to get close to the guy. Trying to figure out what he knows, because I've been getting weird vibes about him for a long time." I looked straight at Clarence. "You know what I mean, right?"

His eyes narrowed, but he didn't say a word. Interesting. This was the first time I'd seen Clarence do the silent-guy routine. I couldn't say I liked it much.

"You looked close to the guy, all right," Kiera said.

I rounded on her. "Dammit, Kiera, do you really believe I'm working for the dark side? I'm fighting my nature, just like you. We're alike, you and I, so you tell me—what side are you on?"

She leaned forward, kicking her feet to the ground, ready to lunge. "I know exactly what side I'm on. And I know what I saw."

"You saw me and Deacon," I said. "You saw me finding out where the third relic is."

Across the room, Clarence hissed in a breath. I turned my back to Kiera and walked to him. "And thanks so much for the support, both of you. I mean, God! I go out and try to do one thing—one really good, solid thing—and you both assume the worst of me."

"You're certain about the piece?" Clarence asked.

I nodded.

"How? How can you be sure?"

The beer in his hand was empty, and I took it from him. This was going to be the tricky part. "I was afraid you wouldn't approve," I said as I wandered into the kitchen. "So I didn't tell you. But I've suspected he knew something for a long time. And I wanted to figure it out on my own." I opened the fridge and grabbed a beer, then looked back toward him as I popped off the lid. "You're probably really mad at me, huh?"

"I'm not happy," he said. "But if the information is good . . ."

"Oh, I think it's solid." I brought the beer back to him. And when I did I made sure our hands touched. And I made sure I looked into his eyes.

And then—*yes*—I was in. And in a split second, I saw it all. The knowledge and innate skill to spin the incantations. The ability to master the map that even now burned on my arm. To find things—relics, vessels, keys, and more.

I didn't find a damn thing about Deacon's legendary key, but I didn't have time to look either. I'd only wanted a peek. Wanted to make certain the incantations came from *him*—from his very essence—and not from a book.

I wanted to make sure that by killing him, I'd gain the ability I needed. That I would truly become an Incantor.

I was certain now.

I jerked free even as he was still howling in surprise and protest.

Barely any time had passed at all, but it was enough for Kiera, and as I thrust my knife forward to strike Clarence, she tackled me from the side, sending my blade askew.

It skimmed over his body, slicing his shirt and drawing a thin line of black, demonic goo, but it didn't kill him. It didn't even come close.

"You idiot!" I screamed as I deflected her blows. "He's a demon. He's a goddamned, fucking demon."

I rolled her over so that she could see, and knew that she believed when I heard her whispered curse. The black goo was proof enough.

But I realized what had really convinced her when I scrambled to my feet—Clarence, his clothing ripping as his demonic form burst free. Wings sprouting. Talons growing.

And angry, buggy eyes fixed right on me.

TWENTY-FOUR

"What the fuck is going on?" Kiera screamed, but I had no time to answer. Clarence was alive. Alive and pissed and seriously deadly.

For the first time in our short acquaintance, I was really and truly afraid of the dude. Because this wasn't my mild-mannered, froggy handler. This was a full-fledged powerful demon. Penemue's right-hand guy.

"Bitch," he snarled. *"Traitorous fiend."*

"Me?" I countered, my knife out as I circled him, trying to guess how he was going to attack. "I'm not the one who lied and pretended to be heaven's messenger. Who the hell are you?" I demanded, because there was *no* way I was believing this beast's name was Clarence.

"I am Clarvek," he said. "And you will join me."

Behind me, Kiera sucked in air. Right then, I wasn't much concerned about her shifting perspective on the world, though. Right then, I simply needed to get Clarvek dead.

"Screw that."

"You are as much a servant of the dark as I am," Clarvek said, his wings spread wide.

"The hell I am," I said, and I lunged at him, reckless and wild, but he'd played the one card that was guaranteed to get under my skin. Because no matter how much I might wish otherwise, the darkness was in me.

And you know what? Right then, I welcomed it. Welcomed the need to kill. The desire to maim. The absolute keening need to take another demon in my hands and suck down its life force.

I had only my blade on me, but I was making the most of it, twirling and darting, calling upon all the demons inside me, all of their tricks, all of their strength.

Even so, I was barely a match for Clarvek. He'd been around for a while, that boy, and he was fast. He lashed out with his talons, his arms now wings that knocked me over in a rush of air and fury.

"Lily!" Kiera had her crossbow with her, and she lifted it now, ready to aim it.

Those deadly claws, however, slashed sideways, knocking the crossbow free and slicing Kiera hard across the face. She yowled, then raced forward, landing a solid kick to his chest. Not that it did any good. He filled his chest up with air, then blew—and Kiera went flying, smashing into the far wall and leaving a dent in the drywall.

She shook it off, her eyes heading toward me, her expression both bewildered and scared.

I didn't have time to reassure her. I was assessing my options. Clarvek might risk killing Kiera, but he wouldn't risk me. He needed me alive. He needed me for my arm.

Which meant that he'd take me. Take me and hole me up somewhere. Lock me away like he'd done Zane, only I wouldn't get a big basement. My cell would be small and cramped and dark and scary. And there'd be no promise of freedom. Instead, I'd get pain and torment and the horror of knowing that my skin was revealing secrets I didn't want displayed.

The very thought was enough to make me freak. And it was *not* going to happen.

No way, no how.

The only good thing about the whole scenario was the fact that because he needed me alive, I could get closer and fight harder than I might otherwise be able to. And I damn sure did. Harder than I'd ever fought, wilder than I'd ever been.

"You cannot win," he snarled.

"Watch me."

I leaped on him then, deciding to just go for it and score some serious points for the good guys. Beside me, Kiera leaped, too. I had my knife out, and despite the fact that I'd managed to get some solid blows in, nothing worked. His skin was like armor, and he was, literally, laughing at me.

"Pretty damn foolish of me to think you were strong. To think you were worthy." He opened his mouth and laughed—

—and I grabbed his tongue, pulled, and sliced.

It didn't kill him, but it damn sure shut him up. And right then, I was taking my victories where I could find them.

Clarvek backed up, howling, then whipped around, sending a thick tail crashing down through my coffee table. I realized what he was doing and lunged for the tail, catching it just as he leaped for the window.

I heard glass shatter, and then felt the whoosh of air as we plummeted to the ground, landing hard in the middle of the asphalt, me on top of the one creature in all the world I hated above all others.

"Bitch," he said, his mentally blasted words reverberating in the air like some demonic public-address system. "We gave you power, and this is how you repay us?"

"Power? You fucked with my life. You set me up to be some goddamned pawn in your stupid game—"

"We made you to be great. You wield the power, Lily. *You*."

"Yeah? Well, watch while I wield it on your fat, ugly face."

Not the best line, I'll admit, but I wasn't thinking clearly, what with the rush of the dark in my mind, racing through my head, urging me to kill and kill and kill.

Oh, yeah, baby. Bring it on.

I lunged forward, but he did as well, rising up on his haunches and swinging around with that deadly tail. It caught me across the middle and sent me flying, knocking me hard against the windshield of a nearby parked car.

"Lily!"

Somehow, Kiera had gotten down to the street, and now she was standing still, her crossbow aimed. She let the arrow fly, even before I could release a scream of protest, and it hit true, lodging in a soft spot between two ribs.

That wouldn't be enough to kill him, though, and she knew it. But she rushed forward with her blade, all set to take him out. To claim this kill as her own.

"No!" I screamed, racing forward, because *I* needed to take him out. I needed his essence, or this whole thing was for nothing.

She turned, baffled, then pissed as I knocked her out of the way. Clarvek roared, and as Kiera landed a hard kick to his groin, I leaped up and thrust my knife hard and firm through his eye and deep into his brain.

He collapsed, his huge bulk melting into goo and revealing a car racing toward us.

I, however, was in no position to worry about what the locals might think. I was too busy doubling over in the street, unable to move because of the force of the essence of a demon like Clarvek.

It was there. All of it. And now I could see it. Now I could *use* it.

"Get in!" The car screeched to a halt, and I looked up to see Deacon looking out from the driver's-side window.

Kiera's eyes went wide, and she shook her head. "No. No way. What the fuck are you doing with him?"

But I had no time to explain. Deacon was already accelerating away, and I yanked open the passenger door and leaped in, barely dodging the knife that Kiera whipped through the air toward my head.

"Where the hell are Rachel and Rose?"

"My home." He turned to me, his expression fierce. "You didn't think I'd leave you alone with him?"

I hadn't thought at all, but now the idea that he'd come to protect me felt nice.

"Did it work?" he asked.

I nodded. "I think so."

"Then do it."

I licked my lips, sliding into my head, searching for Clarvek, for his skill, for his essence. It was there, a knowledge. A trait, and I knew that he'd been given the skill when the prophecy was forged. He'd been made to train the warriors and to bring the champion into the fold. And now I'd screwed all of that up.

I couldn't have been happier.

"Got it," I said, my head overflowing with the strange

words. I sliced my palm, then muttered the incantation that was in my head. A series of words I didn't understand but which seemed to be doing the trick, because as I smeared the blood down my arm, a new pattern arose, one I hadn't seen before. One that, if all went well, would lead to the Vessel of the Keeper.

The rising pattern burned, and I drew another swath of blood to soothe it, then turned to look at Deacon, who had pulled into an alley near the entrance to Zane's basement.

"Go ahead," he said. "We need to know for certain that we're right."

I drew in a breath, then let it out slowly. "Cross your fingers," I said. "And hold on to me." I pressed my other palm down on the mark and immediately felt that hard tug.

The journey was fast and wild, and I landed hard in what appeared to be a strange, glass temple with one wall of water. Behind the waterfall I could see the distorted image of some sort of clay pot, about the size of a coffee can. Other than the glass and the water, it was the only thing in the room.

Having already had some experience with water in these strange templelike places, I pulled a quarter from my pocket and tossed it into the flow. Nothing happened, other than me losing twenty-five cents. Everything seemed safe enough, and I thrust my hand into the flow.

"Do you give your life willingly?"

The disembodied voice filled the chamber.

"I'm sorry?"

"Do you give your life willingly?"

I turned, trying to find who I was talking to, but there was nobody. "I'm sorry. I don't understand."

"The vessel may be removed only by one who gives his life willingly. Do you do so?"

"If I take the vessel, I die?"

"That is so."

"Oh." I considered that for only a moment, because, like the water, I'd faced death in these challenges before as well. "I can do that."

"Agree only if you speak true," the voice said. *"For death is the condition to retrieve the Vessel of the Keeper. Even you, Lily Carlyle, with the blood of eternity flowing in your veins. If you draw forth the vessel, your life will end."*

TWENTY-FIVE

"It's a goddamned suicide mission," I said to Deacon, as soon as I was back in his car. I was breathing hard, exhausted, and frustrated.

And, yeah, I was scared of what I had to do, but I knew I had no choice.

I had to go back.

I had to keep my promise to take care of my sister.

And right now, getting the vessel was the only way I saw to do that.

"Are you insane?" Deacon asked, after I'd explained all of that to him. "You can't die. I need you. The world needs you." He reached over and grabbed my arm. "We need you to lock the gate and stop the fucking Apocalypse."

"Dammit, Deacon, don't you get it? There is no lock.

There is no key. I screwed up big-time. I screwed up the whole goddamned world, but I am *not* going to screw up my sister."

"No lock?" he repeated. "How the hell do you know? Have you tried, Lily? Have you tried looking for it?"

I hadn't, of course. And I realized then that I could. I was the one person in all the world who could find out if the lock existed.

A tiny ray of hope flared inside me. Because the truth was, I didn't want to die. Didn't want that blackness. That nothingness.

Didn't want to be lost forever in the void because I hadn't yet overcome the weight of my sins.

I shook my head, realizing I'd let my mind get carried away. "No. Even if there is a lock, it doesn't help Rose."

"Just look," he said, his voice plaintive. "I need to know."

I took in his face, the fierce determination and the blatant need. "All right," I said. "But no matter what we find, I'm going to save my sister."

A muscle in his cheek twitched, but he didn't argue. Right then, I figured that was the best I could hope for.

I drew inside myself, calling upon this new power over which I had scant control. "Please," I whispered, then drew the blood and recited the words as the incantation filled my head, a musical chorus that filled me up and spilled over into the world.

When I was finished, I thrust my arm out, and we

both peered at it. But nothing changed. My flesh didn't rise. It didn't burn. It didn't even sting slightly.

"There is no lock," I said.

"Bullshit," Deacon countered. "You knew the incantation. There wouldn't be an incantation if there wasn't a lock."

He had a point. "But the arm, Deacon," I said, thrusting it toward him. "My arm finds things. If it's a thing, and it's in this dimension, then I'm the go-to girl. And there's nothing there," I added, shaking my arm for emphasis.

"It's hidden, then. Trapped in another dimension. But it exists, Lily. You know damn well that it exists."

I shook my head, images of Rose filling my mind. Rose in pigtails. Rose at Christmas. Rose with my mother.

And then my mom, asking me to watch after the sweet little girl.

"I have to," I said, hating the way that my voice hitched behind the tears that filled my throat. "She's my priority."

"You save her, and she's still dead," Deacon said flatly. "Do you think the demon hordes will spare her? Do you think Johnson will? She's on his radar, Lily. It'll all start up again. You won't have saved her. You'll have abandoned her."

I winced. "No." I shook my head, not wanting to hear his words, not wanting to believe I could have lost so badly again. "No, no, no."

He pressed his hands to my face, then gently kissed

my forehead. "Don't," he said, his voice soft, tender. "It's not about the gate, Lily. You're mine. I've said so all along."

"Deacon . . ." I wanted him, too. Wanted him desperately. I wanted to win. I wanted to save Rose.

And I damn sure didn't want to die.

I gasped, my body stiffening with a sudden realization.

"What?" he asked.

"I don't want to die," I said, the excitement in my voice undoubtedly mystifying him.

"And I don't want you to."

I squeezed his hand tight. "Go get Rose. Tell Johnson I'm on to the third key. Act incredibly pissed, and tell him you're only telling him so because I insisted, but that you're not going to let him get away with taking the *Oris Clef*. That you're coming, too, and that you'll kill him. Or whatever. Just make it look good. He has to believe I really know where the third relic is."

"And?"

"And get Rose to Zane's. Get her there fast."

TWENTY-SIX

"*Chérie*," Zane said as I burst into his spartan bedroom. He was sitting on his cot, shirtless, the thin material of his sweatpants hugging the tight muscles of his legs. He stood immediately, his hand out to draw me in. "*Ma petite*, you are a mess."

I had to laugh. As understatements went, that one was a doozy. "I need to ask you something," I said. "I need to ask, and if I'm wrong . . ." I trailed off, because if I was wrong, I was screwed, and there really wasn't anywhere to go from there.

"Lily," he said, the accent disappearing as he cupped my chin. "Speak."

"I've killed Clarence," I said. "I've killed him, I've absorbed him, and I'm going to fight them. The demons. The ones who did this to me."

He leaned backward, his expression unreadable. He wasn't, however, lashing forward to lop off my head. Considering the way my luck had been running, that was a mark in the plus column.

"And you come now to me for what purpose? Do you seek to kill me, too?"

I licked my lips. "Not the way you mean."

His eyes narrowed, his confusion clear. "Tell me," he said. "Tell me everything."

I swallowed, then I started at the beginning, my whole story, including the parts he already knew. Rose. Lucas Johnson. Deacon. The *Oris Clef*.

And, most important, the vessel that could house Rose's soul. "We'll come back here once we have Rose inside the vessel," I said. "Then I'll find a demon I can kill, only not with an owned blade." Kill a demon with a blade that hadn't drawn its owner's blood, and the demon's body remained. Only an owned kill reduced the demon to goo. "Deacon knows how to get the soul from the vessel into the body." I licked my lips. "Someone like that goth demon you had me kill," I said, referring to the demon I'd killed my very first day of training. She'd had Rose's eyes, and I'd shown her mercy. And I'd almost died because of it.

"And to do this," Zane said. "To save your sister, you must obtain the vessel. The Vessel of the Keeper."

"That's pretty much the score."

"And to do that," he said, "you must die."

I nodded. "If I die—if I step up to the plate to save

my sister—then any chance of locking the gates to hell dies with me."

He took my arm, lifted it, and gently traced his fingers over my marked skin. "You do not seek the *Oris Clef*."

"Only to the extent it helps me get Rose," I said. "I'm interested in a different key. One that locks. One that seals."

"You are correct, *ma chérie*. You are the only one with the power to find such a key."

He stood, then walked across the room. He stood in the doorway, his back to me, the training room spread out in front of him.

He said nothing, and I waited, wishing he would nod. Would whisper. Would do something so that I didn't have to actually make the request. He wasn't, however, making it easy for me.

I closed my eyes and breathed in deep. Then I stood and went to him, and pressed my hands to his shoulders. "Zane," I said. "I need you."

He turned, his mouth curved in a wry grin. He traced a finger over my lips, making me shiver. "And yet it is another man that you truly need." He leaned forward, then gently brushed his lips over mine. The kiss was sweet and sad, and when he pulled away, I realized I was crying.

"What you ask, *chérie*, I long for it. And yet I dread it."

"I know," I whispered, remembering when he'd told

me he was immortal. Remembering how he'd described the terror that now warred with longing, a desperate craving for the end juxtaposed against a horrible fear of the unknown. "I understand."

He cupped my cheek. "I will do this. And I thank you, *ma chérie*, for setting me free."

My heart squeezed, and I forced myself to stop crying. Instead, I drew him close and rested my head upon his shoulder. "Thank you," I whispered.

Deacon found us that way, arm in arm in the doorway. I felt him before I saw him, and I pulled away from Zane to look at Deacon over his shoulder. He stalked forward and took my arm. It burned under his touch, a reaction that confused me, especially when I looked down and saw nothing new happening with the tats on my arm.

He pulled me toward him as Rose stood in the background, and when I saw her—when I saw *Johnson*—I forgot about my arm.

"Why the *fuck* are we here?" Rose said, only it wasn't Rose, of course.

"The third relic," I said. "We need Zane to get it."

"That a fact?" Johnson said, jutting out Rose's hip and giving me all sorts of attitude.

"Yeah," I said, forcing myself to remember that this was not my sister. "It is."

I realized that without the mouthless Johnson body joining our party, our plan wouldn't actually destroy Lucas Johnson. Considering we hadn't seen the creature, though, we didn't have much choice in the matter. And right then, I honestly didn't care. So long as Rose was free of him, I'd be happy. At least for a moment. And the prospect of hunting him down and killing him at least gave me something to look forward to.

Right then, though, I needed to just concentrate on making this plan work.

Behind us, the elevator doors slid open, and Kiera stepped out, her crossbow aimed straight at me. "Talk," she said. "Now."

"*Ma petite,*" Zane said, stepping forward and slightly in front of me. "What is the trouble?"

"She is," Kiera said, talking to me rather than Zane. "I get what you did," she said. "I saw it. I understand it." Her forehead creased. "And when Clarence changed, I smelled the demon on him." She worked her jaw, and I knew she was battling back the anger and the betrayal. "I didn't smell it before—the bastard hid it somehow—but I caught the whiff at the end."

She whipped sideways, and now her weapon was aimed at Deacon. "Him, though. Him, I've smelled it on from the beginning."

"Kiera, wait." I took a step forward. I couldn't tell her exactly what was going on—not without Johnson learning the score—but I had to at least tell her something. "I promise you. He's on our side."

"Your side? Or mine?"

"Ours," I said firmly. "I swear."

"You know what?" Kiera said. "I don't trust you.

Sorry, girlfriend. I just don't. So I think it's time for us all to sit down and—"

I never learned what we were supposed to sit down and do, though, because Kiera was thrust forward when the floor burst upward, concrete cracking, metal beams jutting forth. The whole room was roiling, as if we were caught at the epicenter of the earthquake to end all earthquakes.

"What the fuck?" Kiera asked, as I reached down to pull her to her feet.

"Him," Rose said, and this time, she looked like my sister—small, and frail, and scared.

"Penemue," Deacon said, his voice deadly. "I think it's safe to say he realizes his lieutenant is dead."

"Shit!" I turned away. I had to get the portal open. Had to get our plan in action. Because we all couldn't travel through my arm, and if I didn't use Clarence's know-how in time, Penemue was going to squash us all like bugs. About that, I was damn certain.

I ran back to the circle that Clarence had drawn for the last two bridges, then began to walk the line. Bits of cement were falling from the ceiling, and the entire building was shaking, as if a large hand had grabbed it and was going to roll the whole building like dice.

I tried to ignore it—the plaster, the cement, the demonic creature clawing its way free from hell. I tried to focus, to concentrate, and to mutter the words that came into my head, trusting that they were right.

As I walked, I could feel the power, the vibrations

from the circle. Vibrations that were *not* caused by the basement falling down around our ears.

A gaping hole had opened up near Kiera, and I yelled at her to get closer. To get in the damned circle.

She lifted her crossbow. "I can hold him off!"

"The hell you can. We're going. Now! Come on!"

As Deacon, Zane, and Rose joined me in the circle, I sliced my arm, letting the blood drip over the symbol carved on the floor. As the walls of the portal began to rise around us, Rose reached over and grabbed my knife, then pressed it to Deacon's neck. "There will be no double cross," he said.

I nodded, hoping to hell he was wrong about that one, and screaming at the top of my lungs for Kiera to hurry, hurry, *hurry*!

She ran, racing toward us, as five long tentacles burst out of the floor.

"Kiera!" I called. "Come on!" She was close, so close, and I thrust my hand out through the portal's walls, my fingers closing around her hand even as one of the tentacles wrapped itself around her leg. "Pull!" I shouted to Zane, even though he'd already gotten that memo and had me around the waist and was pulling with all his might and then—*yes!*—we were in the portal, and Penemue was left behind, and we were hurtling, together, through the blackness.

I couldn't quite believe it, but I'd actually done it, and the moment we landed with a jolt on the slick glass floor of the temple, I was even more amazed. After everything that had gone wrong in my new life as Alice Purdue, one thing had finally gone right.

Astounding.

I looked up to find that Zane had already stepped to the curtain of water. He slid his hand through, and the voice boomed out again. *"Do you give your life willingly?"*

He turned, and I held my breath, afraid his fear had overcome him after all.

As I waited, the air in the temple began to swirl, lazily at first, and then picking up speed. A small cyclone, slowly growing.

Penemue.

I held my breath, afraid the demon would arrive before Zane got the vessel. Afraid that Zane would step back and choose life after all.

As I watched, he closed his eyes. A moment passed, then another. And with every second, the whirlwind increased, and my fear escalated.

"Good-bye, *ma chérie*," Zane said.

And then he slid through the wall of water and disappeared from sight.

TWENTY-SEVEN

The wall of water disappeared, leaving only the vessel behind. On the far side of the chamber, the air still twirled as Penemue attempted to follow us into the temple. I ignored the whirlwind, focusing only on the vessel.

I rushed forward and grabbed it, watching as Rose shifted, edging forward to look, her nostrils flaring and her eyes narrowing.

"That is not the key," she said, and as she spoke, Deacon thrust backward, away from the knife she still held at his throat. He slammed the back of his head hard into her nose, and I winced when I heard the bone shatter.

I forced myself not to react, though. That wasn't my

sister. And in a few minutes, it wasn't even going to be her body.

"You lying little cunt!" Johnson screamed, and at that point I was actually at a bit of a loss what to do. This was all about Deacon. All about demonic essence rushing in where it didn't belong. All about demons fighting for territory in bodies that would burn out too fast from their energy.

And it was all about knocking Rose's soul out of her body and capturing it safely in the vessel.

I had to trust him. Right then, I had no choice but to trust Deacon because he was the one who held my sister's life in his hands.

An eerie yellow glow whipped around Deacon, and I remembered what he'd told me—that before he could leap into Johnson's body, he had to put a protection around his own. For this to work, there could be no empty shell for Johnson to thrust his essence into.

From what I could see, Johnson knew exactly what that glow meant, and as he turned toward me, I saw a hint of fear in his eyes. I relished it, clinging to his fear and letting victory wash over me.

The emotion was short-lived, though, since it fast became clear that Johnson wasn't going down easy.

And if he was going down, he was damn sure going to try to take me with him. And to prove it, he launched himself at me, the knife he still held aimed at my heart.

"No!" Kiera burst forward, knocking me out of the way. I stumbled as Johnson's knife got her deep in the gut. As Kiera's scream of pain and fury echoed in the chamber, he pulled the blade out, then turned on me, and for a moment I froze, undone by the image of my sister coming at me with a knife.

Then he lunged, and the image faded, replaced by hard, cold reality.

I shifted, avoided the blade, but he thrust a leg out and sent me tumbling—and knocking the vessel out of my hands. I yelled and stretched, and though my fingers skimmed the outside, it was no use.

I couldn't catch it.

The vessel landed hard, shattering into hundreds of pieces.

It was broken, and I was furious. I lunged, my rage overwhelming. I'm not at all sure what I was going to do. Maybe choke the bastard out of my sister. But I never got the chance. Because Rose stood there, and threw her head back, and screamed.

Her skin began to move, as if the bones beneath were rearranging. As if I were watching a scene from a horror flick. There was a battle going on, and it was happening right inside Rose.

From the ground, I heard a small gasp, and I hurried to Kiera's side, finding the wound and pressing hard against it. I used her blade to slice my wrist, but I feared my blood wouldn't heal; that it would only buy her a bit more time. The injury was too bad, and she had only seconds left.

"I'm so sorry," Kiera said, her words barely audible.

"Sorry? What do you have to be sorry for?"

"Was wrong . . . about you."

"It's okay," I said, stroking her short hair. "It's okay."

She smiled, almost serenely, as if there were no pain in her world anymore.

"Kiera?"

"It's nice, Lily. There's light. It's peaceful."

And then she was gone. My partner—my friend—gone from this world, and I was cradling nothing more than a shell.

I felt the tears sting my eyes, and realized that despite everything, I was smiling. *There's light,* she'd said. And that, I thought, was worth something.

I cradled her head, realizing that I'd lost more than just Kiera today. The vessel was broken. I'd risked Rose's life, and I'd lost—dear God, I'd lost.

I'd gone out trying to protect her, and once again, I'd failed miserably.

I no longer even tried to hold back. I let loose, and I cried.

As I watched, the body in which that horrific battle was playing out fell to the ground, a bruised and battered mess.

And, very clearly, dying.

I shifted Kiera's head to the ground, then crawled to Rose, my fingers skimming over her face, over her hair. *Dear God, what have I done?*

I looked up to find Deacon back in his body. "Stab

her," he said, his voice deathly urgent. "Stab her now before he can return."

I lifted my knife, then held it there, unable to do it. Unable to end my little sister.

"Dammit, Lily, trust me."

Terror flashed in Rose's eyes, but whether it was Johnson or my sister, I didn't know.

Tears flooded my vision, and Deacon's voice seemed to fill the chamber.

"Now, Lily! You must do it now! Trust me!"

I hesitated only a moment longer. Because dammit, I *did*. I trusted Deacon. More, I knew I had to keep Johnson from coming back.

No matter what I did now, I'd failed. My sister was truly dead.

And with tears streaming down my face, I plunged my knife straight down and into Rose's heart.

I collapsed on the ground beside her, watching as the blood oozed from my sister's body. I felt as dead as she was, and even the scent of blood didn't entice me. I simply lay there, lost, the depth of my failure weighing heavy on my heart.

Beyond Rose's body, Kiera twitched. Then kicked. Then sat up. Her fingers went to the knife wound, her eyes going wide as she looked down to find it healed.

I sat up, my heart pounding. I held my breath, afraid to hope. Afraid to believe.

But then she looked at me, and I saw it in her eyes

before she even said a word. "Lily?" my sister asked. "What happened to me?"

Relief flowed through me, warm and thick like a blanket. I looked up at Deacon, because I really didn't know the answer. All I could do was crawl across the floor to her side and draw her in close to me.

"I pushed her out," he said. "I pushed her out, and while I held Johnson inside her old body, Rose found this new home."

"And Johnson?"

He looked up into the air. "His essence is still out there. I'm guessing he'll find his body and put himself back together." He met my eyes. "Right now, though, he's not a problem."

I looked up at Deacon through tear-filled eyes. "Thank you," I said. "Thank you."

But it wasn't over. Because even as I clung to my sister, the whirlwind picked up speed, finally bursting open to reveal not Penemue, but Gabriel.

"Now it ends," he said, thrusting out his hand and conjuring a force that yanked me across the room and into his waiting arms.

TWENTY-EIGHT

Gabriel held me tight, his grip strong, his massive body giving off wave after wave of energy. My chest was pressed up against his side, and though he held me with only one arm, there was no way I was getting free. He had me, and he had me good.

"Dammit," I said as I struggled. "What do you want with me?"

"What do I want?" he asked, his voice low and rumbly, like an oncoming train. "Ask what it is I do not want."

I stopped struggling, his words both curious and worrisome. "All right," I said slowly. "What is it you don't want?"

"Look," he said, pressing his free hand to my face and staring deep into my eyes. "And see."

The shock of the vision overtook me immediately. There was no barrier, no struggle. He wanted me inside his head, knowing what he knew. Seeing what he saw.

And what I saw was horrible, awful, and oddly, strangely, terribly enticing.

A thousand demons. No, more. A million. Millions upon millions.

All gathered at the gate. All waiting for the convergence.

It was coming . . . coming . . . and they were primed to burst through.

Closer and closer with each tick of the clock until, yes, the stars aligned, the dimensions shifted, and the way between hell and earth was no longer blocked.

They could cross.

They could ride.

They could come and wreak havoc upon the world.

Except they did not, because the gate was thrust open by one who held the Oris Clef. *The one who controlled it, controlled them. A figure, hand raised high, and a knife to draw the blood and press it to the* Oris Clef. *To draw the power and claim the right as holder of the key.*

The holder of the key was royalty, a demon among demons. A legend among the dark.

And as the horde passed through the gate—as the millions descended—each paid tribute with a bow and a promise of loyalty to the keyholder who stood tall and proud in front of them.

A woman.
A queen.
And she was me.

"*No!*" I jerked out, breaking away from the vision when I saw the image of me. "That's not right. That's not true. It can't be true. The third relic was destroyed! Deacon destroyed it!"

But Gabriel was not listening to me. Instead, he moved away. But I wasn't released. Instead, I was trapped within the same swirling mist that had brought him to this temple.

"Stop it! That's not me! Dammit, listen to me! I'm not fighting for the demons. I've been working against them. All this time, I've been working against them. Deacon, tell him!"

Deacon, however, didn't say a word. Instead, his face was a mass of concentration, and I soon realized why— he was the one preventing the swirling mist from taking me away.

Deacon had kept more than his past hidden from me. He had some badass powers, and he was calling on them now. And as I watched, trapped and helpless, I realized why I hadn't been privy to these powers before—because these were demon tricks, and that was something Deacon wanted to get away from. Far, far away.

He was pulling out all the stops now, though, and I

knew that he was doing it for me. And while I hated that he had to dip into the dark, I couldn't deny that the knowledge that he was out there, thwarting Gabriel in an attempt to keep me safe and with him, made my heart that much lighter.

And, yeah, Deacon was definitely doing some serious thwarting. Gabriel's tattooed face was a mask of pure rage, and he thrust both his arms out in an obvious effort to counteract whatever Deacon was doing.

As for Deacon, all I could tell was that he was working hard. I could still see the man I knew, but the effort had cost him, and his skin and bones had shifted, the flesh itself changing color. He wasn't metamorphosing like Clarence had, but there was definitely some demonic mojo going on.

Right then I didn't care. Bring on the demon, if that was what it took. Anything to keep me anchored there.

"Fool," Gabriel hissed. "Do you not see that even now you destroy everything you have strived for?"

"I see myself saving an innocent," Deacon said. "A woman who would save the world, not a demon who would destroy it."

"You do not see clearly."

"I see clearly enough."

"What was it you sought, Deacon Camphire? Was it redemption? I believe that it was."

I could see the anger flare on Deacon's face, but he didn't rise to the bait and answer. He stayed silent, waiting.

"All that you worked for, destroyed," Gabriel said.

"Don't taunt me with what your kind denied me," Deacon said bitterly.

"But cannot your deeds even now redeem you? Cannot what you do today combine with the deeds of the past to earn you what you seek?"

Deacon looked up at Gabriel, and this time, to my horror, I saw interest in his eyes.

"You stole the third relic from Penemue and hid it where it has yet to be found. For that, you were tortured, thrust into the pit, and marked as a Tri-Jal. You would have that torment be for naught?"

"I've made my choice," Deacon said, through clenched teeth.

"Have you? You sought to retrieve the other two relics. Tried to find them for the purpose of destroying them. Tried once more to find a way to betray Penemue and serve the forces of good."

"I failed," Deacon said, even as I fingered the necklace and gemstone that hung around my neck. I understood now how he had known that the caves were in China and how he had known to warn me away from the acid stream. He'd already been there once, and he knew what to expect. What he didn't know then was how to get the box from the water. For that, he needed my blood.

"You wanted to lock the gate. Wanted to earn a place in heaven and shed the weight of the horrors of your past. You failed, though," Gabriel said. "With this woman at your side, you failed."

"It isn't over," Deacon said. "We will still lock the gates."

"'We'?" Gabriel asked. "This woman who craves the dark. Who is fascinated by its lure? By the power it can bring."

Deacon's eyes darted to me, and I wished I could shake my head in denial, but I couldn't. Because everything Gabriel said was true. And if Deacon let me live, he assumed a greater risk than he'd ever assumed before.

"I will lock it," Deacon said. "I've foreseen it. And Lily will help me."

"Visions are tricky things," Gabriel said. "But on the whole, I do not doubt your word. Lily *shall* lock the gate. And as for your redemption, all you must do is choose."

Deacon shook his head, clearly not understanding what Gabriel meant any more than I did.

"*Lily* is the key," Gabriel said, making my knees turn to water. *Me?* Though once I thought about it, I supposed it made sense. The flip side of the prophecy, and all. And it sure as hell explained why I couldn't find the key on my arm even though I knew the proper incantation—my map doesn't find people. And whatever else I might be, I was still a person.

"No," Deacon was saying, shaking his head slowly.

"Yes. It is her—her flesh, her blood—that locks all the gates. Her flesh, her blood, thrown into the portal at the moment of convergence. And you need only lower your arm to ensure your redemption. Lower your arm," he repeated, "and let me take the girl away."

I swallowed, terrified that Deacon would do just that. There was a blur, then I saw that Rose—standing tall and proud with her new pink hair—had Kiera's knife pressed hard to Deacon's temple. "Betray my sister, and I will kill you."

Deacon never even looked at Rose. Instead, he looked only at me. "I would never betray her," he said. And then he jerked away from Rose, and in the same lightning-quick movement, snatched her knife and sliced off his left hand.

"Deacon!"

"I lost my hand a long time ago." He met my eyes. "I thrust it into a stream of acid."

I watched, aghast, as the limb that had fallen to the ground re-formed, shrinking and twisting and turning into what looked like a small, golden cage.

With superhuman speed, Deacon dove for it. And then, before I could even blink in surprise, he threw it straight at my chest.

It didn't, however, hit me. Instead, the thing seemed to have a mind of its own. It bent and twisted and re-formed itself over the gemstone on the *Oris Clef* necklace, making a decorative sort of cage. And the moment it stopped, I understood.

This was the third relic. Deacon hadn't destroyed it; he'd hidden it. And I now wielded the *Oris Clef*, and all the power it promised.

And then, with the same incredible speed, Deacon burst forward, his feet not even touching the ground as he sailed through the mist and tackled me, drawing me out of Gabriel's whirlwind. I was freaked and shaking, but dammit, I knew what I had to do, and with Clarence's powers surging through my head, I called for the portal to open.

It worked. Thank God, it worked, and a portal opened in the floor only feet away. Gabriel raced after us, hand outstretched as he pulled for us, the tug lessened only by the massive power that Deacon had demonstrated. "In!" Deacon cried, and with him and Rose at my side, we leaped inside, the portal closing behind us even as Gabriel's power yanked us backward.

But he was too late. We were in the void.

For the moment at least, we were safe.

It wasn't over, though. I knew that. Not only did he need me to lock the gates, he also knew that I had the *Oris Clef*, and he believed that I'd use it. That I wasn't going to lock out the demons but was going to step up to rule them.

Two visions of my future, and both of them called to me. Dark or light, and I would have to choose.

I shivered, thinking of what I'd seen in his head. The hordes bowing down to me. Worshipping me.

The vision had disgusted me as much as it had foolishly, shamefully, intrigued me and tempted me. To wield power such as I'd seen in Penemue. Could I do that? Did I have the strength within me to stand at the head of the demon hordes? Was my destiny, perhaps, to turn them to good? To help them, and me, find redemption?

Or was I only making excuses to slide into the dark?

I had no idea what the future held. No idea what I would do.

All I knew was that I had my sister back. We were, both of us, free.

I reached up and closed my hand around the *Oris Clef*, this strange relic that was both my salvation and my doom. Despite my uncertain future, I couldn't help but be glad that I'd found it.

Because now I was the girl in charge.

And all I had to do was survive.

Coming January 2010 from Ace Books

The third book in
the Blood Lily Chronicles by Julie Kenner

TURNED

*With her cover blown, Lily goes underground
with a small band of warriors she trusts to help
find the demonic forces who are determined to
unleash the fury of hell on earth. At stake is all
of humanity—and her own soul.*

"Run!"

Deacon's voice cut through the haze in my head, and I realized that the ground was shaking, huge chunks of concrete and lethally sharp steel girders being thrust upward as the earth buckled and snapped.

Except this wasn't an earthquake. This was much, much worse.

I didn't argue, didn't stop to analyze. Instead, I grabbed my sister's hand and tugged her across the undulating floor of Zane's fast-disintegrating training basement. There was only one way out, and we needed to be on that elevator. Right then. Right that very second.

Because I knew what was under the floor—I hadn't seen it, but I was certain.

Penemue. A master demon.

More specifically, a master demon I'd just royally screwed. Somehow, I had a feeling he wasn't planning a nice, reasonable little chat. Instead, he wanted what hung around my neck: the *Oris Clef*. The key that would lock open the Ninth Gate to Hell and give the bearer dominion over all the demons who crossed into the earthly realm.

"Lily!" Rose's shriek was filled with terror, and I turned automatically in the direction she was looking: Behind us, the floor had opened like a sick parody of a flower, concrete peeling away like inelegant petals to reveal a deep pit that reached all the way down into the blackest depths of hell.

"Move." I grabbed her arm and wrenched her back into motion even as I visually scoured the dust and rubble for Deacon.

The stench of sulphur filled my nostrils as the chasm burped vomit green gas. From the black pit in the ground, I could hear a deep, menacing rumbling as what was down there began to emerge—the demon himself in all his powerful, festering, massive glory.

And beyond him, separated from me and Rose by the widening void and the rising beast, I saw Deacon.

"Go!" he shouted. "Just *go.*"

One long, squidlike tentacle shot free of the abyss, then crashed down, shattering the ground as if it were no more substantial than Styrofoam.

"Dammit, Lily! Run!"

I knew I should. Knew I needed to get the hell out of there. But I couldn't. Instead, I stood stock-still, my hand on my knife, my jaw clenched. *This* was the beast who had fucked up my life. This was the beast who had pulled the strings to trick me and make me believe I'd been doing good when really I'd been Evil's puppet.

This was the bastard who'd done that to me, and damned if I didn't want to look in his eyes. Damned if I didn't want to ram my blade right through him. And, yeah, I wanted to wallow in the darkness that filled me following a demon kill, the bitter black that was the price I paid for doing what I was created to do. A master demon like Penemue would be the ultimate hit, beyond anything I'd experienced before. And oh, yeah, like an addict, I craved what could so easily destroy me. But I didn't care. I wanted it. Hell, I *needed* it.

"Lily!" Rose screamed as the tentacle lashed out toward us, coming so close we could feel the breeze left in its wake. She screamed again, the sharp edge of her fear cutting through both my fury and my craving. I took a step backward, abandoning my demonicidal fantasies.

Because the truth was I couldn't end him. Not this beast. Not even with all the power that came from being Prophecy Girl.

He was too much—too massive, too powerful. And even with my supercharged body and über-girl skills, I was no match for him. I couldn't risk losing. Not to him. Not then.

Lose, and he would get the *Oris Clef*.

Lose, and he would use it.

Lose, and Penemue would control all of the demons that crossed over at the convergence. He'd rule the Horsemen of the Apocalypse. Not four, but four billion. Even more. Countless, untold demons that would cover the earth like a plague. With Penemue the master of them all.

Not if I could help it. With Rose's scream still echoing in my ear, I turned, grabbed her hand, and ran, the floor buckling beneath our feet as we stumbled across the room.

"Lily!" Rose stumbled over a length of steel girder rising from the concrete like a sentinel. She slammed to the ground, crying out in pain as the sharp edges of stone and metal sliced through her jeans and cut into her hands.

No time to worry about that, though. I grabbed the back of her T-shirt and hauled her to her feet. "Go!" I shouted. She stumbled a bit, probably not entirely used to her new legs and taller body, but to her credit, she picked up speed and headed toward the elevator, not falling despite the way the floor was buckling and shifting beneath her.

"Come on, come on! Dammit, come on!" Rose tugged on the gate to the old-fashioned elevator, trying to slide it aside, but it was easy enough to see that her efforts were futile. A little fact that sucked big-time, because as far as I knew, there was no other way out of the basement that had once been Zane's prison.

I clenched my jaw, determined not to die. Not when Zane had sacrificed himself, banking on me to step up to save the whole damn world. I feared I didn't have it in me to be the hero that the world needed, but right then I didn't have to find out. Right then, all I had to do was survive.

I pushed in beside Rose and grabbed hold, then gave the gate a good, solid tug.

Nothing.

Well, damn. What was the point of superstrength if you couldn't even open one stuck door?

I spun around, searching for Deacon. I needed his help, but he was still yards away, circumventing the gulf that was opening wider and wider in the floor, sucking everything in—furniture, training ring, weapons—as if it were a black hole. I held my breath because Deacon had lost his left hand, so he had only one set of fingers with which to grip the wall. The gray metal cabinet was still bolted to the wall, and as I watched, Deacon ripped open the door one-handed, then pulled out a crossbow. He met my eyes, then tossed the weapon toward me.

Penemue's tentacle lashed out blindly, knocking the crossbow off its trajectory, but I launched myself sideways and managed to catch it before it disappeared into the abyss. Deacon pitched a quiver of arrows next, and those I caught more easily, then quickly slid the sheath onto my back and hefted the crossbow, already feeling better for the weapon in my hand. My knife was the only thing that would actually kill a demon once and for all, but under the circumstances, I was keen on just knowing I could slow the creature down. Although I have to say, a crossbow wasn't exactly a panacea. Considering the size of the beast fighting its way up through the concrete floor, what I really needed was a missile launcher.

Deacon armed himself, too, then grabbed onto the door and used it to swing himself over the edge of the widening chasm. I held my breath. There were only about three inches of floor left where he was. If he tripped . . . If he needed to reach out and grab something . . .

But he didn't, and once his feet were on firm ground I allowed myself one tense breath. He was steady, but he was hardly safe yet. He stood with his back pressed to the wall, his toes hanging over the ragged concrete edge in a sick parody of a suicidal jumper balancing on a high-rise ledge.

"Deacon! Hurry!" I shouted, as he pushed away from the wall and leaped from the narrow portion to where the ground widened. He landed, steady, and I exhaled in relief, only to feel the sharp sting of cold horror as the tentacle lashed out, circled his waist, and pulled him backward into the abyss.

"No!" I yelled, as Rose cried out Deacon's name.

I don't remember moving, but I was on my belly, my hand reaching out, down into the blackness. Down into where Deacon had gone. Into the night, into the void, into hell.

"Deacon!" I screamed, though I could see nothing in the dark. Not him. Not Penemue. Not even the fires of hell. "Deacon!" I cried. "Deacon! Can you hear me?"

But even as I called, I knew it was futile. He was lost, and my stomach roiled as I choked back bile, willing myself to keep focused and in control despite the fact that my demonic partner had been thrust back into the hell that he'd so desperately longed to escape.

I couldn't think about that just then. If anything, Deacon had bought us time, and I was going to use it. No way was his getting sucked down into hell going to mean the end of me and my sister.

"Come on," I said, scooting back from the abyss and grabbing Rose's elbow. She stood stock-still, her face pale, her lips parted as if she wanted to say something but couldn't quite find the words. "Rose!" I snapped, tugging her back toward the elevator. "Move."

Not that my determination got us any farther. Deacon's demise hadn't magically loosened the elevator gate, and we were still down in the training basement, trapped beside a hole to hell where a gigantic demon would surely reemerge at any moment.

Fuck.

I gave the gate one more futile yank, then kicked the damn thing. It was no ordinary metal we were dealing with. As a training arena for preternatural assassins, the room was chock-full of special protections. How nice.

"Can you make a portal?" Rose asked. "Can you get us out of here?"

I closed my eyes and concentrated, but nothing happened. I'd only recently acquired the skill to create a "bridge" that would take me and my companions through space, time, and the whole nine yards. I'd done it just a few minutes ago, actually, when Rose, Deacon, and I had been racing for our lives. But we'd been returning from a quest for a mystical vessel, and without some object as my goal, I didn't have any way to mentally anchor the bridge.

Which was the long, rambling way of saying that we were stuck.

"We'll figure something out," I said, giving the gate another hard yank.

"Lily . . ." Her voice was low, and far too steady. Which to me meant that she was scared shitless.

I looked over my shoulder—and immediately saw why. A mountainous mass was rising from the dark, like the time-lapse formation of primeval hills. The purple mountains majesty, however, weren't covered with demon slime, and the viscous, snotlike goo that slathered this demonic head made me want to puke.

It wasn't like I hadn't seen scaly, slimy demons before, but the Grykon I'd fought my first day on the job had been more or less my size. A monster, sure, but still manageable.

This, though . . .

The head alone was the size of a Suburban even without the massive, filth-covered horns that extended at least five feet in opposite directions.

His eyes were red with black slits for pupils, and, within the black, I swear I could see the souls of the damned. He had no nose, only what appeared to be a rotting orifice, and green slime oozed out. His skin looked to be as tough as an elephant's hide, and it appeared to be moving, as if living things were sliding around under the flesh.

"Lily . . ." Beside me, Rose whimpered.

"Don't look," I said, pushing her behind me as I lifted the crossbow that seemed utterly insubstantial. "Don't look; don't watch. We'll be fine."

I reached up and closed my hand around the necklace that was the *Oris Clef*, the demonic key that Penemue himself had created and I'd recovered only moments before. The thing had the power to control the coming apocalyptic horde of demons, and damned if I didn't wish I had that power right then. At the moment, a subservient hell monster would be a really good thing.

"What are we going to do?" Rose said.

"Defend ourselves," I said. I raised my crossbow. "Ourselves, and the *Oris Clef*."

So far, our only advantage was that Penemue had slowed down. At first, the building had been crumbling around us. But when Deacon had disappeared, so had the demon's tentacles. He'd returned, but his ascent was so slow that I had to wonder if he was half-in and half-out of some other dimension.

"You need to go," Rose said. "Pick something, use your arm, and just *go*."

I kept my eye firmly on the crossbow's sight. "One, it's not that simple. Two, I'm not leaving you." I'd cozied up to hell—literally—to save my sister, and there was no way I was going to throw her to the wolves. Or the demons.

A long wail emerged from behind me, and we both turned to stare at the gaping hole that was the demon's rising mouth. His eyes were like fire, and his tentacle thrust up, then slammed back down again only a few feet from us, rendering bits of broken concrete into dust.

"Shit!" I cried, bracing my body against the useless elevator. "Something's going on. There's no way he should have missed us."

Something *was* going on, and my heart lifted a little when I realized what it had to be: *Deacon*. He was down there fighting. Buying us time.

He was giving us a gift, and we damn well needed to use it.

"I'm going to check the weapons cabinet," I said.

"Right now?" Her voice was high, squeaky, and terrified.

I didn't expect to find anything to kill Penemue with, but maybe I'd find something to help me open the elevator. For that matter, if I could get to Zane's office, maybe he had some sort of override button. I didn't know. All I could think about was not wasting the chance that Deacon was giving us.

"He'll catch you!" Rose said, as I started in that direction. "He'll knock you in!"

"I'll be careful," I said, but even as I spoke, the tentacle burst free, along with the shoulders of the beast, making the floor buckle and tossing me onto my ass. Penemue lashed out, and it was clear he was aiming right for me. I fired, the arrow shooting true—embedding itself right into that slimy, sickening skull.

Fabulous, I thought. And then amended the thought to *Holy freaking shit*, because my arrow was ejected immediately, thrust out by the intense force of a horrific column of fire.

I threw myself sideways, missing the bulk of the blast, but it still scorched my jeans.

"Lily!" Rose called.

"I'm okay!" I held on to the crossbow as I scooted along the floor, abandoning my plan to head to the cabinet. Instead, I had a better idea.

"Get down," I shouted, then raced toward the elevator, the crossbow aimed at Penemue. "The ground, Rose! On the ground!" The tentacle swiveled and turned, and I dodged it. The head had disappeared beneath floor level, but I needed to see it again, and I took a chance and yelled for Deacon. "Let him go! I have an idea!"

I heard a low rumble like an oncoming earthquake,

so deep and menacing it made my insides tremble. And then the demon burst up, the slime-covered head breaching the shattered floor, as if someone holding him down had suddenly let go and the beast had been overwhelmed even by his own velocity.

I aimed. I fired.

And as soon as the arrow was free, I threw myself to the ground, barely missing the burst of fire that shot from Penemue's punctured skull. The blast shot over both me and Rose, slamming exactly where I'd hoped—right in the middle of the elevator gate.

Bingo.

The gate didn't open, but it didn't matter because now there was a giant hole in the metal mesh.

"In," I shouted to Rose. "Get in!"

Rose didn't need my encouragement. She was already climbing through the hole and calling for me to follow her. I didn't have to be told twice, and I scrambled in that direction, over a floor that was buckling and moving again beneath my feet as the beast surged up, pissed off and determined to stop me.

The damned tentacle shot up again. Only that time it was followed by two more appendages and the entirety of the beast's head. His mouth burst open, and millions of flies emerged, swarming around me, getting in my eyes and my hair and my ears and my face. I swatted at them, ducked my head, and tried to run—tried even harder not to be grossed out—but the truth was, I wasn't fast enough. The bugs did their job, and as I tried to shove through the thick, living mass, I felt something thick and cold lash itself around my ankle.

As Rose screamed, I rolled over, slashing at the tentacle, half-terrified that I'd miss and get my leg, and the other half of me not caring if I lost all my limbs so long as I got free.

It wasn't any use.

Penemue was dragging me back toward hell.

I reached down, grabbing onto the tentacle and trying to pry it off with my fingers. As I did, I looked up, and found myself staring into the demon's face. Into its eyes.

Oh, fuck.

I felt the snap—the sharp tug when I was pulled into another creature's thoughts. Another little gift of mine, and one that I really didn't welcome at the moment, but I had no choice, because I was in and the horror was around me, the fires and the pain and, oh, God, my skin— my skin was burning, the flesh curling, turning to ash as I watched, as I suffered and cried, and then starting all over again, the pain so intense I swear it was alive, and I couldn't do anything except scream and scream and scream and—

Snap!

The connection broke. I'd shut my eyes in terror, the reflex freeing me from the horror. A horror, I knew, that would be mine if I did what needed to be done. If I played the martyr. If I stepped up and saved the world.

I breathed deep, trying to control my trembling.

Dear God, how could I ever find the courage?

"Lily!"

Rose's voice cut through my fear and self-loathing. I didn't need that courage now. Now I just needed to get out of there.

With a fresh burst of determination, I rolled to my side as the tentacle tugged on my leg, this time thrusting my knife into the ground and trying with all my might to halt our progress toward the abyss. I slammed it down hard, shoving it into a crevice in the concrete, then closing my hand tight around it. With my free hand, I grabbed a protruding metal beam, my muscles straining as I tried to pull myself up.

"Nothing's happening!" Rose called. "The buttons don't work!"

Okay, I confess I wasn't completely interested in the state of the elevator at the moment, although I did want my sister to get out of there. Pretty soon, I figured she was going to have plenty of time to escape. Because once the demon had me and the key, it really wasn't going to give a flip about her.

But the other thing I was afraid of was that the demon would realize that she was the way to get to me. Take her hostage, and I was going to be Cooperation Girl. I knew it, and so, I feared, did the demon.

My fears were borne home when the pressure of the tentacle around my leg let up, and I screamed out in both anger and fear as the appendage lashed forward to close around Rose's waist.

She howled, using her knife to hack uselessly at the

tentacle that refused to let go. I rushed forward to join her, thrusting my blade in and twisting, but the demon's tentacle seemed immune to pain.

"It's getting tighter! Lily, oh, God, make it stop!"

I stabbed my knife down deep into the spongy flesh, and started sawing, wishing the blade was serrated, because I was damn well going to saw through all fifteen inches of flesh if that was what it took.

But I had to saw fast, because she was struggling, her mouth open, her breath coming in gasps, and fear pounding behind her eyes.

I was going to lose her. *Oh, God, oh, God.* I was going to lose her. Rose. My little sister. The little girl I'd risked everything—including the Apocalypse—to save.

I felt numb. I felt raw. And I felt wholly and completely impotent.

And then, as her eyes began to dim and I could barely see the dent I was making in the demon's flesh from the tears floating in my eyes, I heard it.

Low at first, and then building up strength. A deep, terrifying wail.

I turned, then saw the demon's eyes go wide, the black shifting to red. I turned back fast, and acting solely on instinct I grabbed Rose around the waist, then spread my legs, my feet anchored inside the elevator, one foot on either side of the hole that had been blasted in the cage door.

It was the right move. The tentacle pulled back, retreating, and trying to take Rose with it.

But it couldn't. Not easily, anyway. Not with me holding on to her.

And damned if it didn't let go.

I didn't completely understand why. All I knew was that whatever had produced that horrific wailing noise had scared Penemue. And he'd retreated into the darkness.

I figured it would be a good idea to get out of there, too. Because even in my limited experience in this world, I'd already figured out that it was a good idea to run from things that disturbed massive beasts from hell.

I slapped Rose's face, heard her moan, and sighed with relief. I didn't have time to do more, though. So I let go and let her fall to the floor of the elevator car. She coughed, and rolled over, and I knew that for the moment at least, she was safe.

I jabbed at the elevator buttons, but Rose was right— they didn't work. We needed out of there, though, and I tilted my head back, searching for the emergency door that was standard in all elevators. Including, apparently, those installed by minions of hell.

I used the broken metal of the cage as a makeshift ladder and managed to get up there, then pulled the trapdoor down. Then I hopped back down and made a stirrup with my hands for Rose to step in. "Can you manage?"

She lifted her head, looking a lot like a girl who badly needed a nap.

"Rose, please. We've got to move."

She opened her mouth, but no sound came out. To her credit, though, she did stand. As she did, her eyes darted toward the hole in the elevator door and out toward the chasm. I knew what she was thinking, because I was thinking the same thing: *Unless I'm dead or broken, I'm getting the hell out of here.*

I held out a hand to steady her as she came over, then re-formed the stirrup for her. "Grab my shoulders," I said.

"I'm okay." Her voice was weak, but she meant what she said, and even before I had time to worry if she'd have the strength in her arms to pull herself up, she was through the hole and I saw her peering down, waiting for me to join her.

I was just about to do that very thing when the tentacle thrust toward me again. I leaped, trying to get through the trapdoor. Rose grabbed the back of my shirt and tugged, trying to help me up, but it wasn't enough. Despite my strength and her valiant effort, the tug of the tentacle that had lashed around my waist kept me from climbing through the escape hatch.

It would have pulled me all the way back to hell with it, if it wasn't for a coal black, winged creature that burst from the gorge. It shot forward as if fired from a cannon, flame dancing over its body, not as if it were on fire, but as if it *was* fire.

And the fire-creature roared straight for us, the flames dissipating as it grabbed me under my arms, and then shot straight up into the elevator shaft, effectively pulling my lower body free of the tentacle, which had loosened only slightly, as if shocked to see the creature.

It slowed enough to grab Rose with its other arm, and then it put on a fresh burst of speed and rocketed straight up, up, up—at least until we jerked to a stop, flipped over, and started moving in the opposite direction. In other words, back *toward* Penemue. Which really wasn't where I wanted to go.

I called out in protest, but it was no use. Penemue was down there, two floors below, and we were heading right for him. The demon's bulbous body filled the elevator shaft, that black pit of a mouth sucking us in, as if we were the very air he needed to breathe. As if we were caught in some damned sci-fi tractor beam, and we were moving backward, toward the gaping maw.

I screamed and struggled in my captor's arms, desperate to get me and Rose out of there. A reaction that was, of course, idiotic, because if I got free, gravity would send me hurtling down into Penemue's waiting mouth. And once that little fact registered in my head, I clung more tightly to my winged rescuer. I didn't know who he was or what he wanted, but at least until he got us out of the elevator shaft, he was my new best friend.

And right then, my friend was fighting dirty.

He thrust his torso and legs up, so that his head was pointed down, and Rose and I were pulled in close to his side. And then, as I watched, he let out a wail that came straight from the deepest pit of hell, and emitted a burst of flame from his mouth so hot that I had to close my eyes and twist my face away. But when it dissipated, I turned back, then sucked in air at what I saw—the entire elevator shaft had melted away, and Penemue had retreated, leaving one burned-off tentacle behind, the flames still snapping at the crispy flesh.

"He will be back." The low voice rumbled through me, rough and inhuman and yet also somehow familiar. My breath caught, and warm fear flowed through me as my mind filled with horrible possibilities.

I had no time to ponder those fears, though. Not then. Not as he shifted direction in the shaft and we began shooting upward, so fast I feared that we'd slam into the masonry and die from massive hematomas.

Not that I had to worry about that. As we approached at breakneck speed, our savior released another burst of flame and melted the floor above us, along with the ceiling above. Handy trick, that.

We burst out into the dead of night, rising high above the city, all of Boarhurst before us and the lights of Boston proper twinkling in the distance.

He dropped down then, and, as my heart pounded in my chest, the beast landed us softly on a patch of grass, his arms releasing us as he stepped back, wings folded, head down, crouched there in front of us.

Beside me, Rose was breathing in and out fast as she scrabbled backward, crablike, away from him.

Me, I stayed put, holding tight to my knife.

But I didn't attack. I knew this creature. I was certain of it.

And when he lifted his head, I saw it in his eyes.

"Deacon?"

Something dark flashed in those eyes, and he lunged, teeth bared, mouth open as if another burst of flame was coming.

Rose screamed, and I tackled her to the ground, then rolled over and thrust out my knife, wondering what the hell use it could possibly be against a demon who could breathe fire as Deacon did.

"Go," he said, his muscles practically trembling with restraint.

I didn't. I just stood there, awed and shaken and—yes—more than a little freaked-out.

"Go," he repeated. "Find the last key. Find it," he growled, "before it's too late."

TAINTED

*Lily Carlyle has lied, cheated, and stolen
her way through life. But in death,
she'll really get to be bad…*

When her little sister is brutalized, a vengeful Lily decides
to exact her own justice. She succeeds—at the cost of her
own life. But as she lies dying, she is given a second chance.
Lily can earn her way into paradise by becoming an
assassin for the forces of good.

It's a job Lily believes she can really get into—but she
doesn't realize that she may not be able to get out.

San Diablo, California.

The perfect place to raise a couple of kids.

And a lot of hell.

Carpe Demon
California Demon
Demons Are Forever
Deja Demon
Demon Ex Machina

penguin.com

M254AS0609